ALSO BY NINO RICCI

FICTION

Lives of the Saints
In a Glass House
Where She Has Gone
Testament
The Origin of Species

NON-FICTION

Pierre Elliott Trudeau

# SLEEP

# SLEEP

DOUBLEDAY CANADA

Doubleday Canada and colophon are registered trademarks of
Random House of Canada Limited

Library and Archives Canada Cataloguing in Publication

Ricci, Nino, 1959-, author
Sleep / Nino Ricci.

Issued in print and electronic formats.
ISBN 978-0-385-68160-5 (bound).--ISBN 978-0-385-68161-2 (epub)

I. Title.

PS8585.I126S54 2015          C813'.54          C2015-901958-3
                                               C2015-901959-1

This book is a work of fiction. Names, characters, places and incidents are
products of the author's imagination or are used fictitiously. Any resemblance to
actual events or locales or persons, living or dead, is entirely coincidental.

Cover and text design: Kelly Hill
Cover art: Alex Colville, *Pacific* 1967. Acrylic on hardboard.
Copyright A.C.Fine Art Inc.
Printed and bound in the USA

Published in Canada by Doubleday Canada,
a division of Random House of Canada Limited,
a Penguin Random House Company

www.penguinrandomhouse.ca

10 9 8 7 6 5 4 3 2 1

Penguin
Random House
DOUBLEDAY CANADA

*In memory of Paul Quarrington*

# PART ONE

# Methylphenidate

A WASH OF CHEMICALS floods David's brain and at once the urge is there, irresistible. What is the trigger, what switch opens the floodgate? If he could find it, he could control it. But even to think of the urge is to bring it on.

"Dad. Dad!"

These are the times it overtakes him: When he is reading. When he is watching. When he is listening. At the crossroads of action and thought, the mind's gathering place, the very place where he lives.

When he is driving.

"Daddy, wake up!"

He hears a thundering like a stampede, he sees chariots, horses. Then the image splinters and there is only the noise itself, jagged and black, until finally the expressway pixelates into clarity and he realizes he has veered onto the rumble strip.

A car is stopped on the shoulder not a hundred metres in front of them. They are headed straight for it.

"Dad, there's a car!"

Afterwards David will never quite be able to sort out his memory of what happens next in any way that makes sense. It will seem as if he has split in two, on one side of him the nuclear blast of sensation, the thump of his wheels, the stopped car, his son's grating terror, on the other an eerie calmness, as if every fibre in him has long been preparing for just such a moment, when everything hangs in the balance. He will be amazed how much data has been left in him by an event that has happened in the blink of an eye. The slant of autumn light through the windshield. The colour of the car, silver-grey, he is heading toward. The look of its driver, a small, dark-skinned man, Middle Eastern or Asian, who has stopped to make a call or stretch his legs or take a leak, as he innocently turns to check for traffic before opening his door only to discover that death is bearing down on him. And already before it comes, David sees the crash, the mess of twisted metal and broken glass and ruined flesh.

He jerks the wheel hard and the car bucks like a wild animal, no longer under his will. His body has braced itself for impact but, impossibly, the impact doesn't come. Instead there is only a suck of air from the far side of the car like the pull of something's gravity, the scream of a horn as David overshoots his lane and nearly sideswipes a passing van. Then, as quickly as that, the danger has passed. As if it had never been. Already the car on the shoulder has receded to a harmless glint in the rear-view mirror.

David's heart is pounding. He digs his little pill container out of his pant pocket and dumps the pills onto the passenger seat, then grabs two by feel and crunches down on them. *Do not chew.* They are bitter like cyanide, like hemlock. But pointless now: he is fully awake.

He can feel Marcus eyeing him from his car seat in the back. "You fell asleep," he says.

"I wasn't asleep." But already David has taken the wrong tack, has responded to the boy's accusation rather than to his fear. "I just closed my eyes for a second, that's all. Because of the sun."

David nudges the mirror to get a better view of him, sees how his shoulders have hunched, how he has balled himself up in his gloom and distrust. He is barely five but already he carries his moods like an adolescent. At the zoo, where they were visiting, he fell into a sulk over a trinket David refused him at the gift shop, and now he will roll this new, larger hurt into the old one, each lending weight to the other. When did he become like this, so vigilant, so hungry for grievance?

David knows he ought to say more about what has happened but is afraid that saying more will only raise the event's importance in the boy's mind. Will only make him more likely to report it to his mother.

"Sit up straight, please. We've talked about that."

A thin line of fire burns a path through David's veins as the drug enters his bloodstream and he feels a panic go through him, nothing like the adrenal rush of the near accident itself but a sense of being vulnerable after the fact, as if by some loop the moment might replay itself, differently. He realizes, suddenly, that his whole body is trembling. It happens sometimes when he is agitated, this loss of control, another of his symptoms.

The sheerest luck has saved him from killing his son.

*Daddy, wake up.*

He casts another look back at Marcus.

"Almost home now," he says. "Almost there."

A hesitation, then the inevitable question.

"Will Momma be there?"

He is never enough. He is never the last recourse.

David lets the question hang.

They merge onto the valley parkway to find it backed up for miles, lurching forward in tiny spurts as the sun sets and the trees along the parkway flame up like an apocalypse in their autumn colours. Julia will be livid that they are so late, that David hasn't called. It has crossed his mind to call any number of times, but each time he has resisted, knowing that she herself will never be the one to call. This is how she tests him, piling up her grievances the way Marcus has learned to. The behaviour of children.

He feels the dull throb of a headache beginning from the spike in his medication. For the next few hours, his heart will pound like a battering ram. He takes advantage of the stalled traffic to gather up the pills still scattered on the seat next to him: stupid to have let Marcus see them, to risk his mentioning them. Right from the start David has kept Julia in the dark, has passed the blame for his symptoms onto insomnia, late nights, overwork, has hidden from her the doctors' visits, the clinics, the pills. That is his default with her now: to hide any sign of weakness, anything that might give her ammunition.

His mind keeps circling back to the instant when the crash felt inevitable, trying to sort out what saved them, though already it is hard to say how much is real in what he remembers and how much is the illogic of whatever dream he had slipped into. A deep brain disorder. That was how Becker put it, his sleep doctor, a fleshy Afrikaner with the hectoring twang of an apartheid politician and the parboiled look of a village butcher. A breakdown in the border that separated waking from sleep. As if sleep were some rebel force that David had let overrun him, leaving him condemned now to live in this place of constant incursion, where nothing was safe, nothing was certain.

A police cruiser squeezes by on the shoulder, then an ambulance. It occurs to David that the loop he has imagined has really happened: somewhere ahead, a version of the horror he has averted is playing itself out. He will drive by and see his own child lying dead, his own double howling in bloodied agony. At the image, something like relief stirs in him, as if only now has he dared it, the sense of a cosmic reprieve, a second chance. This is exactly the sort of thinking he is constantly having to root out of his students, whose notions of historical process don't go much beyond mindless mantras like *Everything happens for a reason.*

He takes out his cell phone and sets it to speaker.

"Just calling your mom," he says to Marcus, and he can feel the boy's mood lift.

She picks up on the first ring.

"Christ, David, where are you? It's past six. Why didn't you call?"

*Why didn't you?*

"We're stuck on the parkway," he says evenly.

"For fuck's sake! I thought we talked about using the cell when you're driving!"

He allows himself the smallest pause.

"We're on speaker, actually."

The behaviour of children.

Into the silence David adds, evenly again, "We had a nice day at the zoo."

"That's just great, David, I'm happy for you. I just wish it would cross your mind sometimes to think of someone other than yourself."

The call leaves David circling along a well-worn path of anger and self-justification. *It's her*, he tells himself, this implacable she-wolf she has been ever since Marcus was born, framing everything he does as a betrayal of his most basic duties as husband and father. The defence has become so knee-jerk in him by now that he seldom thinks beyond it. That she doesn't call because he accuses her of checking up on him, of being controlling. Or because he might be in class, or in a conference, or driving home. Because in a thousand ways, over the years, he has made it known not to call. Probably all afternoon she has been fighting the urge to call him, meanwhile imagining every horror. He has learned that about her, though she doesn't show it, how deep her fears go the second Marcus is out of her sight, how primordial they are, beyond reason.

It is fully dark by the time they reach the source of the holdup. An accident, yes, but less tragedy than farce. A moving van has spilled it contents and sent half a dozen cars into a minor pileup, emergency crews sorting through the wreckage and traffic choked down to a single lane. Debris from the van lies heaped at the roadside etched in the halogen glare of the highway's mast lights, a half-sprung sofa-bed, splintered end tables, ruptured moving boxes spilling clothes, shattered dishes, DVDs. The van itself is farther up, back doors still open, sitting alone at the side of the road as if the accident had nothing to do with it. David makes out two forms, a man and a woman, hurrying toward it in the dark clutching armfuls of salvage.

*Idiots*, he thinks.

Past the bottleneck he picks up speed at once. The red taillights of the cars ahead of him weave through the highway's dips and curves as if riding the air, held disembodied by the dark swath the valley forms against the backdrop of the city. He remembers driving here as a teen in his first car, a reconditioned MG he'd paid for out of his own pocket, the top down and the pedal to the floor while his blood pumped through his veins and the wind roared around him. Back then the valley seemed some hopeful landscape of the future, with the river winding its way toward the lake beneath the flyovers and cloverleaves, and the skyscrapers of downtown beckoning in the distance. Now, he realizes, he is looking instead at the past, that all this is part of an order already in full decline.

There is a clearing near their exit where more than once David has seen deer grazing, as many as a dozen of them. Somehow they have managed to find a corridor here from open country, have been able to thrive in these back-yard-sized patches of bush between murderous highway on one side and the endless concrete and cracked asphalt and brick of the east end on the other. David thinks of them not as some harbinger of a return to the wilderness of old but a sign that nature is on the march, trying to force a new accommodation. All over the city the animals have grown urban, the raccoons long ago but now coyotes, hawks, herds of deer. Meanwhile, the humans grow savage. Jogging past the camps of the homeless that dot the valley, David has seen the scattered bits of offal and bone and matted fur from their kills.

At their exit David steals another look at Marcus.

"Still awake back there?"

Marcus shifts in his seat.

"Are *you*?"

David ought to laugh, feel proud even; it is a sophisticated response. Instead, he hears the voice of Julia. He has the urge to shake the boy, to strike him. He fears that one day, he will.

He remembers the promise he made to himself at Marcus's birth. That he would never do what his own father had done. That he would never make an enemy of his son.

In the darkness, the tree-lined streets of their neighbourhood give off the dead calm of a village. When David was a kid, coming out here to visit an uncle who ran an east-end vegetable shop, the streets teemed with children and grizzled men and old women in black and the yards were staked with laundry lines or with tomatoes and beans. Now, the area is already into its third or fourth wave of gentrification, the houses, mostly two-storey semis on postage-stamp lots, all burnished and bevelled and bleached for maximum value added and their gardens as manicured as Versailles, still with fall flowers in bloom or roses in their second or third flourishing.

David and Julia's place is a standout, a detached Victorian in yellow brick that was built when the tracts east of the valley were still open fields. Of the dozens of places they saw at the time of their move here from Montreal, this was the only one Julia would even consider, though it was too large by half and had never been properly updated. Exactly the sort of place David hated then, fusty and creaky and small-roomed, hemmed in on every side by the inconvenience of the old. David got enough of the old in his work; at home he preferred something more neutral. Clean lines, lots of light, a place he could see his own life in.

Before Marcus, there was this house: it was the project Julia poured all her energies into, all her unspoken resentment at being uprooted for the sake of David's career, this despite his having negotiated a place for her here better than anything she would have got back home. For a while her reputation even seemed set to eclipse his own, her dissertation coming out with one of the more respectable academic presses to critical raves while his follow-up to his first book was almost universally panned, presumably to punish him for the first one's success. By her third year Julia was leveraging enough research money to bring her teaching load down to nearly the same level as David's, though instead of trying to bank a few more publications for her tenure review she instead put the time she'd freed up into the house.

She had become obsessed with restoring the place as closely as possible to its original form, which meant tearing down a mudroom at the back and adding a front veranda, having custom plasterwork done and ordering custom baseboards and period wallpaper, all of this on top of the furnace that needed replacing and the attic that needed insulating and the electrical panel that needed upgrading. David was staggered by the bills coming in. They had bought the place on a pre-emptive bid that was well above the asking price to head off the chance of losing it in an auction, then had sunk the last of his book money into the down payment. When David's second book failed even to earn back its advance, all the reno work had to come right off their salaries. Before his marriage David had always made a point of living large, of picking up tabs, of dressing well, of always ordering the premium wine, but with the money flowing out like water he began to harp on every expense.

At bottom even the money was probably a tangent, every one of their arguments over the house so compromised from the start by other agendas that resolution was never a realistic prospect, maybe not even a hoped-for one. All that mattered, really, was to make a point. For Julia, that this was David's own doing, the price to pay for taking her away from everything familiar, from a place where her life might have been her own; for David, that even casting the move in these terms, as what he had wanted, was just a cover for what he'd been denied. What he had wanted then, what would have made sense, was not a puffed-up chair at a second-rate university in a city he had no wish to return to but an appointment at one of the better schools south of the border. Someplace where ambition wasn't seen as a disease. Where they would have paid him real money. He could have had that then.

His breaking point with the house came over some vintage door hardware Julia had ordered from England, half of it, David thought, stuff his brother could have picked up for nothing from salvage.

"This isn't Daddy's mausoleum on the hill!" David had screamed at her. "Daddy's not paying the fucking bills!"

That was a constant refrain with him at the time, the implication that Julia's extravagances were somehow born of the same old-money contempt that her father—who insisted on pronouncing David's surname, Pace, as *Pah-cheh*, though it probably hadn't been said that way since before David's own father had stepped off the boat—had shown for David from the day he'd first laid eyes on him. And yet at the outset David had taken pleasure in indulging her, still flush with his successes and believing the money would never end. And it wasn't that he had ever really pushed her to seek his brother's services, or that the hardware she'd ordered was much of an extravagance next to what they'd already spent by then. When it had arrived, Julia had come to him in all innocence to show him a lock set from the 1800s whose wooden knobs, carved in a beehive pattern, were delicately canted from the uneven wear of whatever hands had touched them over the centuries. Not in a decade of scouring would Danny have turned up anything that exquisite in salvage. David thinks of those knobs now every time he opens one of the house's doors: after the argument, Julia had returned all the vintage stuff to wherever she'd got it from and had simply left in place the generic hardware the house had come with.

David parks on the street but turns to find that Marcus, uncharacteristically, has nodded off after all, slumped like a shooting victim against the restraints of his car seat. The sight of him asleep like that sparks a complicated burst of emotion in David, a mix of fear and remorse and maybe what for want of a better word he might call love, though that is the part that feels most malevolent, most likely to lead to failure or bad judgment or ill will. Again the image flashes through his head of the stopped car and with it the panic comes as well, even more gut-wrenching now, as though it is only in these incremental waves that he is able to take in the fullness of it. Yet beneath the panic is the memory of that second self who sat steely and clear-eyed and calm, exhilarated, almost, at the crucial instant. Who saved their lives, perhaps, but as if all that had really mattered was the sense, for maybe the first time in months or years, of being fully awake, of being fully alive.

He can't bring himself to rouse Marcus and sits staring out at his house, seeming to see it as a stranger might. The front veranda is bathed in a sallow light that gives way by slow degrees to shadow like the light from a fire, one of Julia's period touches. The veranda had been one of her biggest projects, though only after their blowout—when work on the house essentially ceased, so that to this day it is dotted with little jobs that were never completed—was David finally able to see it as something more than the price tag it had come with. What had struck him as mere frippery at first, its filigreed sconces, its endless balusters and spindles, took on a kind of resonance, of depth. He would look at the veranda and see the homestead the house had once been, this stubborn bit of empire at the edge of the bush. Somehow Julia had succeeded in conjuring that ghost. What was the point of all those arguments they'd had except to rob her, to rob them both, of the pleasure of what she'd accomplished? Why had he come to see the house as something she was taking from him rather than something she was giving him?

*A second chance.* He stares out and can see it shimmering in front of him, a chance at the life he has always wanted. The beautiful house, the beautiful wife, the beautiful child; the successful career. The life that, despite himself, he actually has. And yet even as it sits waiting for him he wonders at the stranger shifting inside him who sees only the lie of it.

At the sound of them at the door Julia comes out of the kitchen and at once bends to take Marcus in her arms, not so much as looking at David. She is dressed in sweats but he gets a whiff of body powder or perfume as if she has changed back from something nicer.

"Did you see the echidna?"

"We couldn't. Dad said that part wasn't open."

"I'm sure it was closed if your dad said it was. You'll see it next time."

David knows he has to speak, make contact, but also that there is nothing he can say that will be the right thing.

"What smells so good?"

"It might have been good, if you'd been here an hour ago."

The dining table is set with candlesticks and wine, the good china. No doubt she has spent much of the afternoon cooking and planning, nursing, against the odds, the hope that it might still be possible to enjoy an evening at home with her husband and son. Time after time David forgets this side of her, her vestigial need to make house, her hope for the restoration of a domestic order that has never really existed. Or he doesn't forget: he suppresses. This is not the Julia he fell in love with; it is not the Julia he married. The Julia he fell in love with was the rising star, the one who loved her work, who could spend hours in the archives poring through letters and journals and laundry lists until the right detail finally leapt out at her. Now it is as if she has cut out that part of herself like a tumour she needed to be free of.

For Marcus, as usual, there is an entirely separate meal, hot dogs with canned beans in molasses. It boggles David how Julia dotes on him but then feeds him this poison. How she trains him to want only that. Pancakes. French fries. Macaroni and cheese from a box. These are the raw materials building the boy's sinew and bone, his brain. It makes David think of the cut-throat contractors his father used to rail against who knocked together whole housing blocks out of cardboard and spit. His father had been a bastard, but at least he'd had standards. None of his buildings looked old the week after they went up. Nor would he ever have allowed to enter his house any of the processed chemical confections that Julia insists on feeding Marcus.

"You have to eat the bun too," Julia says, though it is the punkiest sort of white bread. "And some of the beans."

"I don't like the beans."

David holds his tongue.

"You have to eat some of them. For Mommy."

"Please, Mom. I don't like them."

"Just three spoons, then. For Mommy."

The same ordeal, night after night; the same anger in David that they have veered so badly off course. The anger spirals in him until he has lost all perspective, no longer sure if it is Julia or just the drug coursing through him or if the anger is what he wants, all that keeps him going.

They have hardly exchanged a word the whole meal. David gets up silently when they have finished and starts clearing the table.

"Thanks, Julia," Julia says. "Great supper."

He goes up to his office on the third floor while Julia gets Marcus ready for bed, though he knows how much she hates it when he does this. No point offering help when she is in this mood. The truth, though, is that he is afraid, afraid Marcus will say something, that he himself will. That something will come out of him that he can't take back.

His office is the one room in the house that bears no mark of Julia's restorations. The same desk in aluminum and brushed glass that he had in his apartment in Montreal; a wall of built-ins for his library done in painted MDF. On a top shelf, a row of the various editions of his own work, his only indulgence. None of the little flourishes his fellow classicists go in for, the Romanists especially, the period maps on every wall, the framed coinage, the seventeenth-century editions of Tacitus or Virgil or Livy that belonged to some Cambridge schoolboy. Most of them have a toilet seat from Hadrian's Villa or a collarbone from the catacombs that they've purloined at some point and that they'll bring out like pornography to titillate their colleagues. David had been cured of that impulse early on, when his mother had taken him on his first trip to Rome at age twelve. He had picked up a loose bit of mosaic to pocket as a souvenir while they were visiting Ostia Antica, and the young cicerone who was showing them around had grown suddenly grave, impressing on David what would happen if every tourist took home a piece of the place. It was a lesson that stuck with him.

He checks his email. There is a reminder from Sonny Krishnan about their Monday one-on-one; knowing Sonny, he probably set it up on auto-send the minute they booked the appointment, timed to blot David's weekend. No doubt he is going to try to fob off on David another numbing survey course or hit him up with more thesis supervision or committee work, seeming to have made it his mission ever since taking over as department head to claw back the research concessions David was granted when he was hired. It hasn't helped that David's evaluations have been dipping, or that there have been a couple of incidents that Sonny somehow managed to get wind of. The worst was when he called a student a fucking punk in the middle of a lecture and threw him out of class. This was before his diagnosis, when his symptoms had reached the point where he'd started blanking out in mid-sentence, losing his train of thought or cutting out entirely for a few seconds. After one of these lapses, a football thug logging time for his humanities requirement had made some quip that caused an eruption of laughter around him, and David had lost it.

He had had to put up with one of Sonny's lectures afterwards, delivered in that urgent new-order tone of his that suggested the department, the whole university, was under threat of imminent dissolution, with no room for slippage. It infuriates David how Sonny is constantly looking for ways to position him as some sort of liability when he is still arguably one of the best-published instructors in the department, even now that History has been subsumed within the huge Liberal Studies hydra that Sonny presides over. When he is probably the main reason classical studies haven't disappeared entirely, the only one who has made the effort to keep them current. David has lost count of the number of times students have told him that what got them interested in ancient Rome was some article or post of his that made the connection for them between past and present. That is the Rome David brings to his students, not some dead relic but a place still alive everywhere they look, in their language, their calendars, their government, their laws, in the shapes of their buildings and the concrete they're made of. A place not of yesterday but of tomorrow. That went to the brink of what it meant to be human, then one step beyond.

All of this counts for shit in Sonny's new order.

David hears the water start for Marcus's bath. He logs into his web site to check for comments on his blog even though he knows that he should be making himself present, that with each minute he spends up here he pushes Julia closer to the breaking point. At some point in their marriage the internet has become in Julia's mind a sort of underworld David has given himself over to, a bad side of town where he goes to indulge the degraded parts of himself, the ones for which emotion, human contact, are anathema. That is never how the internet has felt for David: from the start what has thrilled him about it is exactly the sense of connection it gives him, of these millions of threads leading away from him like neural pathways, making him bigger. His web site, PaceRomana, which he has had since before most academics knew what one was, has become a virtual brand. Pace as in David, as in *pah-cheh*, as in peace. As in Pax Romana, the great sleight of hand Rome had managed, making peace its legacy by dint of perpetual war. To tie into the web site David had used the phrase as the title of his second book, the one on Augustus. By then he'd already been happy to start moving away from the brand of his first book, *Masculine History*. It had used Julius Caesar to put forward a theory of historical change whose viral rise to almost cultish currency had quickly been matched by virulent backlash.

No responses yet to his new post. Lately his comments have been plagued by trolling, ad hominem attacks too scurrilous to be taken seriously but too pointed to be dismissed as spam. *Et tu, brute? Get a fucking life! Ex nihilo nihil fit.* From the start there had been no shortage of diatribes against him from all the purists he had offended, but this recent stuff feels different, more personal, more malignant. He finds himself compiling lists in his head of the people who might loathe him enough to expend this sort of energy on him. It could be anyone, of course, some student he failed or colleague he slighted or some anonymous madman out there in cyberspace who has made David his personal anti-Christ, itching to get him in his crosshairs. But certain names recur. Greg Borovic, his grad school sidekick, who cut off all connection with him after *Masculine History* came out. Susan Morales: the last David heard, she was still stuck doing sessional work in some no-name place out West, no doubt convinced David was the one who got her exiled there. Then there is the kid who started all the trouble for him back in Montreal, though chances are he is just some paunchy personal injury lawyer or middle manager by now and has forgotten all about him.

David had run into his old department head from Montreal, Ed Dirksen, at a conference the previous year, ending up face to face with him at a refreshment table before he had even noticed him. It was the first time he had seen him since leaving Montreal.

"My God, David, it's been years! Not that I haven't kept up with your work!"

He looked utterly unchanged, still in the same rumpled suit, still with the babyish cast to his features of someone whose manhood had been stunted. And yet for all the nonentity he had always been, still he had persisted, hadn't simply vanished into the void.

David had to endure several torturous minutes of Dirksen updating him on his former colleagues as if they had all been part of some happy fellowship. Then this.

"Too bad about that unpleasant business." In an almost rueful tone, eyes dipping slightly as if to spare David embarrassment. "But I suppose it all worked out."

He hears footsteps at the base of the stairs.

"I could use some help down here."

He has lost his chance.

He finds Julia staring out the bathroom window seeming withdrawn to a second order of reclusion, one that leaves out even Marcus, who sits playing quietly in the tub with one of his bath toys as if he is merely playing at playing. She might be a stranger to David when she is like this, someone he has never exchanged a word with, never desired, never fucked. After Marcus was born she went weeks in this zombie state— some sort of postpartum syndrome, David figured out afterwards, though at the time it felt like revulsion, utter retreat, as if it had suddenly dawned on her that her marriage, her house, her child, had been a massive error. He often forgets it now, that darkness she slipped into, with him left to take up the slack, not knowing what to do with this child, this being, who cried for hours and hours without reason. Waiting for instinct to kick in, for love.

Julia doesn't turn when he comes in.

"There's two loads of laundry downstairs that need to be folded."

The urge comes to him to apologize, to make amends.

"You okay?"

She gives him a look that seems to draw all emotion back into itself like a black hole.

"Let's not start this right now."

It had been only a matter of weeks after Marcus's birth before Julia had come around, with the suddenness of a genetic switch being thrown. The panicked protectiveness she has had around Marcus ever since makes David suspect that she is still reliving with horror the numbness of those first weeks, when anything might have happened. In this reliving, David has become the enemy, the threat, the bad parent she needs him to be in order to assure herself she is the good one. She caught him nodding off the other day while he was supervising Marcus's bath and it was as if he had dropped the boy into boiling pitch, had shown, in that brief lapse, how little all of this means to him.

He brings the laundry into the living room. His head is throbbing by now from the extra pills he took in the car, from the glass of wine he stupidly drank with supper. It has been one of the hardest things to mask, how badly wine affects him these days, how sharply his intake has dropped. He pops another pill, dry, to stay alert, chewing this one as well, though he has lost all track of how many he is up to. At the end of the month he'll come up short: the pills are strictly controlled, down to the day, no new script until the old one has run its course.

He tunes the TV to one of the news channels, keeping the volume low to head off Julia's reprimand. A car bomb in Baghdad; a drone attack near the Afghan border. Instinctively his mind lays a map of the past over the present, the Arabians, the Parthians, the Persians, trying to match up the fault lines, a reflex from a feature he runs on his web site, "Back to the Future," that connects current events to Roman parallels. These days the connections never feel as clear cut as they once did, the insights never quite as inspired. It isn't just burnout or age: it's the crossed wires from his disorder, the lacunae and gaps that build up each time a synapse misfires or goes astray. Then the energy he spends on these baubles feels more and more like fiddling, when his new book is still just a mess of jottings and his last one, over two years ago, was just another culling of his web posts, light as air. Time and again he has stayed late at the university trying to get up momentum on the new book only to have his brain go to blue screen, waking with a start to find he's been out for an hour or more or has filled the screen with gibberish or has somehow erased a whole day's work, following some dream logic he can't reconstruct. And of course each time he works late he adds a little more poison to his marriage, a little more silence.

A deep brain disorder.

It was the lapses in class that finally sent David in for testing. Two days and nights at the clinic Becker operated near the west-end hospital he worked out of, a warren of narrow rooms and labyrinthine corridors just above a 24-hour Coffee Time. Becker seemed to run the place like his personal fiefdom, the halls lined with his conference posters and a big photo of him hanging in the foyer posed with an ancient-looking Nathaniel Kleitman, the granddaddy of sleep medicine. The sleep rooms were all named after painters, each with its corresponding sleep-themed print on the door, Dali's melting clocks, Goya's *The Sleep of Reason Breeds Monsters*. David got Henri Rousseau and *The Dream*, of a woman reclining naked on a couch like a Titian Venus while around her the jungle rose up and wild animals lurked.

He was prepped in a control room that was a bedlam of cables and ancient equipment and cluttered cubicles. His technician, Nada, kept up a steady litany of complaint about the working conditions as she fixed electrodes to his scalp, letting him know that the country she had come from had not been a backward one, though she didn't name it. His whole time in the place David remained rigged up to these electrodes like a head case, his only contact with the outside world the quick forays he made to pick up bad sandwiches at the Coffee Time and bad coffee he wasn't supposed to be drinking. The clinic stank of other people's sleep, the fecal-and-breath-and-sweat smell of David's half-dozen or so fellow inmates, people he never exchanged a word with but whom he caught glimpses of in the halls in their own Frankenstein gear and heard being tended to in the night as if they were all part of some collective nightmare. More and more the place felt like the inside of his own head, with its hazy half-reality. His dreams were vivid, phantasmagoric, epic battles and travels in time, dreams within dreams where he was above himself like a god, watching himself dream that he was dreaming. He'd buzz Nada in the night to unplug him to pee and then he'd be fucking her or she would be killing him. The whole place seemed steeped somehow in moral ambiguity: the surly technicians from their war-torn countries where they might as easily have been perpetrators as victims; the presiding animus of Becker, who however never once set foot in the place, as if it were a dirty secret he had to keep separate from his public life at the hospital, and who for all David knew had been some sort of Mengele in his former life, had tortured political prisoners or had attached electrodes to the insides of people's brains. It didn't help that David had had to lie to Julia, claiming an engagement out of town, so that he was dogged the entire time by the kind of panic he'd get in fever dreams, the sense of some problem he couldn't solve or critical thing he had failed to attend to. It would have been easy enough for Julia to check up on him; easy enough, if she discovered the lie, for her to imagine the worst yet say nothing.

After the ordeal of the tests, the follow-up with Becker was almost comically anticlimactic.

"We'll start you at thirty milligrams of the Ritalin." In his inquisitor's tone, scowling at David's results as if they had failed to yield anything of clinical interest. "We can increase that, of course, but you must be careful of tolerance."

David asked all the obvious questions about prognosis and cause, which Becker deflected like a guardian of the mysteries. The research had isolated a certain brain chemical that sufferers lacked, though what the chemical did and what caused its lack, to hear Becker tell it, were still matters of purest speculation.

"The brain is a territory more mysterious than Mars, Mr. Pace. The precise mechanisms are not always understood."

David wasn't sure what exactly he had expected. Something larger, certainly, more life-changing, more exculpatory, than a simple prescription, and for a drug that was a mockery, the dirty drug of ADD. A zeitgeist drug, David had always thought of it as, the kind of popular cure of the day, like blood-letting or witch burning, that required appropriate ailments to be invented for it. According to Becker, though, it had been designed exactly for this, for stimulation, its focussing effects just a matter of fluke.

Six months later David is already at twice the dose he started at, his brain awash in stimulants from the minute he awakes in the morning until he burns out at night, when the drug seems to drain from him with the finality of a gas tank going empty. What it gives him in the interim is not some unencumbered alertness but the edgy sense of being constantly goaded, prodded, to stay awake, of hovering over a pit of sleep that only the drug keeps him from being swallowed by. By now he has learned that its stimulant properties are well known, that it is a favoured pick-me-up of soccer moms fighting suburban drift and undergrads pulling all-nighters. Yet still he cannot shed the sense of stigma he associates with it, of damage, even in his own thoughts always referring to it by its generic name, methylphenidate.

For his other symptom, the loss of control, David takes nothing yet, downplaying it with Becker for fear of having his driver's licence revoked. At the outset it was no more than a flutter he'd feel in his brain stem like the brush of a wing at the back of his neck or the intimation of a blade about to fall. Now, though, it is as if a pulse moves through him that shuts his circuits down as it goes, until his body trembles with the

effort of keeping erect and he has to sit, lean into a wall, anything to catch himself. His falling sickness, he thinks of it as, like
Caesar's, though in his case not an epileptic fit but a momen-
tary paralysis, another misfiring, a malfunction of the switch
that shuts the muscles off during REM to keep the body from
acting out its dreams. It lasts only seconds, his mind awake,
aware, the whole time, but his body refusing to respond to it,
as in the dreams of car wrecks he has where his limbs go as
droopy as rubber or the dreams of being attacked, some assail-
ant plunging the knife again and again and David unable to lift
a finger. What sets it off in him, mostly, is anger, as if anger and
dream sit too close to one another in his brain.

The weather lady has come on, a pixie of a woman in a bizarre
1970s-era pantsuit whom the anchor flirts with in a forced way
as if he has been instructed to in order to boost ratings. First the
tally of the dead through pestilence and war; then the latest
word on the coming warm front. David thinks of Petronius's
spoof in the *Satyricon* of the *Acta Diurna*, the daily news sheet
out of Rome that Caesar popularized, the beginning of head-
line news. *Seventy children born at Trimalchio's estate. Slave put to
death. Fire in Pompey's gardens.*

Julia's voice reaches him from their bedroom as she starts in
on Marcus's bedtime reading. Idiot: instead of taking the clothes
upstairs to be with them, he has set himself apart again. Then,
because he isn't there, Marcus will ask if he can sleep in his
mother's bed and she will say yes, despite all her vows to break
him of the habit, so that for the thousandth time David will be
consigned to Marcus's room and the poison between him and
Julia will have a chance to seep into their fibre, into their dreams.
He can make out the dips and swells of Julia's voice as she
reads, its reassuring storytime calm, the emotion that speaks in
it having nothing to do with the words themselves yet just as

clear as they are. She has come back to herself, has come back to Marcus. He feels a rush of gratitude that Marcus has her, at least, is not utterly adrift.

What he felt in those first awful weeks after Marcus's birth, though he hardly understood it then, was fear. It was not that he hadn't wanted a child, that it hadn't been part of the plan from the start, another step on his *cursus honorum*. But then suddenly this blackness in Julia, coming on top of a rough pregnancy in which she had bloated like a whale, hardly able to walk, to sleep, do anything. He had thought of the birth as when some sort of normalcy would return, when Julia would come back to herself, to him, when they'd have sex again, talk, when the marriage would become—in a way it hadn't been yet, not really—a joint enterprise. Instead it was as if she had dropped off a cliff. She couldn't get the baby to latch to her breast, despite all the instruction they'd been given, so that within days her ducts were infected and they'd had to switch to formula. Then it was nearly two weeks before she'd allowed David's family to come, something unheard of. Nelda, Danny's wife, took Marcus in her arms and it seemed the first time he'd been held with a mother's sureness.

David wasn't so infantile at the time as to have used any of this as an excuse for Susan Morales. That wasn't anything he'd sought out or planned, wasn't even really something he'd wanted except perhaps in some left-over lizard corner of his brain. He had got his philandering out of his system before he had married—it was one of the things that had appealed to him about marriage, the thought of all the work it would spare him, the juggling and half-lies, the appeasements, the roller coaster of living through the same precipitous arc of emotions again and again. His only lapse had been a conference hook-up a few months after he and Julia had married that he'd fallen into almost out of habit, as if he had suddenly found himself driving a car he'd forgotten he'd sold. It had been a foolish risk, but if anything he had only felt closer to Julia afterwards, relieved he could put his old life behind him.

Morales was different. The worst of it was that she had come to his office looking for Julia, a new hire who had wanted to work with her but was shy of getting in touch while she was on maternity leave. David ought to have sent her packing; the last thing Julia needed then was to have to hold the hand of some fawning acolyte. But something about her held him—her looks or her youth, the energy of her, like things he was looking at now in a rear-view mirror; her name, perhaps, something as simple as that. He made a joke about it and she laughed, with a Latin openness.

"She's a little sleep deprived right now," David told her. "But I'm sure she'd love to hear from you as soon as her brain's back in working order."

If she had turned and gone that might have been the end of it. Instead she lingered, maybe simply glad of the chance for conversation, for connection. Something caught her eye on his bookshelf and her jaw dropped, as literally as that.

"You wrote that book! The one all the feminists hated."

"Guilty as charged."

"It's so funny the two of you are married. Your wife's work is so different."

There seemed only the logistics to work out after that. A drink in the graduate lounge; the offer of a lift to her apartment; the lies they had to tell themselves at each step in order to get to the next one. She lived in one of the towers of the high-rise ghetto that surrounded the campus. David had offered to pass on to Julia some offprints of her work and he followed her in to fetch them, past the security cameras in the denuded lobby, up through the fetor of ethnic cooking as the elevator took them to her floor. Still lying to themselves even then, still pretending, though maybe the matter had been ordained the minute she had set foot in his office, by her laugh or her smile or her smell, the split-second transmission that scientists said was all it took.

He feels a tingle at his neck and turns to see that Julia is standing behind him.

"Did something happen today?"

He picks up the TV remote and starts surfing.

"Happen where?"

"At the zoo, for Christ's sake. When you were out. He seems scared."

He is looking for turns, the places where he'll be safe.

"Scared of what?"

"I don't know, you tell me! Can you turn that fucking thing off?"

He knows all their battlefields by now, the thickets and swamps, the paths that lead forward and those that only circle back again and again. In a minute they will be shouting, though a thousand times they have vowed not to do this, not in Marcus's hearing. The same accusations, the same gutter language, the same stopping short of anything that matters.

"Don't you see how he plays you?" Continuing to flit through the channels. "Instead of it occurring to you that he just wants to sleep in our bed, right away I'm the bad guy."

What he was afraid of, when Marcus was born, was himself. Not Julia's deadness but his own, the sense of having been stumbling forward like a sleepwalker, wandering deeper and deeper into country he hadn't the vaguest notion how to find his way through. Not knowing, suddenly, what the point of a marriage was, of a family. All the compromises and failures and fights, the constant sense of not measuring up, and then this nightmarish child thrown into the mix, this judgment, this monster of need.

At least Susan Morales was something he understood. Being with her was like every relationship he had had before Julia only more so, dirty and fierce, precipitous, insufficient. The furtive calls and the missed ones, the constant endings and beginning again, the times he showed up unexpectedly at her apartment in the middle of the day and fucked her the instant he was inside the door and the times he didn't show at all. Her always pretending how little she needed from him and his always giving her less than that, until it was hard to tell desire from desperation. A mistake, in other words, from beginning to end, mesmerizing in its destructiveness even while it seemed to hold out the promise of the real life that real life made impossible.

He cut it off definitively within a matter of months. By then this woman who had struck him as so fearless when he'd met her, so self-sufficient, appeared to be dissolving before his eyes. She had never got in touch with Julia, of course. To David she'd shrugged the matter off as more her department head's idea than her own. Yet almost at once she began to feel stalled in her work, missed submission deadlines for conference presentations, became anxious over her teaching, began questioning everything, her accent, her weight, her cooking, her clothes. It was as if he had inadvertently pricked the heart of her, caused some small rupture that was deflating her, bit by bit, to nothing. He didn't tell her it was for her own good that he was ending things, but for once he actually felt that. Later, though, when he learned she had failed her first-year probation and been let go, all he felt was relief. By then the true horror of what he'd done had dawned on him. He had shit in the nest, the unforgivable thing. Each time he went home to his wife, to his son, he carried with him this fecal stink.

Julia is still hovering behind him.

"Do you know how fucking exhausting this is, David?"

He needs the shouting to start, for them to veer off to their familiar set pieces, but instead her voice is hollowed out, as if she has reached the bottom of something.

"I just want to know if anything happened. For Marcus's sake. Just the truth for once, that's all I'm asking. Don't make me beg for it."

This is always the risk, that one of them will step out of the loop.

"And for the record," she adds, "he's in his own bed."

Just the truth. If only he could give her that. If he could get down on his knees and make a clean breast of everything, every failure, every lie, every part of himself he has hidden away. If he could be naked before her, the way he had felt for a time at the outset, what had bound him to her, that she had seen to his core and hadn't refused him.

David's head is pounding, his blood is.

"I'll tell you what's fucking exhausting," he says. "That it's always a witch hunt with you, it's always about scoring points. The truth is the last thing you want!"

The shouting has started.

The irony of history is that it is already over. The crucial moment when disaster might have been averted has already passed. Pompey at Pharsalus. Caesar setting out for the Senate House on the Ides of March.

When the lies started: before he and Julia had so much as set eyes on one another, both of them primed for exactly the mistake the other one was for them. At the heart of the mistake, like some stray bit of viral DNA, some slow-acting carcinogen, was Edward Dirksen. It was under his reign as department head that David had been hired, back before his book had come out and he was still enough of an unknown quantity to have been grateful for the job; it was under him that Julia was brought in for a postdoc a couple of years later, coming back from graduate work in England trailing every sort of accolade after having been a star pupil of Dirksen's as an undergrad. The rumour was that he'd actually had designs on her back then, but David couldn't credit it, couldn't picture Dirk, still a bachelor at forty, with all the sex appeal of a church deacon, ever girding himself for that sort of sexual adventurism.

She was the one who had started things, coming up to him at a beginning-of-term meet-and-greet with the awkward forthrightness of someone determined not to be cowed, long legs stretching like delinquents from her sensible skirt to her sensible shoes. By then he had already spotted her in the department, each time she came in a flutter passing through the place like a shift in the air that signalled a turn in the weather.

"I take it you're Mr. Masculine History."

"I hope this means you're a feminist." Her hair, which she wore long and loose in those days, flashed from dark to red whenever it caught the light. "It would be about time in this department. Even the girls here are old boy."

"What about you? You don't exactly strike me as old boy."

"I guess that makes me your only hope."

In the corner of his eye he had picked out Dirksen making the rounds of the room, playing the host, and yet with the plane of his body half-trained the whole time on Julia.

"I heard Dirksen fought pretty hard to get you back here. I mean, you could have gone anywhere."

She flushed as if he had slapped her.

"I came back because I wanted to come home, actually." She had shut right down. "Dirksen didn't have anything to do with it."

Who knew why he even made the effort after that. Her own stock was as old boy as it came, her father some sort of backroom kingmaker, with a house on the mountain and a pedigree that went back to the Conquest, and her own credentials all of the right sort, with none of the taint that went with David's brand of success. For every good review David had got in the mainstream press for *Masculine History* there had been a snide one in the academic journals, deriding his scholarship or his conclusions or his prose or dismissing his theory as ersatz postmodernism on the one hand or mere reactionism on the other.

He sent her flowers after the dig about Dirksen. It was the sort of gesture she might have felt obliged to scoff at, yet he saw how she brightened despite herself when their paths crossed again.

"Next time instead of sending flowers, just don't act like an asshole."

He made a point of taking matters slowly with her. Coffee in the middle of the day at dingy places in the student ghetto. A couple of foreign films at the Cinémathèque. Trying to avoid the usual crash-and-burn, not daring to so much as touch her, hazard a kiss, until some signal was clear. What surprised him was how much he *liked* her, how unfamiliar this felt, as if being with women until then had been simply a matter of compulsion. They had more in common than he'd expected—food, films, a zero tolerance for pretension; dead parents. Her mother had died the year before she'd gone overseas, around the time his own father had.

"She essentially drank herself to death. All my father's fault, of course. You'll understand when you meet him."

He hung on the word "when."

"With my father it was cigarettes."

"Looks like substance abuse runs in our families. Remind me never to have children with you."

Then on an overnight trip for a book event he ended up bedding a graduate student who'd been assigned to look after him. Nothing to do with Julia, he told himself, but when he met up with her for supper on his return it was as if the smell of the woman was still on him.

"You know, I'm not sure I've got this straight." In a tone he hadn't heard from her before, diamond-tipped, glittery with sarcasm. "Are we just being collegial here, is that what this is? Because if meanwhile you're off fucking every bit of tail you can get your hands on, I'd like to know. Just in case someone asks."

He felt sure if he told her the truth she would throw him over then and there. For once he was frightened. For once he didn't feel he already had an eye on the exit. When he'd slept with the girl, it was Julia he'd pictured.

"It's not as if I haven't thought of you every night since we met. Let's just say I know myself by now. That there's patterns I fall into."

"Well." He could feel her relenting. "It's not like all the choices I've made have exactly been stellar ones either."

She was the one who had ended up making a confession then. It turned out that the rumours about her and Dirksen were true: there had been a brief dalliance between them in the summer after she'd graduated. David could hardly believe it. From her terse description of it he gathered it hadn't come to much more than a couple of half-abortive mercy fucks, but still he was floored. He couldn't get the thought from his head of Dirksen's fumbling exertions, of her allowing them.

"You have to promise you'll never breathe a word of this, not to anyone. For his sake. Something like this could wreck his career."

That was the night she came home with him, with these things that shouldn't have mattered, that he should have been able to laugh at, banging around in his head. He couldn't give a shape to the emotion pumping through him, jealousy and guilt but also a kind of outrage whose object he couldn't make out.

"I feel so foolish about it now," she'd admitted. "But at the time he seemed different. Promising, in a way. A bit like you, really."

He let that sit.

"I guess you ruined him."

But she hadn't caught his tone.

"I sometimes wondered that. He was so mortified afterwards. We both were, really."

Then she was there with him in his apartment. All the days and weeks of anticipation, of getting to know her, seemed now only like obstacles he had to overcome. He made a show of being rough with her because he thought that was what she wanted, feeling the whole time that he was playing at being himself. Afterwards she lay with her face turned away from him into the pillow, finally naked next to him, as beautiful as he had hoped, yet still somehow obscure to him.

It took him an instant to realize she was crying.

"What is it? What's wrong?"

"Fucking hell," she said, letting out a laugh. "I swore I wouldn't do this."

"Do what?"

"All of this. Sleep with someone I work with. With someone like you."

*Someone like you.* A bounder, a striver, a climber, a cad. Someone in whom the impulse to cut and run was as instinctive as breathing. Whose only ethic was the practical one of what worked. He heard all of this and felt cut to the quick and somehow set free. Felt seen, in a way he seldom had.

"The worst of it," she said, "is that I practically had to beg you for it."

He would have liked to have told her everything then, every doubt and fear, every hatred, every callous act.

"It won't be the last time you'll beg." He pressed up against her and they fucked again, harder, and this time it seemed that the obstacles were kicked clear.

All the things he had planned to tell her back then. His father, his brother, his women, his crimes. How precarious everything felt to him sometimes, the whole edifice of his life, nothing that a good solid blow wouldn't shatter to its foundations. How all his success seemed built on sand, on a book that was just a rehash of the same tired sources and a theory that had started out as a joke, a poke in the eye of the sacred cows of the day that he and Greg Borovic had come up with on one of their late-night benders.

Back then he thought he had all the time in the world to speak of these things. Ten years on, he is still waiting for the right opening.

They are both shouting now, David has managed that, has hit the right buttons, inching their volume up bit by bit until they have drowned out the TV and filled the room. This is what he has turned Julia into, this shouter, this shrew. What she has made herself for his benefit, her way of giving him, again and again, a second chance, because the alternative would be to see through him.

"Don't you see how you do it? How every word to him you're turning him against me? *I'm sure it was closed if your dad says it was!* You're basically telling him I'm a liar."

"Are you serious? Are you even listening to how ludicrous you sound?"

"Don't turn this back on me. I'm not an idiot. The place was fucking closed, full stop! Not because Daddy said it was."

What keeps him going in this is that the anger is real, that there is always this pressure chamber of resentments and hurts he can tap into instantly, until the rage is all he sees. Until he feels he will burst with it. That he has a right to, as if any emotion this violent must be justified.

They both become aware at the same moment that Marcus is standing at the foot of the stairs. Julia takes him in her arms so quickly that there is no role for David except as the perpetrator, exactly the one he deserves.

"I'm sorry, my little munchkin." She is close to tears. "It's nothing. We didn't mean to scare you."

"You were fighting."

David sees it as soon as she takes hold of him, how much fear is still in him.

"My God, you're trembling. What is it, Marcus? What is it? What are you scared of?"

David catches a look from him that is like a trapped animal's. Those split seconds of terror on the highway are in it, but also the understanding that he must say nothing, that that is his father's unspoken imperative. How is it that the incident has remained so vivid in his five-year-old brain when it was so fleeting, so near to incoherence, that even David, afterwards, had to struggle to make sense of it?

"Jesus Christ, David, he's terrified, what did you do to him? What is it, Marcus? Tell Mommy."

He is just a child. None of this, David can see, is about manipulation or piling up grievances, only about fear. About not knowing which way to jump. Which side is safer.

Any second now, he will have to choose.

"Cut the hysterics, for God's sake. He's probably afraid because we're fighting like animals. If you want to know the truth, he was upset because I didn't buy him a plastic penguin or some bloody thing he wanted at the zoo. That's what all this is about. That's what the big trauma is, that he didn't get his fix. Another addiction you've managed to pass on to him. Every outing I take him on, that's all he cares about, what we're going to buy at the gift shop."

He is trying to veer off again toward the familiar, the well-worn. Except that Marcus knows nothing of these patterns, of this collusion. He only knows what he knows.

"It wasn't that," he says. "It wasn't the gift shop."

David feels the same sense of foreboding he'd felt on the highway, sees the next moments unfolding before his mind's eye as if they have already happened.

"What was it, Marcus? Tell Mommy. Don't be afraid."

"Look," David says, "what's the point of this exactly? Haven't we traumatized the kid enough for one day?"

"Tell me, Marcus. What was it?"

An awful pause. There is a flash of fear in Marcus's eyes, and David can't bring himself to try to stop him anymore.

"Dad fell asleep."

For an instant, Julia is confused. Clearly this is nothing like what she was expecting.

"Fell asleep where? What do you mean?"

Before Marcus has had a chance to answer, David can see understanding beginning to dawn on her.

"Fell asleep where?" With more urgency now. "In the car?"

Marcus's eyes have clouded. He seems suddenly to have realized that no side, after all, is safe.

"In the car, Marcus? While he was driving?"

Marcus won't look at her.

"I thought so, but Daddy said no."

"But what happened? Did he close his eyes? Did he go off the road?"

"There was a noise. But Daddy said no."

"I hope you're enjoying this, Julia. Talk about traumatizing."

"He says you fell asleep! Where was this? On the expressway?"

"I didn't fall asleep, for Christ's sake. I got distracted and hit the rumble strip. The noise must have scared him."

"So why didn't you bring it up?"

"What, that I hit the rumble strip?"

"You knew something was bothering him!"

"Look, I thought it was the gift shop. I didn't realize the thing had affected him so much. I hadn't even thought of it again till he brought it up now."

"But he says you fell asleep. Why would he lie?"

"He didn't say I fell asleep, you did!" He puts this so forcefully he almost convinces himself it is the truth. "This is how you operate. You let him know what you want him to say, then you get him to say it."

"Don't twist this, David! Did you fall asleep? Why would he think that?"

"Maybe he was sleeping himself and the noise woke him up! He's a kid, for Christ's sake. Kids get confused."

"He hasn't fallen asleep in the car since he was two. Not once."

"That's such bullshit! He was sleeping when we got home. It shows how much you know your own son."

He can still get to her this way when he needs to, can still touch the spot in her that is afraid, above all, of being a bad mother.

"Is that true, Marcus? Did you fall asleep?"

Marcus shrugs, stares at the ground, seeming to sense the trap David has set for him.

"Why are you making such a big deal of this?" David says. He has introduced enough doubt, perhaps, to bring them back from the edge. "Why are you putting him on the spot?"

Julia takes the boy in her arms again, holding him with a fierceness that brings the moment on the highway crashing to the front of David's thoughts again in all its enormity.

"Let's get you back upstairs," she says. "We'll put you in Mommy's bed. Just for tonight."

David feels no sense of reprieve when she is gone, only of pointless deferral. Sooner or later, even despite herself, even wanting, like David, just to forget, to move on, she will tease from Marcus the telling detail from which the rest will follow. The pills. The stopped car. It is how her mind works, what she does. Right from when he first knew her he has feared this skill in her, how she unlocks whole histories from what appear the smallest irrelevances.

The TV is still on. All this time it has kept flashing through its own separate stream of images like some oblivious house guest, carrying on its self-absorption while the house comes down around it. A deer stares out from a car ad and David feels tears well up in him, he hardly knows why. Another misfiring. They happen more and more, these emotions that surge in him though he can't trace their source, the memories that shimmer yet stay out of reach. It is as if they are there but the bridge to them has been scuttled. Or he reaches a spot where there are too many turnings and no way to choose among them, to distinguish what is real from what he has read or seen in a movie, what has actually happened to him from what he has dreamed. The breakdown of borders.

Becker had given him a copy of his sleep-study report, half a dozen pages of jargon and statistics and charts that for weeks

David resisted putting his mind to. He didn't want to know, didn't want to make his affliction more real by paying attention to it. Now, bit by bit, he has begun to inform himself. He has been surprised at how little he has known about sleep given how much time he has spent at it, though even the experts, it turns out, don't have much of a clue. One thing is sure: it is infinitely more complex than David has imagined. He has always thought of sleep as a kind of zero to waking's one, with the occasional dream thrown in like static, when it is a place as varied and shifting and strange as the ocean floor, moving through permutations that have as little to do with each other as with waking itself. REM and NREM; theta sleep and delta sleep; the alpha flatlines and jagged spindles and K-complex spikes that are like the creak and moan of the brain shutting the door to the outer world. Out of these a shape emerges that is called the architecture of sleep. As if sleep were an apartment building or boarding house, a warren of different rooms each with its own grizzled denizen keeping his own hours and his own rules, the wired dreamer in the attic, the plodding slow-wave oaf in the mouldering basement.

That is what David sees now when he thinks of sleep, these secret lives going on in him that his waking self has known almost nothing of. Except suddenly these other selves are on the move, leaving their curtains open, their doors, shuffling ceaselessly through the halls until it seems they must burst out into the light of day. Sometimes as he is falling asleep he hears them trudging into his room, sees the shadow of them at his bedside, feels the weight of them as they settle onto his chest to take him over like succubi, like alien abductors. He tries to flail, to scream, defend himself, but cannot move.

The terror he feels then is real.

From upstairs, silence. Perhaps Julia isn't returning, has had enough of him or has simply fallen asleep next to Marcus.

Another throb of emotion: how he had fought her, in the first years, over having Marcus in bed with them. They would spoil him, he said; they would never be free of him; they would stunt him in some irreparable way. When the truth was that those were the purest times for him, Marcus's little body between them smelling of milk and sleep. Hardly daring to give in to the love in him then, afraid for it, that it was too fragile a thing to risk exposing.

It doesn't bear thinking about.

He takes up the remote again and surfs. Shopping channel. Cooking channel. Family channel. History. What passes for history these days: reality shows, conspiracy theories, proofs of alien abductions or of biblical truth. Animations of battle scenes where squirts of blood spatter the screen. Doomsday documentaries: this one, a countdown of likely scenarios—pestilence, war—for the end of days.

David feels an unpleasant grinding in him like a gear not quite slipping into place. It is the thought of his book, the new one. A doomsday book, in its way, one he has been planning practically since childhood, since Ostia Antica, in fact, when that same young guide who had admonished him over the piece of mosaic—really just some smooth talker the concierge at their hotel had hooked them up with, probably a cousin of his in need of quick cash—had painted a picture for David of the town's rapid decline after the fall of Rome. More than a little fanciful, it later turned out, though the image had stayed with David, of this bustling port town of hundreds of thousands reduced to ruins almost overnight. That sense of the transience of things, mysterious and bracing. How in an instant humans could revert from the civilized to the savage.

That is the book he has always wanted to write, about that reversion, not just at the fall of Rome but across all of history, like something embedded in history's DNA. He should have started in on it years ago, right after he'd finished the Augustus book, when the whole end-of-civilization rage hadn't kicked in yet and he would have been seen as a trailblazer. Instead he has wasted his time churning out stopgaps. He wouldn't have admitted it back then but the fiasco in Montreal had spooked him, exactly when he should have been bold, when he should have been striking out into new territory. Even the Augustus book, by the end, was just him playing it safe, trying to shore up his bona fides, with the result that he'd been crucified both inside the academy and out.

On the screen, they are at death by machine. Armed robots march in the background while Stephen Hawking warns in his computer voice of the day when computers will exceed humans.

Back when these so-called learning channels were still running programs of substance, one of them had actually optioned *Masculine History*. David had signed the deal only a couple of months after starting up with Julia, when it had seemed a final assurance that every problem was behind him. For once he had even managed to sustain a relationship for longer than a dirty weekend, had proved he was not just some sociopath, that he was capable of real connection. He kept waiting to grow tired of Julia, for the flight instinct to kick in, but instead he awoke every morning with the same thankfulness that he hadn't yet wrecked things. It might have been nothing more than hormones—he has read about that, how at a certain point the nesting instinct kicks in, in men as much as in women. But at the time it felt like arrival. Like coming to the end of a hard road and being able to rest.

When his father had been diagnosed at the start of his doctorate David had felt rudderless, in the grip of feelings that pulled in so many different directions he thought they would tear him apart. He had been in the midst of his comprehensives, up against deadlines for his dissertation proposal, for research funding, for the whole course of his future, yet once it was clear his father was dying, once David no longer had his defiance of him to spur him on, it felt like all volition had left him. There had been one awful night when he had wept like a child at how little his life seemed set to amount to for all his ambitions. And yet he had got through. Had managed barely into his thirties to reach a pinnacle most academics wouldn't get to in a lifetime.

With the TV deal even Julia's father finally deigned to take notice of David, inviting him and Julia to dinner. Not at his house, which David wouldn't see the inside of until after the wedding, but at his club, a fusty place downtown all oak and velour and padded leather where they were served overcooked salmon and underdone vegetables and where some months later, having failed to scare David off, her father would insist on holding the wedding reception, complete with cash bar. David had expected someone more turned out, not this barrel-chested scrapper, a big man a good three inches taller than David with a shock of white hair that looked like it had been trimmed with a weed-whacker and a plaid sports jacket a good half-century out of fashion. But he was sharp, the sort of man who dared you to underestimate him.

"Here he is, our *novus homo*," he had greeted David, what the Romans had called those striving plebes who had managed to scrounge a place among the patricians.

That was how the evening unfolded, in these smiling assaults, Julia looking on the whole time like an amused spectator. Away from her father she was scathing about him, but up close David could feel the dark lines of force that bound them.

"You'll get used to him," she said afterwards. "He just needs to claim his territory."

Julia, too, had been quick to claim her territory, right from the start giving up any pretense of hiding their relationship at work, lingering in his office, taking his arm in the halls, planting her stakes. The truth was it pleased him to be taken possession of like this. He could see they were the envy of the department, in the untouchable way of celebrities or royalty, as if there was the sort of rightness to their coming together that put aside the usual pettinesses and rancour. Then the more open they were, the sooner Julia would be free of any lingering residue of Dirksen. For his own part, Dirksen had taken the hint early on—there was no more mooning at her office door, no orbiting at a distance, just his nods and smiles and quick retreats as if he were trying to make himself invisible. David figured he had come around like everyone else had, was probably even happy for them. They were both his protégés, in a way, even David, whom Dirksen had pushed for when he'd been hired and had always shown a paternal protectiveness toward.

The television deal brought another wave of buzz around David's book and another flurry of speaking invitations, some of them from big-name universities in the States. More than once he was asked, with the sort of discretion that suggested serious intent, whether he had any plans for a move. The idea grew more compelling the more he thought about it. Even the B university back home had approached him, with an offer of a tailor-made cross-appointment. Nothing like the money he might get south of the border, but with course relief and a decent research budget.

He made a point of following up on every query and of shaking the right hands whenever he was on the road, telling himself he was merely finding out what was out there even while a part of him was already living an imagined future of doubled earnings and halved teaching loads. He didn't breathe a word of any of this in the department, not even to Julia: he had too much at stake to risk involving her at this stage, still more than two years short of tenure and with plenty of detractors who would be ready to force his hand if any rumour got out that he was thinking of jumping ship. What made sense was to wait until he had decided definitively before bringing the matter up. Maybe even to wait until he had an actual offer; it would be easy enough then to negotiate something for Julia as part of the deal. That was his secret vision, to come to her with an engagement ring in one hand and a fat offer from a prestigious American school in the other. This despite all the evidence he'd had by then of her attachment to the city, the friends she'd had since kindergarten, the old haunts she'd taken him to, her secret devotion to her insufferable father. Somehow he shut all that out, drunk with his own possibilities.

He was just on the verge of expressing interest to a couple of places when Dirksen waylaid him in the hall one day as he was coming back from class. By then Dirksen had drifted so much to the edge of David's field of vision that he had to keep reminding himself to actually take notice of him.

"I've got a student of yours in my office who wanted to see you." Smiling, a bit quizzically. "Just a small matter, I think."

David didn't think anything of it—it was just like Dirksen to take in wandering strays like that and make sure they were tended to. The student was a hulking plodder from David's Late Republic seminar who never said boo in class, sitting hunched in Dirksen's office next to a hippopotamus of a woman decked out in bangles and shawls as if she had just come from a Bedouin wedding.

"I think Maddy and his mother have a question for you about his final paper," Dirksen said, and there it sat on his desk, a big

B minus on its cover page that David had awarded it, as he recalled, only because he couldn't be bothered with the work of justifying the lower grade it actually deserved.

The woman was rummaging in her purse as if searching for some round of cheese or bottle of wine she had brought to propitiate him.

"Professor, please." She had pulled out a newspaper clipping, which she laid with great ceremony next to the essay. "I can show you."

It took David an instant to recognize the clipping as one of his own articles, a review he'd done recently for a local paper of a book on the Roman dictator Sulla. A couple of lines near the end of it had been carefully underlined in pencil.

David felt a shiver at the back of his neck.

"My son, he says you are famous. That you are writing a famous book. I tell him, he is lucky to have good professor. For good professor, he can work harder. He can learn more."

Already David was finding it difficult to follow her. What threw him off was this deference, which did not waver the whole time she was making her case.

"You see, you write, 'Good work,' only that, no mistakes. But only B minus! He is trying for lawyer, my son, on the test, is good, but here only B minus. Then I see in the newspaper, where you write, is like Maddy! If famous professor can write for the newspaper, why only B minus?"

David's temperature was rising. He wished Dirksen had had the wherewithal to spare him this. He was sick of students assuming that anything in their papers that didn't have a big red circle around it was essentially flawless. Of parents coming to beg higher grades for their unremarkable offspring in the hope of getting them into law or medicine or a Harvard MBA.

The woman was urging the newspaper clipping on him, but he wouldn't take it. Dirksen was still sitting there like a lump, his vicar's smile plastered on his face.

"I beg you, Professor. Maybe can be B plus or A. To help him for lawyer."

"You can't expect him to get a fucking A just because he copied something he probably heard me say in class!"

The woman started back as if David had made a swipe at her. In the corner of his eye, he saw Dirksen go white.

"No, Professor Pace." It was Maddy. He was the only one who looked unfazed. "I remember, I came up with the idea myself. Not that I would have if I hadn't been in your class. I mean, you're the one who taught us to think like that."

The room had started to warp and shift. He shouldn't have said *probably*, shouldn't have left room for doubt. He shouldn't have said *fucking*. He shouldn't have given shape to an accusation that hadn't even been made yet.

Dirksen was finally stirring to action.

"I think we understand your point, Mrs. Hakimi." In a soothing tone David was actually grateful for. "Why don't you let us discuss this on our own and see if we can't find a solution."

"Yes, Professor, thank you, I thank you!"

All David could see by then was a great black maw opening up before him. The matter came down to a short passage at the end of his Sulla review comparing a recent corruption scandal in the city to one in Roman times. A throwaway, really, just David acting clever, but of strikingly similar gist to an idea Maddy had developed at some length in his paper. Even the wording had echoes, David saw them at once. There was no chance Maddy had lifted the point from the review, which had come out only days earlier, after the essay had been marked and returned. One of the few margin comments David had bothered to make on the paper had singled out exactly the passage in question. "Great analogy," he'd written. "Good work."

David sat staring at the evidence after the duo had gone, unable to take it in.

"There's no way that kid came up with this on his own! I distinctly remember discussing it in class. Either that or in a private meeting with him."

But already he was scrambling, contradicting himself, until he wasn't even sure anymore what the truth was.

Dirksen, to his credit, hadn't expressed the least hint of judgment in any of this, not even over David's outburst.

"Let's not lose our heads." David could feel himself clutching at Dirksen's calm. "It sounds like all they're looking for is a grade review. Why don't you let me give the paper a read and we'll see if we can't find some way for everyone to come out happy."

When Dirksen called him back into his office the next day, however, all his assurance was gone. One of the boy's other professors, it turned out, a Renaissance witch David had never got along with, had got wind of the dispute and had pressed Dirksen for details.

Dirksen wouldn't meet David's eye.

"I held her off, of course, but you have to understand this complicates things a bit, there'll have to be some sort of follow-up. The boy must have talked to her after he left here. I suppose if you'd given him a bit more hope." All the judgment Dirksen had withheld the previous day seemed there now. "The important thing is just to put your case together so we can keep this out of your tenure file. To spare you any awkwardness down the road."

David wanted to scream. He already knew by then that he had nothing to prove he was in the right, no class notes that might clear him, no record of a private meeting. Not even his own

confidence: the truth was, he'd reread the paper and been surprised, stunned really, at how cogent it had suddenly sounded.

Over the smallest thing—a couple of lines, it could happen
to anyone—he was looking at ruin. Word would get out, it
always did, and all his options would vanish, and meanwhile
the matter would sit in his file ready to bite him again when he
came up for tenure. Maybe some zealot would have managed
to dig up dirt on *Masculine History* by then and David would be
confirmed as a serial plagiarist, lucky to land a sessional job in
the back of beyond.

The worst of it would be the humiliation. The look on his
colleagues' faces. On Julia's. The smirk on her father's.

He was ready to beg, even to Dirksen.

"Ed, you know how it'll look if something like this gets out.
The kind of stain it can leave."

Some shadow flitted across Dirksen's face, of compassion
maybe. For some reason David thought he was thinking of
Julia, of his own transgression.

"Let's not get ahead of ourselves." Forcing a smile. "I'm sure
in a couple of weeks the whole matter will be behind you."


David is falling, scrambling for handholds, hurtling toward
solid ground or just the realization that there is no solid ground,
only space without end. Then he opens his eyes with a jerk: he
has nodded off. Five minutes? Twenty? He can't say. When he
drops out like this his head fills with such a rush of images
he has the sense that months might be passing, whole lives.
Another of his symptoms, that his dreams light up like the
Milky Way the instant he closes his eyes as if all along they have
been reeling there at the back of his thoughts, waiting for dark.

On the Doomsday Channel the countdown has reached
number one: death by warm front. Animals changing their

habitats; flowers blooming out of season. Hurricanes, forest fires, floods. Great sheets of ice fall into the sea while satellite maps show Florida, London, Bangladesh disappearing beneath the rising tides. The stuff of nightmare. Of history.

The irony of history: that in the long run, it hardly matters. Ice caps spread and recede, continents drift, tumours the size of the moon split away and it is all just the blink of an eye on the way to final extinction. There is something comforting in that, liberating. In their deepest selves, David suspects, apocalypse is what people long for, to be freed of all caring, all restraint.

What he'd felt when he'd left Dirksen's office was something like that freedom, a rush like heroin going through him or poison, the sense of his ties to the world being cut. The worst would happen and all the disguises he had made for himself, the careful lies, would fall away. Even Julia: this wasn't something she could forgive him for, not really, he had already convinced himself of that. She needed him to be the golden boy, the star, not this blemished thing.

Then the instant he'd accepted the worst, the way forward was suddenly clear. All he had to do was act, to stop his dithering and forge ahead with the plans he had already been setting in motion for months. Now, at a distance of years, he suspects he might have invented the entire crisis just to galvanize himself into action, imagining himself at a precipice when chances were that the whole matter would have blown over even if he had done nothing. In any event he had proved Dirksen right, in the space of a couple of weeks managing to put the whole fiasco behind him, on his own terms. By then he had proposed to Julia and had brought her around to the idea of a move; he had quit his job and landed a new one. With his resignation there was no real point to any sort of inquisition beyond the practical one of the boy's grade, which, without the least qualm, he bumped up to the A his mother had asked for.

David had been proud then of how well he had arranged things, had thought himself bold, the master of his fate. He had managed to talk Julia into the move through a blend of seduction and coercion, taking her out to a resort in the Townships for a weekend getaway with a big diamond ring in tow and making her promises and telling her lies, framing the move as a matter of getting better terms for the both of them, of catching the tide. By then he already had a firm offer in hand from the university back home, the only place he had called, in fact, using the interest from the States as leverage but never really following up on any of it. This was his concession to Julia, was what he told himself, just as he told himself that his strongarming—that he hadn't hesitated, for instance, to put her tryst with Dirksen into the mix, probably what had broken her in the end—was all to the greater good of their relationship. Now, though, he sees that he was just using Julia as a cover for his own fears. That what would truly have been bold back then would have been to be honest, to have shown her the whole of himself as he had wanted to from the start.

He still remembers the stupid pleasure he took announcing to Dirksen that he was leaving.

"You have a good job here, David. Don't throw it away."

Certain then that he was making the right choice, that he was averting exactly the sort of plodding mediocrity Dirksen himself embodied. Yet ever since the run-in with him the year before David has been haunted by the feeling there was something he'd missed. More than once he has dreamed of being with Dirksen in his office again, everything the same, the tidy desk, the ordered shelves, yet more fraught, as if layered over with all the things David never knew that he knew, the deception and self-deception, the animal reflex, unavailable to the conscious mind, that is ninety per cent of every act. Dirksen, too, is amorphous in this way, himself and not, some question hanging between them that is never spoken but is like the very air they breathe, ubiquitous, forgettable, life-and-death.

David doesn't know what to make of these revisitings. Since the onset of his disorder his dreams have grown increasingly pressing and vivid, yet if there is some insight they are trying to impart, David has yet to piece it out. From the sleep literature he has gathered that the thinking on dreams is as all over the map as on sleep itself, that Freud was utterly mistaken in them or only slightly so, that they are merely the brain's desperate attempts to make sense of its own chemical twitches during sleep or a kind of spawning ground for consciousness itself. That they have something to do with firming up memories though in a way that subtly changes them, adding neural links that shift their associative streams according to a logic beyond the conscious mind's reach. All night long, perhaps, this secret reconstruction work is going on in David's head, his nighttime selves rejigging the experiences that his daytime one regards as the very stuff of his life. To what end? To make better sense of them? Or simply to fit them to the lie of what he thinks of as himself?

David had never really suspected Dirksen's motives back then, never wondered why he had called him into his own office rather than sending the boy to David's, whether he was as much in the dark as David was about what was coming or already knew the noose the boy's mother would dangle and sat calmly waiting until David had put his neck in it. Even the story of the other professor who had come to him could have been pure invention. David had stolen his woman, after all, and knew things that could have destroyed him. Not that Dirksen was the type who could ever have schemed so brazenly, but then who knew what under-selves of his own he employed to hold intact the smiling innocent he no doubt believed himself.

David wonders now if he would ever have proposed to Julia at all if Dirksen hadn't been a factor. When he did, actually getting down on one knee to give her the ring, Julia's face cycled through a dozen different emotions in an instant.

"You've got to be kidding! Pace the player is proposing? Let me get my camera! Who would believe it?"

In the first years of their marriage Julia used to tell this story with that same mordant good humour, as if this enterprise they had embarked on had had exactly the sort of grand beginning that boded well. Eventually her version of things overwrote David's own until his memories of the weekend faded to mere impression. All that sticks out for him now with any vividness is a single image, of some animal crashing through the winter deadwood behind them as they were walking through the woods and Julia half-turned with a look of dread that for a split second seemed directed at him.

The sound of footsteps.

"What kills me is that you thought I'd never notice. That you could just keep putting me off with the same stupid excuses."

The doomsday show is winding down. Images of abandoned cities, of empty highways, of desert and waste. The earth without people.

"What kills me is that you'd lie about it as if it were some kind of threat to your precious manhood. That that's more important to you than your own son."

"If you'd noticed," he says, "why didn't you ever bring it up?"

"For fuck's sake, David. Is that really how this is supposed to work?"

On the TV, a view of the earth from space that gradually pulls back to take in the moon, the other planets, the Milky

Way, as the screen fades to black. Against the blackness, a man-on-the-street voiceover. *We might be the lucky ones, in a way. We'll get to be there at the end.*

Julia picks up the remote and kills the power.

"You don't know how close I am right now to just walking out the door with him."

"Please don't dramatize for once. Don't make me out to be some kind of monster."

"What are you, then? Tell me. Because sometimes I look at you and I don't have a clue. I really don't."

"It's just a sleep disorder, Julia, not a heroin addiction. It's not like I can't control it."

"So it's true, then. You fell asleep. Christ, David. Jesus fucking Christ."

He sees himself through the prism of her own horror and suddenly can hardly make sense of himself. The truth is that driving home from his late nights at the university he has drifted off any number of times, even now with his meds. And yet has persisted in the notion that he is in control. That he is safe.

"I didn't say I fell asleep. Don't twist things."

"So what is it, then? Did you or didn't you? Ten fucking years I've been waiting for one honest word from you. Here's your chance."

"Don't do this, Julia."

"Did you fall asleep? Yes or no?"

He should never have given her the least opening.

"It's always the same with you, isn't it? It's always about making me feel like shit."

"You risked his *life*. Do you understand that? Who does that to his son?"

"Don't start high-grounding me because of your own garbage. I'm the one who's been waiting ten years, if it comes to that. It's like every fuck-up of yours is a payback, the house, your job, even our son. Do you remember what you were like? I swear, every time I went to work I was afraid you were going to drop him in front of a subway. Talk about monsters."

"Thank God I had you to cover for me. Thank God you had my back."

"Don't rewrite history, Julia. I was the one who had to feed him, who had to change him, who had to walk around with him for hours when he wouldn't stop crying because you were off in one of your zombie states. Let's try to stick to the truth."

"The truth? Are you serious? Is this really where you want to take a stand? Are you that much of an asshole? There are a lot of things I've been willing to forget, believe me, but not this one. Whatever little scandal it was that you were hiding when we moved here, for instance. Or whatever little trysts you've had on the road. All the passes you've expected me to give you for the sake of your bloody career when you know as much as I do you've just been spinning your wheels ever since we moved here. But not this one. This one takes the cake, David, that the best you have to offer for what a good parent you've been is that when I needed you most you were off fucking some junior lecturer. Am I understanding you, David? Is that what you mean by the truth? And then all these years you've had the gall to go on about how I've abandoned my career. You *fucked* my career, David, that's what happened to it. You fucked it."

The room recedes. He has the impression again of seeing himself from the outside, not as the person who has managed to rise up every morning all these years as if his life had a semblance of normalcy and meaning but as some despicable stranger, a scoundrel, a beast.

"There's your truth for you, David. If you ask me it looks like shit. That's what I'm covered in every day. And yet I still keep thinking you'll change, if not for me then at least for your son. But you'd rather kill him than change. That's who you are."

David sees Marcus then, watching them again from the top of the stairs. He has heard everything. Years from now, this day, this night, will still be emblazoned in him.

He wants Julia to stop.

"It's like we're just burdens to you! We're just things that get in the fucking way. In the way of what, David? What is it you want?"

What he wants is to scream, to throttle her, anything to make her stop. To be free of this part of him he has never asked for, has never understood, for whom all of this, his marriage, his home, his child, is a living death.

"Why are you still even here, David? Why?"

He is on his feet, needing to smash something, flee, though he feels the flutter at the back of his neck and then the knife drops and he is falling. Inertia keeps him pitching forward, a dead slab of flesh, to upend the laundry, the coffee table, the DVD rack, the TV, a great flurry of destruction.

*Fuck, fuck, fuck,* he howls, though all that comes out is a wordless yammer.

"What is *wrong* with you?" No trace of sympathy in her voice, of any connection. "What is *wrong* with you?"

When he hits the floor it is only his body that stops, the rest of him continuing to hurtle out into empty space.

## Fluoxetine

DAVID STANDS ON THE back terrace of his brother's new house looking out to a yard that is the size of a park, and is landscaped like one, with rocky knolls and a pond, a circular greenhouse, a stand of trucked-in twenty-year-old evergreens that must have cost five, ten thousand a pop. Danny has cheated code on the fencing by topping it with a good two and a half feet of tight-weave trellis, so that all that is visible beyond it are the upper boughs of his neighbours' own trophy trees and the upper gables of their equally monstrous houses.

In the middle of the yard is one of those circus-sized trampolines that have become the suburban rage, Marcus hovering beside it watching Danny's two boys show off their acrobatics. He is all angle and bone now, thin as a Holocaust survivor, and as far as David can tell without physical skills of any sort.

David glances at his watch.

"Marcus, don't just stand there. Jump on!"

David's mother sits straight-backed and silvern on a padded lounge chair looking as out of place as Marcus does. Not for her the villas of the north, with their deserted sidewalk-less streets, their lunar silence, far from the bustle and grind. David's father had built a place out here in the first wave of immigrant exodus, but she had sold it within weeks of his death and moved back to the city.

She is staring out hawk-eyed at Marcus. Any minute now, David can feel it, she will start in on one of her rants.

He checks his watch again.

"For Christ's sake, David, we've still got the whole afternoon." He has had to endure the humiliation of catching a ride with her here. A court order prevents him from driving on a highway with Marcus. "Anyway, what can she do if you're late, call the police?"

"It's not worth the energy, Ma. Believe me."

"Each time you give in you show you're weak. And she takes more."

She's losing it, is what it is, thinks she's the matriarch in one of those TV series about the mob or Imperial Rome.

"It's called family law, Ma."

Ever since the divorce a contempt has come into his mother as if this were the greatest failure for a man, to lose his woman. She was always the one who had *got* him when he was young, who had shared his own sense of ambition for himself. Now, every word from her has some dagger in it.

"What you never understood is she's just like her father. There's only one way to deal with people like that. To show strength."

David holds his tongue.

Danny comes out of the house flourishing a tray of bruschetta. Even now, into their forties, something flinches in

David whenever he lays eyes on his brother. To look at them you would never know they are twins, Danny a good six inches shorter than him and with a slightly stunted look as if his body had turned in on itself. Nearly two pounds separated them at birth. The story was that David had tried to starve Danny in the womb, like those animals that killed off their siblings to boost their own survival odds.

"Davie, you get the tour yet? Ma, did you show him around?"

"Show him what? We just got here."

It has taken David nearly a year to get around to seeing the place. He was expecting the usual ersatz monumentalism, some big-box eyesore built to within an inch of its lot lines, festooned with arches and electrocoated in ceramic. Instead he has found something of an entirely different order. He did a double take when his mother pulled up to the place, the facade a complicated fretwork of cantilevered stone and wooden beams and two-storey windows like something out of Frank Lloyd Wright.

"This is Danny's?"

"You'd know if you ever came out here."

What David can't get over is that his brother has had the vision for such a place. Before this he was living in a three-bedroom bungalow near their mother's condo in the north of the city that was the essence of the second-generation dead end, crammed with children and memorabilia and too-heavy furnishings.

"Let me get you a beer, Davie. I've got a nice local label, you're gonna like it."

"Think I'll pass for now."

"What's the big deal? It's not like you're driving."

He can't tell if Danny is mocking him or just being literal. No doubt their mother has already passed on to him some convoluted version of David's disorder from the bare-bones one David has had to give her to explain his need for a ride.

"It's because you sit at a desk all day instead of getting your hands dirty," was her analysis. "Your father used to get by on five, six hours of sleep every night. Then in the day, he did what he had to."

David's eye keeps going back to Marcus. Always when he looks at him now he sees only deficiency, all the things about him that need fixing. Always when he is with him he feels the same impatience, that he is waiting for their time together to truly begin in some way or maybe simply for it to be over, he hardly knows which.

Jamie, the older boy, grabs hold of his little brother and makes as if to toss him on top of Marcus. Marcus flinches and Jamie pulls short at the last instant, laughing.

*Asshole.*

Danny is nodding at the patio tiles.

"What do you think of that stone, Davie? Ever see anything like it?"

It is all David can do not to march out and wring the boy's neck.

"What is it, kryptonite or something?"

"It's local marble, if you can believe it. From just north of here. Used to be big once but you have to look for it now. We bought a little quarry of it a couple of years ago. Like Carrara was for Augustus, right? I was thinking of that when I bought the place, about what you said in your book. How he changed Rome from a city of wood into one of marble. That stuck with me."

David is taken off guard. So Danny has read one of his books. Has read the second one, several hundred copies of which David had had to toss into the recycling when he moved out of the house because he couldn't even give them away.

He makes a show of looking at the stone, salmon coloured with streaks of grey, but can't manage to form an opinion of it.

"Looks great," he says.

"You should come up there one day, I think you'd enjoy it. I picked these pieces out myself, on the spot. Don't you love the colour?"

David's brain feels like a sheet of glass, ready to shatter at the next word that reaches it, the next shaft of light.

"Is there a bathroom I can use?"

"There's half a dozen of them. Take your pick."

In the bathroom David pulls out his pill pod and downs a twenty-mig tab of Ritalin SR and a cap of fluoxetine, chasing them with a handful of water from the sink. Whenever Marcus stays over he hardly gets a minute's sleep, so that the next day he is a basket case. The extra fluoxetine—a.k.a. Prozac, another in his growing list of repurposed zeitgeist drugs—is in the hope of quelling the shudder he keeps feeling in his brain stem that presages one of his collapses. It isn't likely to help: the drug needs days or weeks to rewire his circuits before it kicks in, though in the usual way of these crossover brain drugs no one seems sure why it works at all.

Three years after his diagnosis his pharma regime is still stunningly hit and miss. Becker, for all the banker's parsimoniousness he showed at the outset, has been happy to ply him with every sort of psychotropic, pushing his dosages to the upper limits with each new cocktail as if he were an expendable specimen in a rat trial. Phenethylamines and tricyclics; drugs to boost his serotonin or his dopamine or his norepinephrine; a so-called smart drug promising seventy-two hours of wakefulness at a stretch; time-released drugs with delivery systems as sophisticated as an ICBM's. The smart drug, modafinil, had sounded promising: another fluke, stumbled on by chance, mechanism unknown, but already in wide use among pilots and soldiers, emergency doctors, academics looking for an edge. David, though, got pounding headaches on it, and nothing like the kick he got from the Ritalin. Worse, he couldn't focus, couldn't see the big picture. He'd spend hours redrafting a single paragraph over and over, then be unable to choose among the dozen different versions he'd come up with. Maybe it was just that he was too hooked on the Ritalin by then, though who knew anymore what was him and what was the drugs taking him over.

The Ritalin is what he has stuck with, juggling various formulations—immediate release and sustained release and extended release—with the vigilance of military deployments and cycling in substitutes on the weekends to keep down his tolerance. He might almost feel he was managing if not for the constant thrum at the back of his neck these days ready to fell him like a taser charge at the least spike of emotion. All day long he is fighting himself, pumped up on his meds but having to stifle every reaction to keep from collapsing. It isn't just anger anymore but almost any heightened state—elation, amusement, excitement, fear. Bit by bit he is having to strip away everything that drives him, that makes him alive. Becker's response has been merely to keep upping his Prozac, from five migs to ten to twenty to forty, though the drug seems only to have sped up the process of extinguishing the person he thinks of as himself.

He takes a seat on the toilet to give the drugs a chance to kick in. A powder room, Danny called this one, though it is probably twice the size of the den that serves as Marcus's bedroom in the condo David now calls home. Everything is top of the line, the fixtures, the lighting, the cabinets, the faucets. The counters and floor are in a glossy space-age material of brilliant white that gives the room an otherworldly look, like a film depiction of a place in heaven or in a dream.

The realization is coming over David that his brother is rich, at a level he would never have imagined. Danny had gone into the business right out of high school, had doggedly stuck with it through the real estate crash, through all the legal troubles, through their father's illness and death. When their father died David had figured the company was about five minutes short of receivership. Yet somehow Danny has managed to survive. Not just survive: to thrive. To grow rich. David, meanwhile, has been reduced since the divorce to a one-bedroom condo downtown that, ironically, was part of a deal he'd made to relinquish any claim in the family business when his father had made Danny a partner.

This was something David hadn't reckoned on going into the divorce, how much it would cost him. Even though he was told by everyone who cared to offer an opinion that divorce was a fight in which there were no winners except the lawyers, still he forged ahead and committed every error, animated by what in retrospect seems to have been a kind of derangement. He wasted a lot of money up front on idiocies, taking his lawyer's advice that he not move out of the house because it would prejudice his claim to Marcus but then paying for an office downtown to have a place away from his students to work and maxing out his credit cards on restaurant meals and dry cleaning and hotel stays. Then right from the start Julia's father had got into the act, calling in chits from every quarter to make sure Julia was properly lawyered. Almost weekly, David was served with some new motion or disclosure order. The worst was the forensic accountant her father set on him, who made his every smallest excess seem the sign of a criminal profligacy.

If David had been smart he would have accepted from the start how outgunned he was. Instead, with each setback he dug in his heels, firing lawyers and hiring new ones, firing those and representing himself, somehow convinced at each stage that if he fought hard enough it would prove he was in the right. One by one, the judgments went against him. He was forced to move out of the house, was left on the hook for both child and spousal support, was assessed a big whack of Julia's legal fees because of motions of his own that the court deemed frivolous. Through a couple of loopholes Julia's lawyers even managed to get almost the entire value of his condo thrown in as common property, though he'd had it for years before the marriage, so that when the final balance sheet came in, what Julia ended up owing him for his share of the house—the house she had insisted on, on which she had indulged her every whim, that had cost him every penny he had earned from his books—had barely been enough to cover his legal bills.

The sucker punch was custody. Julia got sole, which meant final say on everything, and managed to limit his access to three weekends a month. He had gone to great lengths to fight her on that one, had brought in experts, dredged up the postpartum episode, forced Julia to go in for psychiatric testing, yet the asshole judge—the same one who had issued the injunction against his taking Marcus on the highway—completely turned the tables on him, going so far as to cite concern for the boy's safety on account of David's disorder. The whole system seemed rife with this sort of hypocrisy, demonizing fathers under the guise of being progressive when it was just the worst sort of mother worship, of old-style family-values conservatism. The same hypocrisy he had had to put up with his entire marriage: for all his dereliction, all his mistakes, it was Julia, from the start, who had set the boundaries, who had closed him out from what she'd claimed as her realm until it held no place for him.

Now, though, he finds it hard to connect to the self-righteousness he felt then, hard to piece together his actions in any way that makes sense. He can barely fathom how they ever got through those long nightmare months when they were both still in the house, all the work of negotiating bathrooms and breakfasts and bedtimes, school drop-offs, of murdering every emotion, every memory or image of the different people they had been to each other before this hate. Then all the while having to pretend to believe that they could make Marcus believe that all this was normal, that it was possible to pass through such devastation and come out whole.

His ass has gone numb from the toilet seat. He should have chewed the Ritalin the way he used to, though with the time-release tabs it is like mainlining, like jabbing a needle directly into his brain. Instead he has to hide from his family like a child nursing a grudge. Not that telling the truth is an option. *I popped out to take my Prozac and Ritalin.* He could mention as well the boxes of Viagra he has at home, Becker's answer to Prozac's libido death. This is what his life has come down to, this unholy zeitgeist triumvirate, three drugs whose brand names are like banners for the times. Meanwhile, just to feel alive, he has to search out ever more extreme forms of stimulation, has to drive faster, watch more violent movies, surf porn for the hope of an erection that isn't medically induced.

"Hey Davie!" Danny calls. "You fall asleep in there or what?"

He can hear his mother's snort of laughter.

"It's like the time he fell asleep in that greenhouse, remember that, Danny? Jesus, I hadn't thought of that in years! Even back then he was falling asleep. Your father gave him such a smack!"

David's blood rises and he feels his face go slack, feels his head dip. He is like a dog on a choke chain, leaping forward, teeth bared, then slammed back, forever trying to find the still point between too little and too much. Then each time he thinks he has found it, the right pills at the right times to get through the morning slump and the afternoon one, to not keep him up at night, the right mix of stimulation and restraint that will keep him sharp, in control, on his feet, it seems to shift.

By now David knows that the problem is his sleep. Little by little, Becker has warned him, it is coming undone. *Losing integrity*, was his term. The evidence is there in David's sleep graphs, the early-onset REM, the light sleep that refuses to deepen, blips that at a glance might appear mere variations but are like the fault lines in a structure that won't hold. Every night, it seems, a labour unfolds in his head as vast as the night work of Caesar's armies building their fortress camps as they marched. What gets built by it, what risks dilapidation with each oversight, each cut corner, is his mind. David has read by now of the role sleep plays not only in memory but in almost every mental function, from solving problems to improving his squash game; in repairing the neural wear and tear of the day; in helping to hold intact the sort of unified self that makes it possible to face the world. The more he learns, the more Becker's vagueness about prognosis feels like a matter of discretion rather than hedging: David can do the math, the damage all this lost work will amount to as it accumulates night by night.

Whole nights go by now when David feels he hasn't slept at all, has merely been wandering in some middle state that is less sleep than waking dream. Marcus appears beside him or Julia does, he imagines holding them or hurting them, he can't tell which, then awakes to his sheets twisted into knots, his pillows knocked across the room. Or he finally sinks into deeper sleep, with the suddenness of a stone dropping to the bottom of a well, then finds himself at his kitchen counter on some mission he can't reconstruct or pissing into a corner of his couch with an animal precision, just here and not here, as if it made all the difference. It has happened more than once. Confusional arousals, Becker calls them, like surfacing too quickly from a dive, though he doesn't rule out a dozen other possibilities, each with its own taxonomy and dangers. The disorders of sleep, it turns out, are legion; one by one, as David's sleep betrays him, they appear at his door like lost relations he has to accommodate.

Once, before the breakup, he awoke to Julia slapping at him in a daze of confusion and fear because he had struck her. The bruise on her midriff where he had hit her persisted for days.

There are those who in their sleep have sexually assaulted their own children. A man who stabbed his wife forty-four times with a kitchen knife, then rolled her into their swimming pool and went back to bed. One who drove across town to murder his in-laws. One who smashed what he thought was a dangerous animal to the floor and woke to find he had killed his own son. The strength people have in sleep is mythic, superhuman. They let nothing stand in their way, no obstacle or restraint.

Whenever Marcus stays over, David goes through the apartment after he is asleep making his special arrangements, barring the balcony door with a cut broomstick, shifting tables and chairs to block the usual passageways, setting out stacks of books, strips of masking tape, in the hope of startling himself if he wanders. So far, it has been enough to be vigilant, to be afraid. Sleeping in half-hour bursts, an hour at most; doing tests at each waking to make sure he is truly awake and not merely dreaming he is, checking a clock, for instance, since clocks tend to malfunction in dreams, or picking up a book, since books tend to read as gibberish. Staring into a mirror to make sure the person who stares back is himself. It is madness, of course, he can't go on like this; he knows that the more he cheats sleep, the more voracious it grows. The whole time Marcus is with him he feels it massing in his head, waiting to swarm; the whole time he feels angry, indiscriminately, because he is tired and because he wants the boy and wants him gone and because it will never be enough now between them, will never be right. Angry because he is angry. Because even in affliction, even with his mind no longer his own, he cannot help simply being himself.

The sunlight hits him like an assault when he returns to the patio. His mother is still going on about the greenhouse.

"Where was it, David? It was that little park, what was it called? Some kind of botanical gardens. Your father used to love that place."

Danny looks over at him.

"Everything okay, Davie?"

"I guess the bruschetta didn't agree with me. I remember in Rome they used to call it *toast*, as if it was some kind of American fast food."

Only now does David notice that Marcus has actually joined his cousins on the trampoline, the three boys locked arm in arm bouncing in unison, higher and higher. Jamie is whooping it up, urging the other boys on. As they reach the top of a bounce, he goes eerily silent and David feels his heart lurch, afraid of some mishap or trick. But then Jamie lets out another whoop and they land without incident, easing back on their rebounds until the three of them have collapsed on the mat in a jostling heap.

"Way to go, Marco!" Jamie says.

Marcus is grinning from ear to ear, maybe the happiest David has seen him in years.

"Looks like he's a natural on that thing," Danny says. "Too bad you can't get one for the condo."

"Yeah, I'll put it on the balcony."

He must have got on the minute David left the scene. This is what his son looks like without him, David thinks, just a normal kid having fun.

"It was in the east end," his mother says, a dog with a bone, "I remember that. With a creek that went through it, you boys used to race little sticks in it. It was always the joke that you had to let David win."

It isn't just the lies she comes out with these days but that no matter how farfetched they are, David still ends up having to make some sort of space for them in his head. He remembers the greenhouse incident vividly but isn't about to start scrapping with her over the details.

"Maybe it started back then," she says, "did you ever think of that? Maybe you should have Marcus tested."

The place is surely still out there somewhere, though it has never occurred to David to try to track it down. What his father liked about it was the market garden, a big outdoor patch where they grew herbs and vegetables and greens. He had befriended a custodian there who used to give him seedlings from the greenhouses for his garden at home, and they would talk about plants with what to David sounded like a secret language, coded and strangely intimate.

Once, on one of their visits, David got separated from the others. Or he wandered off on purpose: he couldn't have been more than five at the time, yet already the wilfulness had grown large in him. His father was leading them along some path like the paterfamilias he was when David noticed that the door to one of the greenhouses had been left ajar. Somehow he managed to drop behind the others and slip through it. He still remembers the pleasant cushion of heat that hit him, remembers the smell, unlike any smell he could have named. There were trays of seedlings laid out on benches and at the end of them a heap of straw of the sort his father used to protect his vines in winter and to bed his fig tree, which he would tip into a trench and pad with the straw, then bury beneath a mound of earth.

All this comes back to David with utter clarity. Maybe his mind is not so far gone yet after all. But then as soon as he thinks this, his memory starts to clot. He must have lain down in the straw and fallen asleep, though all he remembers is a sense of unfurling, of respite, that seems as much a wish from the present as a memory of the past. Then opening his eyes to Danny grinning down at him, and the custodian and his mother. Waiting for some reward to take shape, for his mother to bend to take him in her arms, and instead his father wrenching him to his feet right there in front of the custodian and giving him a backhand to his head that was like a brick smashing into it. Just as his mother has claimed.

*Don't try something stupid like that again. You ruined things for everyone.*

Even in his silence, his mother has won. All he can see now is that he got what he deserved.

Nelda has come out to call them for lunch. David grabs at Marcus to roughhouse him as he comes up from the yard and sees how his eyes go at once to Jamie as if seeking permission from him.

"Fun stuff out there," David says.

"It was all right." Already he is retreating back to his shell. But then he adds, "Can we come here again next weekend?"

"Of course we can." Letting himself forget that he has already traded the next weekend to Julia. That the last thing he could face is another ride up here with his mother.

He puts an arm around Marcus to lead him into the house and can feel him relax a bit against him. Maybe this is all he really wants, his father's approval. For David to be the one, for once, to bend and take him up.

They eat at a dining table that is a huge kidney-shaped slab of unpolished stone that looks as if it has arrived straight from whatever mountainside it has been carved from. Around them the ground floor stretches like the flight deck of the USS *Enterprise*, half walls and jutting appurtenances dividing it by a kind of gestalt into virtual rooms and the ceiling rising up in a series of intersecting planes to the two-storey atrium, whose massive windows suffuse the entire floor with light.

Nelda brings out the food. She has barely stepped out of the kitchen the whole time David has been here, a real throwback, the sort of wife men used to have to make a trip back to the old country to find. Cooks and cleans, raises the kids, does the company books. Exactly the sort David would never have gone for.

"You better tell Danny what he has to do when they get home," his mother had said to David at the wedding. "Don't expect Nelda to know."

She doesn't take a seat until everyone has been served. She gives Danny a look.

"Did you show David the house yet?"

"He got waylaid." It is growing obvious that all of this matters to Danny a lot more than David would have guessed. "We'll do a tour after lunch."

Even the meal is a showpiece, with a nouvelle salad topped with gorgonzola and figs and a risotto laced with white truffle. David is sure his mother will never go for this stuff.

"I feel like I'm on the Cooking Channel," he says, to give her an opening.

But Nelda is beaming.

"Nelda spent a few weeks last summer at one of those cooking schools in New York," Danny says. "You can imagine the grocery bills since then."

"New York. I'm impressed." The last time David was in New York was well before the divorce. "I guess Danny must be eating like a king."

"Idiot." The word hits him like a bullet. "She didn't do it for Danny. It's for the restaurant."

He has to stop himself from lashing out. It comes to him, suddenly, what he has been hearing in his mother all morning: the voice of his father.

"What are you talking about, Ma? What restaurant?"

"Danny didn't tell you?"

"Danny's opening a restaurant?"

"Not Danny. You think he has time for that? Me and Nelda."

"We've been meaning to bring it up," Danny says quickly. "Just a sort of hot table, really. Like in the old days. Now that the kids are getting older. It's always been a kind of dream for Nelda."

David's head is spinning.

"I can't believe this." That, indeed, is his feeling, that none of this makes sense. "Do I even belong to this family anymore? Was anyone ever going to mention any of this?"

The whole table seems to brace itself for some inevitable escalation, for David to be David and try to bully everyone into a proper state of contrition. Except that he can't trust his lips to form another word.

"Don't make a big deal of this, David," his mother says. But some of the hardness has gone from her. "You've had your own problems lately. It's not like you've been around."

"We bought a building in town that we're fixing up," Danny says. "We can drive over later if you want. I think you're going to like it."

Somehow they get through the meal. At least he hasn't ruined things for Marcus by making a scene. Nelda has gone to the trouble of preparing a separate dish for the children, spaghetti and meatballs, and Marcus, for once, following his cousins' lead, is actually eating what has been set in front of him.

"I'll bet all his mother feeds him is hot dogs," David's mother says. "Look at him, skin and bones."

Danny gives Marcus a wink.

"What's wrong with hot dogs? You used to make them for us all the time."

It was to spare everyone the spectacle of this sort of inanity, David always told himself, that he avoided these people the whole time he was married. Marcus, though, is lapping it all up like some orphan suddenly discovering what a family is.

The boys have cleaned their plates.

"Is it all right if we show Marcus our rooms, Uncle David?" Jamie says.

The deference sends a twitch of shame through him.

"Just don't get him hooked on some computer game or his mother will have my hide."

The last time he and Julia had felt anything like a family had been on an all-inclusive they had done with Marcus on the Gulf the winter before the breakup. Their hotel turned out to be a disaster, an awful shopping mall of a place on the strip that looked out to a narrow sliver of beach eroded nearly to nothing by a string of recent hurricanes. Somehow, though, they had managed to make things work. Julia scouted out a five-star place where the beach hadn't been affected and every day they'd take a taxi there, eating their meals à la carte at the hotel restaurant and spreading the tips around so the staff turned a blind eye when they used the facilities. Marcus befriended a couple of boys his own age and David would watch him building sandcastles with them at the water's edge and think: *It isn't too late.*

Their last day they took the ferry out to a nearby island, renting a golf cart in the little town there and following the coastal road until the low-end resorts and beach houses gave way to deserted scrubland and rocky shoals. David turned onto a dirt side road looking for a turtle-breeding station that was marked on their map but they ended up instead at a narrow strip of beachfront hemmed in by a wall of matted brush.

The beach was littered with shells.

"Can we stop?" Marcus said. "Can we collect some?"

He went along collecting shells in his sand bucket while David and Julia followed behind. David reached a hand out for Julia's and felt grateful when she didn't resist him.

"What do you think?" he said. "Could you see living here? No more department meetings, no more theme birthday parties."

"You'd get bored in a week. You need to be on the circuit."

"I could do the circuit right here. Take the golf cart out for a spin every morning."

"Right." But she was laughing. "And leave me doing the laundry by the river with the other *chicas.*"

Julia spotted a speck of some sort out at sea, then another, and they tried to make out whether they were dolphins or whales. They couldn't have spent more than a minute or two looking out, but when they turned back to the beach Marcus was nowhere in sight.

David's stomach dropped.

"Jesus, David, where is he? Marcus!"

His mind went at once to the dangers, the water on one side, the bush on the other. Who knew what the currents were here, maybe dangerous rip tides. And then all the abduction stories you heard, what better location than this if they'd been followed?

Julia was already out in the water, thrashing through the shoals looking for who knew what. The beach fell away steeply here and in a matter of steps she was nearly up to her waist.

"For God's sake, where could he be? Wouldn't we have heard him if he'd gone in the water?"

David remembered the public service ads they used to run of the sound of a child drowning: perfect silence. If a current had taken him, they were lost.

"My God, David, what should we do?"

"Keep searching the water! I'll search the shore!"

The shingle of beach stretched no more than half a dozen metres before coming up against brush. He tried to make out footprints, but the beach here was mostly shale.

It was possible they had been targeted right from the moment they'd stepped off the ferry, that someone had waited for just such a chance. He knew Julia would never recover if something had happened to him, would be ruined, they both would.

"Marcus!"

Then he saw it, a narrow path through the dense growth and, faintly, what looked like footprints. Already he was doing the calculations in his head, how much money they could raise in a hurry, who they would go to.

Something moved in the thicket of shadow ahead of him.

Marcus was crouched in a clump of ferns like an animal evading capture. A million emotions collided in David.

"For the love of Christ, Marcus! Didn't you hear us calling you? What are you doing here?"

He seemed afraid to get up.

"What were you thinking? Answer me! Why were you hiding?"

He was shouting now, had pulled the boy up by his arm and dragged him out to the open.

"Don't ever try something stupid like that again!"

Julia was running toward them.

"What are you doing? You're hurting him!"

"He was just hiding there, for fuck's sake! We're going out of our heads and he's just hiding there!"

"Let go of him, you're hurting him! Did you ask him why he was hiding? Did you do that?"

All he could see was his anger, like a burning wall he had to pass through.

"Ask him what, for Christ's sake? I could see for myself he'd done it on purpose! We're shouting like idiots and he's hiding there the whole time like it's some kind of game!"

"But why would he do that? Why?"

"You tell me! Because I don't have a fucking clue!"

"That's right, you don't have a clue! Whose fault is that? Whose fault?"

The day was ruined after that; the entire trip was. The family had atomized along familiar lines, a clean break. David didn't even bother trying to find out what Julia might have managed to glean from the boy about the incident. He didn't want to know, didn't want the excuses, the lies. Didn't want to have to think how differently things might have gone if he had simply taken the boy in his arms.

"Davie, you with us? We better move on that house tour if you want to have time for the visit."

He realizes he has blanked out. Microsleeps, Becker calls these episodes, a sudden drop in his brainwaves from alpha to theta for seconds or microseconds, long enough to lose a conversational thread or crash a car.

"I think I'm going to give the restaurant a miss."

"Not the restaurant. I meant Dad. Ma, did you tell him at least?"

"It's not for me to tell him. It's for him to know."

"Come on, Ma. I wouldn't have remembered myself if you hadn't reminded me."

"Don't lie for your brother's sake. Every year you've gone with me."

David's brain hurts. More than anything, he wants the day to be over.

"Could somebody please tell me what the fuck we're talking about?"

"You see?" his mother says.

"It's no big deal, Davie. We were planning to stop by the cemetery, that's all. To pay our respects. It's twenty years today."

*Twenty years*. The number staggers him. Sometimes he still feels the man at his back as if it were yesterday.

Twenty years from now, maybe this is what David will be to his own son, just this darkness, this tumour.

"Can we get going, at least? Who knows what the traffic will be getting Marcus home."

He must have had his reasons. Some impulse he couldn't shake. Or maybe he had turned to see his parents walking hand in hand and it had hurt him in a way he couldn't have named, the danger and the hope of it.

Danny puts a hand on his shoulder.

"Just a quick tour of the house, then we'll go. Who knows when we'll get you out here again."

The house goes on forever, with more square footage than their whole city block had back in their old west-end neighbourhood. In the basement there is a second kitchen, a second family room, a wine cellar; an entertainment centre with a cinema-sized projection screen. The floor, of polished concrete, is lined with radiant heat.

"All geothermal," Danny says. "Thought I'd do my bit for the environment. They had to drill halfway to China to put the pipes in but it practically puts us off the grid."

"I guess you'll be set when it ends, then."

"What's that exactly, Davie? When what ends?"

"Civilization as we know it."

Danny doesn't miss a beat.

"I figure that ended a long time ago, brother. Strictly the law of the jungle out there. You should know more than anyone."

David might almost be pleased by all of this if it didn't feel like something set against him. Right from childhood his relationship with Danny has always felt like a zero-sum game, just a certain portion allotted to them that they must forever fight to get their share of. Even when Danny got picked on in school there was always a part of David that was relieved, as if whatever Danny got, he himself was spared.

Danny takes him outside and leads him to what looks like the facade of an entirely separate residence, jutting out in a big bay from the side of the house with its own double-doored entrance and trellised courtyard. The courtyard feels utterly private and self-contained, with no sightline to the front entrance or the back patio.

"You could live here and never know there was a whole other house attached," Danny says. "That was the idea."

From his bated air David senses they have come to the real object of the tour. Inside, the facade's bay has been mirrored to form a big diamond-shaped space, with a kitchen to one side and a sitting and dining area angled around it. It takes David a few seconds to figure out what is so eerie about the place: it is like a miniature of the house their father built when he moved the family out here, specially designed to fit its odd-shaped ravine lot.

"All right," he says. "I'll bite. Is this where you put the au pair? The mistress?"

"Come on, David. It's for Mom."

"You've got to be kidding! She'd have to be dead before she moved out here."

Danny shifts. "I guess she didn't say anything, then."

"What, do you think she's going to move up here to look after your kids? She loves it downtown! I don't know if you actually got her to agree to this, but if she did she's just stringing you along."

"She's already sold the place, Davie. It closes in a couple of months."

David feels the hum start at the back of his neck.

"I get it now. It's about the restaurant, isn't it? You figured you'd get the condo money out of her so Nelda can have her little amusement."

"You don't know what you're talking about, David."

He turns to see that their mother has come in behind them.

"Don't I?" Just wanting to lash out now, to do damage. "What did your condo fetch? A million? One five?"

"Don't start this, David. You won't like where it ends."

"At the truth? Is that what you mean? You both made it sound like you couldn't rub two cents together when Dad died but now look at you, with your restaurant and your monster house. I didn't see it then, how you closed me out."

"Closed *you* out?" his mother says. "You didn't ask about the money back then, did you? You didn't want to know. You had your scholarship or whatever, that was all that mattered. You had your condo. Why do you think I sold the house up here, really? Do you think I cared about going to museums or the theatre? Do you think I cared about shopping?"

"Ma," Danny says. "Just stop. We don't want to do this."

"Tell me, David. Why do you think?"

He has made his scene after all. And so will get what he deserves.

"Because we needed the money, David, that's why. We needed the money. Who paid for your condo, did you ever think of that? Did you think it was free, just because your father built it? You knew all the problems he'd had with that building, all the buybacks we'd had to do, but you didn't ask. You didn't want to know."

She has done it again. Now this is the version of things he will have to live with, that will become the truth.

"It's like you've been holding this over me just so you could throw it in my face! Why didn't you just say something back then, for Christ's sake? I would have signed the thing over in a heartbeat for all I fucking cared!"

"You think I wouldn't have asked? It was only for Danny's sake that I didn't. He fought for you then, if you're looking for the truth."

Danny won't look at him.

"That was years, ago, Ma. Why hash it out now? We just did what Dad wanted. We just did what was right."

He didn't want to know. All these years he has gone along thinking that he was the one who had always had the upper hand.

History has shown that whenever twins stand in line for succession, one of them has to die.

"As far as I'm concerned, Davie," Danny says, "this conversation never happened. Let's not let it wreck the whole day."

They leave the kids behind with Nelda and drive to the cemetery in Danny's SUV. The vehicle reeks of luxury, leather seats, drop-down video, in-dash GPS. David sits in back, the first time he can remember being in the back seat of a car since he was a teen.

"You still driving that fancy import?" Danny says.

The fancy import that he had had to return to the dealer when the lease expired because he couldn't afford the buyout.

"Strictly subcompact these days. Thinking about the environment."

"Yeah, right."

David feels sleep coming on as soon as the car is in motion. It was how he used to put Marcus to sleep when he had colic, driving the valley parkway for hours at a stretch. Something about the movement and white noise, people said, the containment of the car, like being back in the womb. Maybe it is the same for David, the same sense of regression.

He slips a hand into his pocket and feels by shape for a tab of ten-mig immediate-release.

Danny's eye goes to the rear-view.

"You okay back there?"

"Just wondering when the movie starts."

"Don't joke. Half the time Nelda and Ma sit in the back when we go out so they can catch up on their soaps or whatever. Makes me feel like the frigging chauffeur."

They ride past houses built like Palladian villas and Disney castles, one after another, with huge fountains out front or mile-long driveways with enough interlocking brick to pave the Appian Way. Like Rome before the fall, when everything got sloppy and big, the roadways out of the city lined with the monuments of all the middlemen who'd got rich bilking the provinces. Back when their father moved them out here, this whole zone was still farmland—that was probably what drew him here, the prospect of looking out from his back garden to open country like some aging Cincinnatus. By the time he died, the cornfields beyond their ravine had already given way to the road and sewer works of another development.

This is always the first image of his father that comes to David, of him tending his garden, though it wasn't something he himself ever showed an interest in. That was Danny's job, to show an interest. David's was to resist at all costs, to pile up grievances. Over stupid things, he sees now, things that hardly mattered, and yet at the time it felt like his whole being depended on this unreasoned defiance. At one point he even started imagining to himself that his father was some sort of imposter who had wormed his way among them, taking his cue from the story his mother used to tell of how they met, when she was working for an uncle's construction company and he came looking for a job.

"I had to fake everything for him, all his papers. He didn't have so much as a library card."

David used to do furtive searches of his father's bedroom drawers, his closet, his desk, looking for he didn't know what. Some clue, some proof he didn't belong to them. There were occasional handwritten letters from Italy but he could never decipher them; there were photographs, mostly of job sites but also older ones of people he didn't know, their surfaces cracked, their edges oddly serrated. It took David years of looking at maps before he found one that showed the town his father's passport listed as his birthplace, up in the lake district. Later he would figure out it wasn't far from Salò, the town where the Germans had set up Mussolini's puppet republic after the Italians deposed him. For years, right into adulthood, the idea persisted in David's mind that his father had had some connection to it, on the basis of nothing, really, given that his father would have been all of seventeen by the war's end.

The irony now is that David can hardly remember more than a handful of real confrontations between the two of them. The worst had been when he had broken into one of his father's work sites with some of his friends and crashed a forklift into a foundation wall, ending up riding home in the back of a police car. His father hadn't said a word, had simply pulled off his belt when the police were gone and lit into him, the whole time David thinking, *Now everyone will see what he is.* And yet the truth was that this kind of violence was rare in him. That was the summer of David's trip to Italy with his mother, which might have been a twisted compensation for the beating, though it felt more like his father simply giving up on him. In the fall, Danny started joining in on their father's hunting trips, as if the implicit partitioning of him and Danny between their parents had finally been formalized. David can still remember the blackness that used to go through him when Danny returned from those trips, the feeling he had missed out on some rite of passage, something that might have given a shape to the violence in him.

"You can just see the top of it from here, Davie, the one in fieldstone."

David has blanked out again. They are on the bypass that skirts the old town centre, which is just visible beyond an expanse of golf course and new housing.

"Used to be an old mill, if you can believe it. We're trying to get it back to what it was. Maybe you could swing around with Mom next weekend to have a look. Jamie was saying Marcus asked if he could come up again."

"Yeah, sure. I'll have to see. I might have something planned."

They go past their old neighbourhood, a stretch of modest split-levels and bungalows that from the highway looks almost bucolic now, the sterile, unbroken lawns of the old days having given way to actual landscaping and full-grown trees. Beyond it, though, instead of the open vistas, there are only more houses, and then the strip malls and fast-food drive-throughs, the stadium-sized reception halls, the big-box plazas. A place without a centre, David thinks, but then it comes to him that Danny's mill is the centre, where all of this, all this progress, got its start. Back in its day it was probably as much of an eyesore as this sprawl is, spoiling the river and the view.

"Looks different out here now, doesn't it?" Danny says. "I know you guys in the city look down on us but you won't get a better espresso than here, never mind the chain stuff downtown."

Even the cemetery looks nothing like David remembers it, hemmed in by highway now and the entrance marked by a big arching gateway. Several mausoleums in polished stone rise up near the entrance like condo buildings for the dead, with glassed-in fronts that look into double-storeyed lobbies complete with seating areas and potted plants. Beyond them is a row of family-sized crypts, each with its elaborate statuary and rusticated flourishes. At least their father had had the grace to die before this sort of excess had become the norm, his own grave in an older section where the same arched slabs stretch row after row like the cookie-cutter gravestones of war cemeteries.

Their father's stone, in rose-coloured marble, bears a porcelain cameo of him from a few years before he died. It is a shock to David how young he looks in it, how striking, rugged and lean like a leading man from the 1950s. The headstone is a double one, their mother's name already etched out eerily next to their father's and beneath it her birthdate followed by a dash, as if the span of her life since his death has been merely a malingering.

Danny has dropped the back gate of the SUV and pulled out four shot glasses and a bottle of Courvoisier from a plastic bin. He pours a generous splash of the brandy into each of the glasses.

"What is this?" David says.

"Has it been that long? Come on, Davie, we always do this, every anniversary. Don't tell me you don't remember."

"He doesn't remember because he's never been here," his mother says.

"That's not true, Ma. He always used to come."

Danny passes the glasses around. He pours the extra one one over their father's grave, like a priest anointing a penitent.

"To Dad," he says, raising his own glass and knocking it back. From out of the bin he pulls a box of Montecristos.

"Davie, drink up, you look like you're going to bust a gut. Don't you remember how every weekend he used to have his cognac and his stogie? No matter what was happening, he had to have his little island of *me* time. The cigarettes were a habit but the cigar was something else. It was an occasion. Something holy."

None of this jives with what David remembers of their weekends. What David remembers is the air of threat hanging over the house that there would be some new incident, some provocation.

Danny holds out a cigar.

"Keep it as a souvenir if you don't want to smoke it. It's twenty years now, Davie. At some point you have to make your peace."

Even his mother has lit up. The smell pulls at David, though he can't make out where it is leading him. With cigarette smoke it is different: twenty years on and the least whiff of it is still enough to call up his father as surely as if he were standing before him.

"If he wanted to make his peace," his mother says, "he'd have done it by now. He never cared about family, not really. If he did, he'd still have one."

Danny goes white. "Ma, you're not being fair."

"I'm just saying the truth, that's all. He is what he is."

David turns away. He downs his cognac and sets the glass in the bin, then wanders off along the row of tombstones.

"You go too far sometimes, Ma," he hears Danny say.

"Never mind too far. It's the only way to make him hear. Your father knew that."

The surrounding graves read like a street plan from the old neighbourhood in the west end, the half-familiar names, the half-familiar faces staring out from the porcelain cameos. Bouquets of flowers in various stages of decay spew out from metal urns set into the bases of the graves. David remembers his mother once railing against all the rotting flowers, seeing them as some kind of desecration. As if they could matter. As if any of this does, these rites for the dead still as steeped in unreason as the ancestor worship of the Romans, with their death masks and their house shrines and their offerings of cake and wine to appease the underworld's demons.

David had not made it in time for his father's last moments. There was a call one morning from Danny at the hospital saying he was close to the end, but by the time David arrived from downtown he was gone. He had visited a few days earlier and his father had still had the indestructible air of someone who might go on for months yet or years, though he was reduced by then to little more than a sack of bones.

David was left alone with him while his mother went down to eat.

"Call the nurse," he said. It was hard to tell by then what was his old hardness and what just him conserving his breath. "I need to get out of this room."

The nurse hooked up a tank for his oxygen and David wheeled him out to the hospital garden. The sun was out, one of the first warm days, and a forsythia bush was in full bloom and around it a bed of tulips, also yellow, so that the effect was like a child's papier-mâché model of a sunflower or of the sun itself. David parked his father next to the flowers thinking, *This is what you won't have*, hardly knowing whether he meant it in anguish or in spite.

"You finish school yet?"

David had cause to wonder afterwards if this had been his father's stab at some sort of reconciliation, though at the time all he let himself hear was the familiar contempt.

"Not yet, Dad." He had started his doctorate by then, but this was a level of detail he would never have gone into with his father. "A few more years still."

His father grunted.

"Always a few more." Pause. Breath. "I hope you know what you're doing."

"I'm doing what I like, Dad. I'm doing what I want."

"I know what you want. You want me dead."

David felt his whole body go weak. To answer him would just be to fall into his trap.

"Take me back. I don't want your mother to worry."

It was their last exchange.

After his father died David left almost at once for Rome, to do research for his dissertation. He remembers that time now as if it were part of some different life he had led. The ochre-coloured walls of the university, the cavernous lecture halls, the midnight walks past the Pantheon and the Campidoglio and the Colosseum; the smell that he remembered still from childhood, of sweat and car exhaust and history. By mid-October the tourists had gone and he had the city practically to himself, wandering the Forum from morning to dusk until he had covered every inch of it, every ruined temple and state house, every heaved-up back alley, every shop. The weather had been perfect for touring, day after day the same cloudless skies, the cool mornings, the dry midday heat, the long sunsets with their light like the last gasp of the fallen world. And the whole time he had felt, for what seemed the first time in his life, utterly self-sufficient, complete, with no sense of striving beyond that of immersing himself in his work. The clearest mark of the change in him was that he hardly so much as looked at a woman his entire stay, though in his former life it had felt like his very being had depended on the ceaseless job of coupling and disengaging.

He gave barely a thought to his father. It was as if every trace of him had been stripped away with his death, as easily as that. Then one week he rented a car to visit some Roman sites in the north of the country and his second day out he passed a direction sign on the expressway listing a name that seemed to come out of a dream: his father's hometown.

On impulse he took the exit. Soon the flatlands of the Po had given way to gloomy foothills that felt still as raw and lost to the world as they might have been when the Gauls had scrounged their living among them. He had to stop for directions at every village, each one more insular and becalmed than the last, with the same central bar with a few thatch chairs out front, the same old men who would argue and contradict and fail to come to consensus.

After hours of driving he reached the town. It was bigger than he'd expected, sitting on a slope that overlooked a river valley and spread along a series of switchbacks that tentacled out at every curve into spruce-looking residential enclaves. He passed houses in pink and yellow stucco, children in pressed uniforms, balconies where women had set out their linens to air or old people sat watching television or playing cards. There was a jewellery shop on the main strip, a shop that sold baby clothes; there were pedestrians, cars, a cenotaph, two sets of traffic lights. At the bottom of the town, a factory that made hardware for windows and doors, its parking lot packed, its loading bays bustling. A display board in the lobby window showed off its wares, beneath the motto "From our house to yours."

The town was nothing like David had imagined it. Or rather, he *hadn't* imagined it, except as a backdrop to his made-up histories, vaguely rundown and miserable and grey, not this burgher's town practically Swiss in its air of prosperity and self-satisfaction. Yet somehow it felt more sinister in its ordinariness than the colourless place of his fantasies. He stopped at a public phone to check the directory and there they were, half a dozen listings under his own family name, he had only to drop a token into the phone and dial the numbers. He thought of showing up at some stranger's door, of seeing his father's face again, of having it seen in his own, and already felt steeped in lies. Felt that whatever he was after would only recede the more he sought it.

He got back in his car and drove on.

It is getting late. He can feel his guts starting to tighten at the prospect of the shouting match with Julia that his mother has made clear she will make no effort to avert. This is how she guards her place at the centre, by sowing dissension in every quarter, dividing and conquering. Who knows if she hadn't done the same between him and his father. "Just between you and me," she used to say, when she'd given him some special indulgence or concession. "Your father doesn't have to know."

Without realizing it he has wandered halfway across the cemetery.

"David, we're waiting for you!" his mother calls out. "Then you complain you're in a hurry!"

Riding home he can't get the cameo of his father out of his mind, staring out from his grave so hearty and hale.

"You know what it is," his mother says. "It's because you weren't there at the end. That's why you can't make your peace."

"Ma, don't," Danny says.

"I'm just trying to help him. It has to weigh on him. Even Nelda was there, you weren't even married yet."

"For Christ's sake, Ma, it wasn't his fault. It's not like he had a cell phone or anything back then."

"Your father was waiting for him, you could see it. That's why he held on. And then he couldn't wait."

*You want me dead.* What if that had been a chance his father had offered him, something to push past? What if the only real obstacle between them had been that they'd both clung to the same insoluble lump, their stupid pride?

He had slept at some girl's place that night, which was why Danny hadn't reached him until the morning. "A couple of hours, maybe," was what Danny said. "It's hard to tell." David showered and shaved, ate his breakfast. Got stuck in traffic. The whole time in a sort of fugue state, outside of himself, pretending not to hear the voice at the back of his head telling him that if he was lucky, he'd be too late.

"Davie, don't listen to her, it wasn't like that. It was his time, that's all. You came as fast as you could."

David sits silent.

By the time they get back to Danny's, David feels wound up like a caged animal. He hears a movie blaring from the basement, probably one he'll end up catching grief over from Julia, and starts down to get Marcus, the unreasonableness swirling in him, looking for an outlet. All he needs now to make the day complete is to blow up at Marcus over some trifle.

A war movie is raging on the projection screen but the boys aren't attending to it. Instead they are huddled on the floor with a furtive air around some object Jamie has apparently laid out for them.

"Marcus! We have to go."

They start at the sound of his voice and David sees what it is they are gawking at. It is so far from anything he has expected that he can't quite process it at first. Some sort of replica or toy, he thinks, though it is so convincing-looking, right down to its dull metallic sheen, that he feels a shiver.

The boys have gone silent.

"Nice piece. Mind if I take a look?"

He takes it up from the wooden case it sits in. The instant he feels the solidity of it, he knows in his bones it is real.

He tries to keep his voice even.

"Where'd you get this thing?"

"Grandma gave it to me. She said it belonged to Grandpa."

The shiver has become a throb. It is as if the clue he searched for his whole childhood has suddenly been handed to him.

"She gave it to you?"

"She said it wasn't loaded or anything."

It is not much larger than the palm of his hand. The grips on the handle are embossed with a logo done in an elaborate Gothic script, though what strikes David is the rough machining of the rest, the metal ridged and notched as if some last finishing pass has been skipped. The only markings are a tiny one above one of the grips like a silver mark and a serial number above the trigger guard.

The boys' eyes are riveted on him, Marcus's as much as the others'. On impulse he drops the gun's magazine. The dulled copper heads of several bullets show in it.

The boys stare open-mouthed.

"Ma! *Ma!* Would you get down here please? Danny, you might want to see this!"

By the time everyone has gathered, his mother is already in full denial mode.

"You and Danny had guns when you were younger than he is! What's the big deal?"

"Did you think to ask his parents before you gave it to him? Did you think what might have happened if he'd taken it to school to show his friends? A loaded handgun?"

Nelda flushes.

"My God, Danny. A loaded gun."

"Who knew it was loaded, for God's sake? I took it out on the balcony and pulled the trigger and nothing happened, so I figured it was safe. If it isn't working, what difference does it make if it's loaded?"

Danny has taken over. He pulls the slide back on the gun and jiggles his pinky around in the chamber, then peers into the barrel.

"What were you thinking, Ma? This isn't something you give to a kid."

"I just wanted him to have a keepsake, that's all. Something of his grandfather's."

Danny eases the bullets out of the magazine and sets the gun back in its case.

"Sorry, son, I think we'll have to turn this sucker in. It's not like the old days when I used to keep my Winchester out in the garden shed."

Somehow, in this gutless scolding, it seems their mother has prevailed again.

"Why do you have to turn it in?" she says. "It's ours, isn't it? Just keep it for him until he's older."

"It doesn't really work that way, Ma. I mean, where did it even come from? It doesn't even have a brand name on it. Don't tell me he brought the thing with him from the old country."

"You know how he was. The past was the past. He used to

keep it at the top of the closet, that's all I knew. I didn't ask questions."

David wonders how he could have missed it in all those years of prying. What dark theories it might have confirmed for him if he had found it.

"Why don't you let me take it in?"

"Nah, Davie, it's no trouble. I know people here."

"That's why it should be me. The word goes around someone from the tribe brought in a gun, right away all the old bullshit gets trotted out."

"Let him take it, Danny," Nelda says. "Just the thought of it here even one more night—"

"Fine, then. Just don't shoot yourself with it. And Marcus, not a word to your mother about any of this or we won't see you again till you're twenty-one."

David takes the bullets as well, dropping them into a jacket pocket. He can feel Marcus eyeing the gun case as they walk out to his mother's car.

"When are you going to take it in?"

It is out of character for Marcus to break a silence like this.

"I dunno." All David can think of is what the gun felt like in his hand. "Maybe tomorrow. Why do you ask?"

"Just wondering, that's all."

Clearly Julia's prohibitions against guns haven't stopped Marcus from being fascinated with them. David, too, though he had hidden it, had been drawn to them: more than once he had snuck Danny's Winchester or .22 out of the house to hunt groundhogs and squirrels or to shoot out the windows of an abandoned factory near their place. A couple of times, though it boggles his mind to think of it now, he had hidden himself on a hill overlooking the uptown expressway extension and taken potshots at the licence plates of passing vehicles.

In the car, he sets the gun case at his feet.

"You know, I'm thinking they'd probably let me keep the thing as long as it's registered. It's a family heirloom, after all."

"Keep it for what?" his mother says. "What do you need it for? You said you'd turn it in, so turn it in."

He shoots a complicit look at Marcus in back.

"Listen to yourself, Ma. You were the one who wanted to keep it in the family."

He is anxious to get home so he can try to trace the gun's origins. So he can hold it in his hands again.

He presses his feet to the case, keeping it close.

David opens his eyes to darkness, fighting to get his bearings like someone awaking to the sound of a threat. He is in his mother's car still, alone; he has fallen asleep.

The car is parked in front of Julia's house. Clearly his mother has taken it upon herself to come here directly instead of letting him collect his car at her place and bring Marcus down on his own. Because of the time, she'll say; because he fell asleep.

She and Julia stand talking in the sallow light of the front veranda with what seems a grotesque complicity, as if he were some problem child they were consulting over. Marcus, meanwhile, is nowhere in sight, spirited away from him without so much as a goodbye between them. David has half a mind to waltz into the house to claim his due. *His* house, a part of him still thinks of it as, maybe more now than when he actually lived in it. The house he bled for.

He feels the gun case at his feet and thinks, *Fuck it*.

Julia actually takes his mother's hand in both of hers when they part as if she has saved Marcus from certain death.

"Please don't do that again," he says when his mother returns. "Please don't humiliate me like that in front of her."

She doesn't fight him. It feels like the first concession she has made to him the entire day.

They drive up to her condo in silence. His mother takes the parkway for a stretch but then cuts up through a complicated series of backstreets that she manoeuvres with practised ease. Maybe she isn't losing it after all. The truth is that David hardly sees her enough anymore to be able to judge. That there hasn't been any real connection between them for years, probably, since before his marriage at least. Since his father's death, in short, though he has never admitted as much. He remembers standing in the rec room of their house after he died watching her pack things for her move and thinking that all this was dead to him now, that he wanted only to be gone, free and clear. That he didn't want to know.

She had given him a box of photographs then from their Italy trip. For years he had carted them around with him with each move, going through them for probably the first time only when he moved into the condo after the divorce. Half of them were from a visit they'd made to her hometown in the south, of people and places he had barely any recollection of now, the rest from the couple of weeks they'd spent as tourists in Rome. Of these the bulk were from their visit to Ostia Antica, mostly close-ups of him and his mother that had surely been taken by their young guide, who appeared in none of them. His mother looked younger than he remembered her, girlish, almost, but elegant, dressed in a form-fitting sleeveless dress she had probably picked up in one of the high-end shops that flanked their hotel in Rome. It was something she had fostered in him, an appreciation for style, taking him shopping downtown at the end of every summer to pick out his clothes for the fall. "Danny doesn't care," she would say. "But you know what it means to look good."

From Ostia Antica there was a shot of him and his mother at the Thermopolium, with its fresco of food and wine and still-intact bar; another of his mother laughing at the picnic lunch their guide had laid out for them in the courtyard garden beyond it. His mother had been different those weeks in Rome. The whole time of her marriage David had never once heard his father raise his voice against her, had never seen him be anything other than the gentleman, attentive, indulgent, everything that David knows he himself has never been to a woman. Yet in Rome it was as if his mother, too, was suddenly free of some shadow, some darkness.

She turns into the visitors' lot at her building and pulls up next to the no-options hatchback David picked up used after the divorce.

"David, don't think I don't see it. Don't think I don't know how hard all this stuff has been for you."

There is sympathy in her voice but also something deeper, more wrenching. Disappointment, perhaps. For a moment he sees the woman she was on their Italy trip, remembers the thrill of waking with her in their hotel room to the buzz of Vespas in the street, the rattle of storefront shutters. Remembers sitting in that courtyard in Ostia Antica in the tawny afternoon light, wishing they'd never go home.

"You don't have to worry about me, Ma. I'll manage."

"Because you've done such a good job so far. I'm saying this with the best intention, David. Don't let whatever it is you're going through wreck your life. You're not young enough anymore for a second chance."

In his car he sets the gun case at the foot of the front passenger seat so he can keep an eye on it. He heads downtown, but when he reaches his cross street he doesn't turn, unable to face the prospect of making a meal, of eating it alone. His place still has such a provisional air, like a temporary stop en route to some other, fuller life. One he has so far been unable to imagine.

He considers crossing the river to eat at one of his former haunts in the old neighbourhood but the thought only fills him with bitterness. Instead he keeps driving until he hits the lakeshore, then follows it out past the condo towers and hotels, the badlands of the old port, until he comes to the turnoff for the spit. It has been years since he was down here, though in the old days it was like a gathering place for the tribe. Maybe a hundred trucks a day came through then, from every contractor in the city, edging the spit out bit by bit into the lake with the city's detritus. The rumours always swirling about this one who had snuck in a load of car batteries or asbestos or that one the lead-laced dirt from some old factory site; and then the other rumours, about mob hits and bodies in concrete. A couple of union men disappeared when David was a kid, guys David himself had seen speak at the local union hall when his father had taken him and Danny there, and the story had always been that they were pushing up dandelions down at the spit.

Already from the entrance gate, at the bottom of a desolate zone of industrial warehouses and empty lots, the place looks unrecognizable. What was once a moonscape of shattered concrete and jutting rebar now, in the dark, gives off the lush silhouette of a nature preserve. A chain has been drawn across the roadway to bar entry but no one has bothered to lock it. David unravels one end from its hitching post to pass his car through and reattaches it behind him. A beaten track leads him past stands of poplar and willow; walking trails lead off into darkened bush. Through his open window, a lake smell and a racket of crickets and of frogs, who bellow and moan in the dark like fiends in heat.

Somehow, out of this garbage heap, nature has reclaimed

her own, only the occasional lump of concrete or brick pushing up through the roadway giving any sign of the tons of detritus and waste that lie underneath. The road winds past ponds and lagoons that glimmer in the moonlight like ancient tar pits. Something scuttles across his path but he doesn't make out what, a shadowy mass whose eyes flash in his headlights before it melts back into the bush.

Gradually the vegetation thins and gives way to the familiar blight of old. Bulldozed earth rutted with truck tracks; staggered heaps of rubble that stretch off toward the black of the lake. He has reached the spit's festering edge. He parks by the water, a highway of moonlight stretching out in front of him. Nearby a backhoe sits parked against a half-levelled pile of debris with a logo on the door he remembers from childhood, from one of the old-boy operations that even back then the city tended to favour.

He takes out the cigar his brother gave him and lights it, sucking the smoke right into his lungs, wanting to feel the burn of it. The smell teases at him again and then it comes back to him, the image of his father in the back yard with his cigar, though he isn't sure if he is remembering or if his mind has merely conjured the image from scratch, is trying to give him the past he might have had if he'd been different, had cared about different things, had bothered to see them. The past he might have wanted. He has learned from his sleep books that even the waking mind is a place of merest invention, winnowing the billions of points of data the universe emits every second down to the handful of isolate bits it needs to create the dream it calls the world. All the rest, all the excess that the brain has no use for, the colours it doesn't register, the smells and sounds, the inconceivable worldviews and extra dimensions, are like the universe's dark matter, invisible, unknown, though the very pith and meaning of things might reside in it and every accepted truth be overthrown. David wonders sometimes if the fraying he feels at the edges of himself is this dark matter worming its way in, demanding accommodation.

He takes up the gun case and opens it on the passenger seat next to him. On his phone he does a search of the two letters, PB, that make up the logo on the grips: Pietro Beretta. Another quick search and he has located the factory, in Gardone Val Trompia. Not thirty miles from his father's hometown, in the heart of what was once Mussolini's puppet republic.

David's blood is racing. It is as if the fantasies of his childhood have turned real. He keeps up his searches, trying to pin down some explanation for the gun's crude finish. He is amazed at the gun lore available at a touch, encyclopedia sites, chat rooms, auction sites, videos, feeling the same disjunction as when he'd started surfing for porn, the sense of these alternate worlds out there in the ether in which the dangerous, the forbidden, the deviant have assumed the bland normality of stamp collecting or trading recipes. He comes across a video of a spectacled man with the look a children's show host demonstrating a Beretta M1935. "Ever wonder what kind of handguns the Italians were making in the 1930s?" In smiling detail he explains how to load, cock and fire it, getting off eight rounds in as many seconds.

His father's gun is a match for the M1935 except for the lack of markings and finish. Then on an auction site David finds its double: the same rough machining, the same industrial-grade serial number over the trigger guard. *A great addition to any Nazi pistol collection.* A write-up explains how the Germans, who commandeered the Beretta factory under the republic, ordered it to dispense with aesthetics to speed up production, the guns marked only by the seal of the special inspection unit the Germans instituted to ensure the guns still met their standards, the Quarto Ufficio Tecnico.

David, almost trembling, lifts his father's gun from its case and holds it up to the cabin light. He squints at the tiny mark on the frame: a *4* over the letters *UT*.

The feeling that goes through him seems to have little to do with his old suspicions and theories, is more like a sudden sense of his father's presence, as if, across the decades, the gun has connected David to him like a dark thread. All those years that he spent dreaming up infamies for him. Yet even if he'd had the evidence in his hands, it hardly would have mattered. It wasn't accusation he was after but connection. Something that said to his father, *We're the same.*

*You want me dead.* Who could have seen that in him if not someone like him?

He drops the gun's magazine and squeezes the bullets in his pocket back into place. Loaded, the gun feels more real, more itself. Such a strange object, designed for one purpose, to kill, yet oddly compelling, maybe even more so in this state of raw incompletion.

David isn't sure how he has reached a point where his own life has become a place he dreads returning to. His family, his shoebox apartment, his work. He is well into his fourth year of effort on his doomsday book but it has yet to coalesce, so that he has started finding every reason to avoid it, to waste his time on frivolities. Then every time he comes back to it he feels it eluding him like his memories do, his thoughts, his very life.

He pulls back the slide on the Beretta the way the video has shown him to draw a round up into the chamber. Now the hammer is cocked and the gun is ready to fire, as simply as that. His heart is pounding. He keeps expecting the throb in his brain stem, the familiar slackening, but it doesn't come. Instead he feels a strange calm, a focus. As if he has found it, the still point between too little and too much.

He points the gun out the window and sights targets in the moonlight. A fluted column. A shard of ceramic. A metal pole.

The windshield of the backhoe.

*Bang.*

A blast of flame and a noise like his head exploding, the gun bucking in his hands as if to rip them apart. It takes his brain a second to realize that he is the one who has pulled the trigger.

The backhoe's windshield looks like the Milky Way, an intricate web of tiny cracks.

*Bang.*

The windshield shatters.

His ears are ringing, the bones of his hands feel unhinged.

He targets the gas tank.

*Bang.* Then again.

There is no explosion like in the movies, only the smell of gas. He ought to go, might have been heard, but instead he takes up his cigar and sits smoking, feeling clearer than he has in months, feeling awake. The cigar slows down time like some menial but essential task, tending a garden or watching a child.

When he has smoked it down to a stub he tosses it into the dark. At the gate he replaces the chain behind him when he has passed through, no looking back.

## Sodium Oxybate

"NOT IF YOU'RE TENURE-TRACK," David says, and she laughs.

They have moved to the living area by now, she to the couch and he kitty-corner to her in the club chair. The dregs of the meal that they picked up from the high-end caterer down the street litter the table behind them and the city stretches out in front, lit up in all its frigid majesty right down to the lake through the ceiling-high windows. The view is the one feature of the place that still makes it bearable for David, more than just a cage for his reduced life.

She is wearing the same nunnish dress suit in ash grey, collar tight, hem past her knees, that she'd worn to the hiring committee's pre-interview dinner. Maybe it is the only good thing she owns. Or maybe, like then, she is trying to avoid any charge of sexual provocation, though, like then, all David can think of is the dark wisp of her body beneath it.

He reaches for the last of the pinot noir.

"More wine?"

"I dunno," she says, going suddenly girlish, "I'm pretty tipsy already."

He fills her glass nonetheless and makes a show of topping up his own, though he has hardly touched it.

In the courtroom of his mind David is already making his excuses. Surely no one could accuse him of premeditation; no one could say he has done anything more than follow her cues. As much as anyone, it is Sonny Krishnan who has landed her here. He was the one who pointed out, at the sad little wine-and-cheese he put on for her after her hire, that the place she'd rented downtown was just a few blocks from David's.

"Oh!" she'd said, with panicked brightness. This was the kind of creepy personal data that Sonny regularly trafficked in, to let people know he literally knew where they lived. "We should get together for coffee or something! Since we're so close!"

David had gone out of his way to avoid the least hint of predatory intent, arranging to meet in the dead middle of a dead Sunday afternoon at a coffee bar that was more or less at the midpoint between them, steering clear of the Saturday even though it was Marcus's weekend with his mother. What he expected was an hour or so of insipid conversation while she tried to gauge when she could politely make her excuses and he tried to hide his dirty thoughts. Only in his fantasies had it ever occurred to him he might actually have a chance with her—she seemed too clueless, too unspoiled. It was part of her appeal, that someone like him would be so far outside the realm of what she knew as nearly to defy comprehension.

Somehow, though, their coffee ended up stretching on until the light outside had started to fade and the windows of the coffee shop had grown steamy. David trotted out his usual

Sonny anecdotes and she didn't balk, laughing at them with a lightness that seemed to take the malice out of them.

"I'm getting the feeling there's something between you two."

"If you mean, do I hate his bloody bureaucratic guts, then, no, I think that would be putting the matter too strongly."

"But he's always saying such nice things about you!"

"You've got to be kidding."

"No, really! Like you're the star of the department and all that. He really said that."

"The thing you have to realize about Sonny is that every move he makes is part of some master plan. Mind you, nobody has figured out what it is yet. In fact, no one knows the first thing about Sonny. I can't even tell you if he's married. I can't even tell you if he's straight."

"Oh, definitely straight," she said.

"Wow. So I guess someone's been putting the moves on you."

She laughed.

"Just good gaydar, that's all. Though he did ask me to come in to see him before the faculty meeting tomorrow. To go over my paperwork, was how he put it."

"That's definitely code, coming from Sonny. Nothing gets him going like paperwork."

David kept waiting for the glance at her watch, the mock-surprised exclamation, the little moue of disappointment at having to go. Instead it was as if she was at his disposal. She asked about buying food in the neighbourhood and he offered to introduce her to his local catering shop, whose menu he practically lived on.

"I was going to pick something up for supper there, actually. If you wanted to join me."

As easy as that, one step leading to the next. If there was any deceit in this it was surely just the mutual self-deceit of any seduction, that level of knowing and unknowing that gave the mind permission for its own complicity.

She slips off her shoes now and crosses her legs beneath her on the couch with a slightly boozy primness, a stretch of black-nyloned thigh flaring out.

"People are a lot more open here," she is saying. "Back there it was like, the profs were using White so everyone had to. All that stuff about metaphor, I don't know, it just seems such a cop-out."

"Maybe you're just afraid he's right. It's not as if history comes with its own storylines. If it did we wouldn't need historians."

"But isn't that like saying there was no Holocaust? Isn't it like saying we're just making it all up?"

"Of course we're making it up. I bet the two of us, right now, couldn't even come up with a version of the afternoon we could agree on, never mind the Holocaust."

Something flashes in her eyes, as if he might actually make her try this in earnest.

"Our thoughts would be different," she says, "but not the facts."

"Let's do the facts, then. How long did we spend at that coffee shop drinking overpriced lattes?"

"That isn't fair. I was too caught up in the conversation."

"Right answer, but it doesn't let you off the hook. What about the name of the catering place we went to? Or the address? Or mine, for that matter?"

Now she laughs.

"Those are trick questions. Anyway, all I'd have to do is look them up."

"Exactly. Enter the historian. You've proved my point."

She laughs again. When she laughs she seems most herself, most innocent.

"Very clever," she says.

He grabs a cigarette from the pack on the coffee table. In less than two years he has gone from the occasional nighttime smoke to nearly a pack a day, a development that has both astonished him and given him a perverse satisfaction.

"So," she says. "I was wondering. If the things I heard about you in the department are true."

"Do you mean about what a bastard I am? Or about how washed up my career is?"

"I mean about the hire! About you pushing for me."

"If people are saying I pushed for you," he says, "I doubt they mean it as a compliment."

A pinprick of panic shows in her eyes. It is clear she hasn't understood yet the nest of vipers she has landed in.

"I never know if you're joking or telling the truth."

"Are those the only options?"

"So are you saying people hate me? I don't understand what you're saying."

"Hate's a strong word. Though I'm guessing one or two of the women aren't especially pleased."

"Why would that be?" But she perks up a bit. "I mean, it's not like I'm a threat."

"That's not how *they* see it."

She seems smart enough to realize that pressing him for more would just look like narcissism.

She reaches for his cigarettes.

"You mind?"

"Hardly. Nothing makes addicts happier than dragging other people into their addictions."

"The scary thing is you're serious."

"The scary thing is you think I'm not."

That she knows he pushed for her, that she has made it a point to let him know that she knows, means the spectre of quid pro quo hangs over them now. He isn't sure whether this helps him or hurts him.

She turns to take a light from him and her hair, of blackest black, falls forward from one of her shoulders straight as falling water. His hand brushes against it and a charge shoots through him that begins right at the base of his cock.

In his fantasies he has already lived this moment, has crossed over a dozen, a hundred times from this sort of accidental touch to what comes next. Has run a hand along her midriff, along her ass; has slid her panties down and licked her clit. Has fucked her again and again, in his half dreams and dreams and awake until the line between what he has imagined and what is real has grown thin.

She has nearly emptied her wine glass again.

"Let me top that up for you," he says, and gets up to grab another bottle before the line frays.

On paper she barely even made his long list. Graduate work at a couple of B-level universities out West; a postdoc at a place in New Mexico that had the unmistakable whiff of last resort. Her dissertation, some sort of revisionist look at aboriginal first contact that he hadn't been able to bring himself to do more than power-skim, was exactly the sort of topic-of-the-moment irrelevance that drove David to distraction. Out in the real world Indians might still be living poor and forgotten and dispossessed, but in the academy they were king.

It was Sonny, again, who had to take the blame for turning him. Sonny was the one who had instituted video calls during hires, as a way of reducing the number of candidates who had to be flown in for a final vetting. This despite all the research that showed judgment went out the window once physical appearance became a factor. You could confess to war crimes in an interview or recite *The Protocols of the Elders of Zion* and it wouldn't matter a lick as long as you dressed well and had good teeth. Case in point: as soon as David set eyes on Jennifer Lowe, she rose straight to the top of his pile. From the surname he had been expecting some thick-legged Highland girl or mousy Wasp, not this tan lotus child. No doubt the name had come down from a Lau or a Liu that had got mangled in the immigration lines; either that or from whatever genetic interloper accounted for her delicious hybrid look. He tried to prise her background out of her at the pre-interview dinner, whose alcohol-fuelled purpose was exactly to ferret out all the compromising personal data that couldn't be asked about in the actual interviews, but she grew awkward.

"Oh, you know. Small town in the middle of nowhere. Very boring." And he pictured her serving hamburgers and wonton at the single Asian restaurant in one of those godforsaken prairie towns that were all grain silo and big sky.

David had signed on to the hiring committee only because it had seemed the best way to break Sonny's balls over the service hours he insisted on bleeding out of him. The last thing Sonny wanted was to lose control of a hire. Now it became a sort of game for David to see if he could push Jennifer Lowe through right under Sonny's nose. Everyone knew that half the committee was made up of Sonny's plants, who right from the start had made clear who the Brahmin's chosen one was. David's strategy was to foment resentment behind the scenes among the straggling others and so harden them in their own alternative choice. When the inevitable stalemate resulted, it was easy enough to bring Jennifer up the middle as a compromise, even though she had made it through to the short list based on little more than tokenism.

In the kitchen David tops up his meds with ten migs of immediate-release and uncorks a Californian from the emergency cache he still keeps on hand. Jennifer, in her stocking feet, has got up to browse his bookcase. The wine seems to have softened her around the edges like a layer of wash in a watercolour.

He fills her glass where she has left it and drops down onto the couch next to her own emptied spot.

"Any bites yet on the dissertation?"

"Oh, yeah," she says, a little too quickly. "I mean, I've had some good readers' reports. I guess I'm just waiting for the right fit."

Translation: her first choices have turned it down. It wasn't that the thing was actually drivel, as he recalls—it was more the earnestness of it, the grating sense of an agenda behind every line.

"Have you tried for funding? It's hard to get a commitment these days from a publisher without five or ten K on the table."

"Yeah. I don't know. Sonny suggested that too. I just sort of feel—"

"What, did he offer you something from the slush fund he keeps to make sure his pets stay in print?"

A tiny pause.

"I didn't know I was one of his pets."

"Be careful or you will be. That's how he gets you, by making you think he's your best friend. Then before you know it he has so much over you, you can't even take a shit without asking his permission."

"What does he have over *you*?"

"Nothing. That's why he can't stand me."

Some of their earlier lightness is gone. Jennifer, with her back to him, moves on to the glass-doored cabinet that holds his collectibles. Exactly the sort of stuff he used to make fun of, pocket-sized eighteenth-century college editions of *Bello Gallico* and *Bello Civili*, thick leather-bound tomes from the library of Esquire This or *Egregio* That. He feels vaguely exposed, as if she'd stumbled on his porn stash or old disco collection.

She pulls out his 1618 Taubmann edition of Virgil, one of his best pieces.

"I picked that up in a used bookstore in Miami Beach, if you can believe it."

She runs a hand over the leather binding, which is original, rare for a book this old, elaborately tooled in acanthus leaves and heraldic motifs.

"Just think of who's held this over the centuries," she says.

The truth is that David hardly glances at these books after the first thrill of ownership has passed. Then the longer they sit there on his shelves gathering dust the more they feel like an accusation. All he can think of is how bit by bit they disintegrate in the apartment's shifting air and shifting heat like dead things, things no longer in history.

"Look," he says. "Don't let my cynicism corrupt you. Sonny's fine, really. You'll work things out with him. If he's putting money on the table, my advice is to take it and run. That's what we'd all do. I'd do it myself if he ever actually offered me any."

"He doesn't offer you any because you don't need it to get published."

"He doesn't offer me any because he knows I'd eat my own children before I'd go begging to him for it."

Any minute now, he suspects, she will check her watch, force a smile, make her moue. He wishes he hadn't let himself want this, hadn't started thinking of it as a real possibility.

"This one looks like it's been through the wars."

She has managed to sniff out the collection's ur-text, a battered Petronius he picked up for a song back in his student days in Rome, half the spine missing and the marbled front board thickened and warped from ancient water damage. As she opens it a folded sheet falls to the floor.

"Oh! Sorry!"

It takes David a moment to realize what it is.

"It's nothing," he says. "Just some notes."

Before he can get to it she has already bent to collect it.

"Not notes," he corrects himself. "A translation. Something I did years ago."

"It's something dirty, isn't it? Isn't that what the Romans are famous for?"

"Not dirty, exactly. Worse than that. I wouldn't risk reading it if I were you. The last person who did turned to salt."

But she is already scanning the page, her eyes growing brighter by the instant.

"Wow," she says. "You translated this?"

"More or less." In fact he had spent weeks on it when he'd first come across it as an undergrad, scouring every other translation he could get ahold of, rethinking every word again and again. Year after year he had come back to it, trying to get it just right. "You could say there was some sampling involved."

"I bet you can't recite it."

As soon as she says this he feels the poem recede into one of the dark pits that pock his brain now, though he had thought it encoded in his very DNA.

"Tell you what," he says. "Why don't you read it to me."

The flash in her eyes again.

"Seriously?"

"Why not. I'd like that."

"I don't know," she says. "You'd have to close your eyes. Otherwise it'd be too weird."

"Got it. Closing them."

The second he does so he feels foolish, avuncular, old. But already her voice has started out of the blankness, tentative, like someone crossing a rope bridge over a chasm.

> God, what a night
> What a soft bed, what hot loving we had,
> Our bodies mixing like rivers in our mouths.
> I said goodbye then to the merely human.
> So began my destruction.

He can still remember the jolt the poem had given him when he'd first read it, the feeling of a sensibility so familiar, so bracing, so new, it was like a message from his own future. In the silence after she finishes it seems she is feeling the same jolt, that sense of someone speaking to them across two thousand years as if from yesterday. Then he opens his eyes to her standing there in front of him like a deer in headlights.

"I can't believe I read that to you. I mean, it's so intimate. It's so *sexy*."

"You read it beautifully," is all he says, though what sticks in his mind is how she paused the briefest instant before the last line as if already looking back to the wrong turn.

What David wouldn't give simply for the chance to fuck someone again as if he really meant it. The Prozac messed him up: he has been off it for months already yet still feels some remnant of it coiled up inside him like a dormant strand of viral code, awaiting the trigger that will revive it. It wasn't just that his sex drive had flatlined but that sex itself had grown suddenly repugnant, as if he'd undergone some nightmarish conversion. All he could see was its grubby absurdity, its pathetic gropings and sick commingling of flesh. The worst was that beneath his horror at his unmanning he sensed a relief, a small unclenching in him at having this thing that had been shackled to him all his grown life, his own animal self, finally cut loose. He started searching his mind then, going back and back, before the Prozac, before the disorder, before the death-in-life of the last years of his marriage, yet could never seem to get back to a time when the sex, for all that it had driven him, wasn't already compromised somehow, already tainted. Not with Susan Morales or the mindless fucks of his youth; not even in the heady first months of infatuation with Julia, when he'd thought he had finally joined the human race. All he could see was compulsion, a darkness that had run through him like a death wish.

He has begun to match Jennifer glass for glass by now, stupidly, possibly fatally, and they have polished the Californian and moved on to a Barolo he has been keeping since before Marcus was born.

"Marriages end," he says, rounding out a long, ill-considered ramble on his ex which he can no longer remember the starting point of, "but divorce lasts the rest of your fucking life."

"But there must have been something good! You must have loved her!"

"Christ, watch your language. You know what love is, don't you? I mean, medically? It's a psychosis. It has the same chemical signature as schizophrenia, I shit you not."

He is running on pure bravado now, without plan, at once desperate to keep her here and wishing she'd go, and so spare them the aftermath of whatever train wreck it is they are headed for. Her puking into his toilet or passing out on his couch; him nodding off in mid-sentence or suddenly spazzing out in one of his fits. Or worse, the two of them falling into bed and fucking in some pale simulacrum of what he has imagined, both of them blunted with wine and him fighting the whole time to stay hard. By now he can no longer ignore the small dark bead of self-destructiveness in her, reassuring, in a way, something that joins them, yet also setting off every alarm, like a siren call to his most depraved under-selves. Like permission.

"You?" he says. "Any marriages yet? Lesbian hook-ups? Psycho-killer ex-lovers?"

Her laugh, a bit too ready now, too compliant.

"Nothing that exciting, sorry to say. Just your typical boring academic."

Barely a foot and a half of couch separates them at this point, Jennifer still in her lotus squat though growing more and more askew, now her hem riding up, now some kink making her shift a butt cheek or thigh. Meanwhile the wine wears away at his brain, blurring its borders. He sees himself lean in to her to take her wrists, slender as a child's. Sees her pinned beneath him as he thrusts.

She reaches to the coffee table for another cigarette.

"You must want to quit. I mean, after your father."

"Quit?" He has no memory of mentioning his father. "But I'm just getting started."

He gets up to empty the ashtray so he can pop another IR. If he isn't careful, he will lose it. If he isn't careful, he'll slide into some twilight self like a Jekyll and Hyde.

Jennifer is blowing smoking rings, big ones and little ones that ride out on the room's invisible currents like Morse code.

"I just hope you're not going to drop dead on me all of a sudden or anything."

"If I do it won't be from smoking. Smoking goes in more for long and lingering than sudden death. Lots of time for regret."

"Not that! I mean those pills you keep taking. If they're like nitroglycerine or something."

It seems all evening long, while he has been imagining himself the soul of discretion, she has been seeing right through him.

"Nothing that exciting, sorry to say." Then instead of putting her off he adds, "More recreational, as a matter of fact. If you're interested."

Again, in her eyes, something sparks, and he knows he has taken the right tack.

"I guess it depends what they are."

Without a word he brings a small mortar and pestle over to the coffee table and starts crushing ten-mig tabs into a powder.

"I don't believe it! You're like a pusher! Is it some kind of Oxy or something?"

"Even better. Methylphenidate. Also known as Ritalin."

She lets out a guffaw.

"Kiddy coke? You can't be serious! What, did you skank it off your son?"

"How do you know I have a son?"

"There's a picture of him right there on the bookshelf. He looks just like you."

David can't bear to leave Marcus on the hook.

"Unfortunately, the boy is perfectly normal. I have to buy the stuff off the internet like everyone else."

When he has ground the pills down he spreads the powder into lines on the coffee table with the edge of his cigarette pack. He can feel in her now what he recognizes in himself, the addict's quickening. He rolls a twenty into a tube and holds it out to her.

"I'm not going to end up naked and comatose in an emergency room, am I?"

"Safe for children," he says. "But if you do, just remember this phrase: *informed consent*."

She hovers over the table an instant as if steeling herself for a dive before finally sucking a line up into one of her nostrils. The briefest pause, then she switches sides and does another.

"This is so wild. Whoever thought I'd be snorting lines one day with the author of *Masculine History*?"

"I wouldn't have taken you for a Roman history buff."

"Are you kidding? Not that that even mattered with your stuff. I mean, what you had to say about empire, I tell you I was shitting myself when I found out you were on the hiring committee! I was sure when you read my dissertation you were going to think I was some kind of plagiarist."

The comment pulls him up short.

"You know what they say." How far had he got in the thing, really? Forty pages? Thirty? He can't even call up the title. "Plagiarism is the highest form of flattery."

"But wait, wait! That's not what I meant!" She is already speeding. "I mean, I meant it, but it's not what I wanted to say! It was the writing! How you made it feel like you'd actually been there or something! What was that quote you gave? Otto von Richter. Otto von Ranke."

"Leopold."

"That's right! Leopold von Ranke! *Only to show how it actually was.* Isn't that it? I mean, it gave me goosebumps! That said it exactly! Never mind all the theoretical bullshit about how you couldn't say anything for certain. I mean, otherwise, why bother? That's why I wanted to come to you. Why Sonny suggested it. Because you were such an influence."

He feels a twitch.

"What does Sonny have to do with it?"

"Oh! Sorry! I mean. I thought he'd mentioned it! Since you brought it up!"

"Brought what up?"

"The dissertation! Sorry! You asked me about it. I just figured that's what you meant. I mean about you working with
me, he thought you could help. I should have said from the
start! Shit! I just thought, I don't know! You're not angry, are
you? He said you gave it such a rave he just thought you'd be
willing to help clean it up a bit. Maybe get it to one of the bigger
publishers. It sounds so awful now! Like I've been scheming or
something! Tell me you aren't angry!"

He bends to do a line. The twenty is still warm from her
touch. He ought to just take her this second, right here on the
couch. Surely no one could blame him. Quid pro quo.

No doubt Sonny has engineered this whole scenario, right
down to playing on his prurience, to knowing the fantasies that
run through his head. Sonny who has stripped him by now of
every last vestige of privilege; who has gone out of his way to
make him a pariah. Not that David gives a flying fuck what
people think of him, and yet it wears at his being, the false
smiles, the whispered asides, the going day after day without
a single warm look, a single connection with someone he trusts.

He has left Jennifer hanging.

"Don't be silly. How could I be angry at someone who
quotes Ranke back at me?"

*Only to show how it actually was.* Hard to imagine that he'd
actually believed that crap once, that he had been that naive,
when even the past afternoon, the past hour, seem already such
a chemical and hormonal blot, a hopeless tangle of layered
duplicities and veiled intent.

He does another line, then passes the twenty to Jennifer.

"I don't know," she says. "I'm pretty wired already. Maybe
I shouldn't."

If she had made the least move to leave then, if she had been
that obvious, he would have hustled her out the door in a

heartbeat, making promises of every sort of the help he would give her that he would then drag out for months or years until they had come to nothing. Instead she gives him a sidelong look that reminds him of Marcus, how he'll not quite turn to David in a moment of unsureness as if seeking his permission.

"I wouldn't worry about it. It wears off pretty quickly this way."

Another look, another pause, then she bends to the table.

The fog of the wine is already lifting. He watches her as she bends, her dress tightening against the small of her back, the round of her haunch, and the images flit through his head of what he has done to her, what he will do.

What has replaced David's Prozac to manage his falling fits is sodium oxybate, a sleep drug that enjoys the singular distinction of having been approved for prescription use even while remaining classed as a banned substance. Danger of hallucinations, of seizures, of suicidal ideation. Danger of respiratory depression. Of coma. Of death. Its real infamy, though, rests on its having, like Ritalin, an active street life, where as gamma-hydroxybutyric acid—a.k.a. GHB, Georgia Home Boy, Liquid Ecstasy, Fantasy, Everclear, Salty Water, Easy Lay—it is a favoured drug of raves and of heightened sex for its pleasant buzz at lower doses and of date rape at slightly higher ones, when it induces a few hours of coma-like unconsciousness before being excreted from the system as water and $CO_2$, leaving no trace of itself except a small black hole of oblivion in the brain.

For David, that oblivion is what now passes for sleep. Two doses a night of a viscous solution as salty as the Dead Sea, one at bedtime and the other three or four hours later when the first wears off, which it does with the abruptness of a light clicking on in his head. In the interim he is like a dead man, often waking stiff from lack of movement still in the same pose as when he closed his eyes. Becker had mentioned the drug a couple of years earlier when it was just coming off its approvals, but it had struck David as too sketchy then. Another drug that had been repurposed, this one originally used as an anaesthetic, before the dosage range between efficacy and death had been deemed too narrow; another one whose precise mechanism was unknown. Then on top of the absurdity of having to wake in the middle of the night to take something to sleep, there was the long list of contraindications, nearly two hundred of them, everything from muscle relaxants and cold pills to hand sanitizers and rubbing alcohol. Next to it, Prozac had seemed as safe as Pez.

That, though, was before David had reached the lower circles of Prozac hell. Beyond the cluster bomb Prozac had lobbed into his sex life there was also the ongoing demise of his sleep, which had become such a carnival of bizarre acrobatics that it had ceased to give him anything like respite. The sleepwalking and confusional arousals, the bouts of paralysis and repetitive movement, the pissing into corners; and then the constant tossing and turning, the sense of hovering the whole night in a hallucinatory purgatory in which his dreams had so much of the nagging insistence of the waking world that he arose exhausted from them. It was like a slow descent into madness. David made the connection to the Prozac only after he came across a couple of studies that linked it to insomnia and REM cycle aberrations, possibilities that Becker had failed to mention.

"Yes, perhaps there is some effect," Becker said dismissively. "But you must also accept that this is normal for your condition. This deterioration."

Who knew what normal meant in this context, given the general level of ignorance in brain medicine, whose remedies by then had begun to strike David as little above the level of reading entrails. There were a hundred billion neurons in the brain, each in constant communication with as many as ten thousand of its neighbours, in an intricate language of chemical exchange that had been built up over hundreds of millions of years. Pumping indiscriminate drugs into this scheme by trial and error to target some barely understood short circuit amidst some barely mapped network of dense neural wiring was like using Agent Orange to cure a case of leaf blight. David had given up thinking about the knock-on effects of his ongoing regimen of drugs, the incalculable tiny shifts is his brain's chemistry that like the flap of a butterfly's wings had surely already altered the very essence of him in ways he would never know.

At least with the sodium oxybate his sex drive has revived and he has even been able to cut back on his stimulants. Able to get through a day without collapsing each time he loses his temper or tells a joke; to get through a night without smashing his bedside lamp or pissing into his kitchen sink or opening his eyes to find himself standing half-naked in the cold on his twenty-sixth-storey balcony. The drug apparently works by boosting slow-wave sleep, though there is some question whether what it induces is actual sleep or only an eerie synthetic version of it, something that reads as sleep in the monitors but that at a deeper cellular level might be an entirely new state of consciousness, unknown in nature. Studies in humans and in mice have shown that the drug can bring on in subjects who are still awake the same slow-wave patterns once thought distinctive to deep sleep. It has already happened a number of times to David that he has got up to pee in mid-dose and has suddenly found himself thrashing against the walls or crawling on the floor stuck in a mindset altogether unfamiliar to him, feeling purposeful and awake yet utterly unable to get his bearings. It is as if he is conscious, lucid, yet somehow blind, half his brain still in darkness or each half inaccessible to the other as in those epileptics whose brains had been split in experimental surgeries.

The drug is ringed round with security protocols that make those of Ritalin look like high school. David has managed to double-dip on his Ritalin more than once without being called on it, cadging scripts from his family doctor when his supply from Becker has run short and getting them filled at independents rather than through his regular chain so they wouldn't show on his file. That isn't something he could ever pull with his sodium oxybate. Only a single pharmacy in the country is authorized to dispense it, sending a shipment by courier every thirty days, the deliveries scheduled by a rep from the drug company who calls him on day sixteen or so of every cycle and who repeats her name in full each time she calls, Emmanuelle Gattuso. She speaks in a slightly accented but thoroughly uninflected English, avoiding the least foray into the personal, as if she is being closely monitored. Always she begins by asking how many days' worth of medication he still has on hand, a question that used to throw him into a small panic because it felt like a test, especially as, more than once, she had pressed him on his answer as though to suggest he was lying or had made a mistake. Now, instead of trying to guess if a partly filled bottle has three days' worth of drug in it or five, he has put a thirty-day repeat on his desktop calendar and simply counts back from the end date for each cycle to arrive at the number that Emmanuelle Gattuso herself has surely already worked out by exactly the same method. In this way he often shows a bit of a surplus each month, as the pharmacists tend to err a few grams in his favour with nearly every bottle, though

David wouldn't be surprised if this, too, were part of some scheme to test his trustworthiness.

In any event he has been putting the surplus to good use. A few times a week, when the mood hits him, he takes a small starter dose a half-hour or so before sleep and stretches out on his bed to masturbate. At first he couldn't understand why the drug was considered such an aphrodisiac when all he felt was a kind of pleasant drowsiness. Bit by bit, though, something has been unleashed in him, until these sessions have become almost an addiction. In the usual way of sex it is less what happens in his body that matters than in his head, the different place the drug takes him to, leading him on like some force outside of him in the way that dreams do or the first rush of images that goes through his head just before sleep. Up unfamiliar stairwells, down unfamiliar halls, into rooms where every speakable and unspeakable act is permitted, anything that can be imagined or abhorred.

He has set out another round of lines but has lost all track by now of how many they are up to. At some point his father's Beretta has made an appearance, after Jennifer started going through the drawers in his living room cabinet and found the one that was locked.

"This is the one I have to see! The stuff you hide from your son!"

She'd expected porn, maybe, though had looked thrilled to discover the Beretta instead.

"You're shitting me. Just don't tell me you're a serial killer or something because that would really wreck the whole evening."

It had been easier than he had expected to get the thing registered and have himself licensed. A police check; a weekend course on gun safety; a couple of exams any seven-year-old could have passed. He kept waiting for the gun to get tied to some mob hit or war crime but the paperwork went through without a hitch. Afterwards he joined the gun club north of the city where he'd taken his safety course and started driving out a couple of times a week to fire rounds.

Jennifer pulls back the slide on the Beretta the way David has shown her and whips around like a gunslinger to her reflection in the living room window. She pulls the trigger. *Click.* In his mind's eye David sees the window shatter and the two of them sucked off into the night as into the vacuum of interstellar space.

"Shit. I really thought it was going to go off."

"You should come out with me to my club sometime. We could go after the faculty meeting tomorrow. It's always my favourite time to go."

David has spent much of the morning at the club, shooting until his arms were numb, until his whole body ached. The buzz of it lingers for days sometimes. By now he has gotten good enough not to embarrass himself, able to manage consistent two-and-a-half-inch clusters at twenty-five yards. When he is peering into his sights, the world falls away. There is only his finger on the trigger, only the bullet barrelling forward like his own will. It is better than any brain drug, the only time when every fibre in him feels fully awake.

Jennifer is picking off imaginary foes, faking kickback with each shot. *P-tew. P-tew.*

David checks his cigarette pack: empty.

"I'm wondering if you're as wired as I am," he says.

She picks off the glass door that guards his collectibles. She picks off his flat-screen. The picture of Marcus. *P-tew.*

"Look at us," she says. "Look at us. It's so fucking weird. It's like I'm in ancient Rome with David Pace. So *decadent.* I always loved that word. What was it you said about Roman art? I mean, it was fucking brilliant."

"If I said something about Roman art, then you have my permission to shoot me."

"Not tonight, silly! In your book!"

"Whatever I said, I take it back."

"About realism. How they got to a level that wouldn't come back till the fucking Renaissance and then they just got bored with it! It's like, in fifteen years they covered fifteen hundred. That's where we are now, isn't that what you're always saying? *We're* the fucking Romans! Everything has to happen so fast or we're bored out of our tree. Ritalin, don't you see? It all fits. Attention deficit."

Cigarettes. But then the thought of the thousand obstacles he will have to negotiate to get some while he is bouncing off the walls like this, the door fobs and keys, the buttons in elevators. The thought of leaving Jennifer alone here with a cocked Beretta and a half-box of ammo in an unlocked drawer.

*P-tew.*

"You know what?" he says. "I don't know the first thing about you. Why is that exactly? I mean, apart from the fact that I'm an insufferable narcissist prick."

"But you know everything about me. You read my dissertation, right?"

"By that logic, I'm Julius Caesar."

"I always thought of you more as Augustus."

She plops down in the club chair gangster-style, legs spread, the Beretta loose in one hand like an apple she is about to bite into.

"Listen," he says. "Why don't I give us something to slow us down a bit."

"Something good, I hope."

The phrase goes through his mind: *informed consent.*

"Something you'll like, I think."

She trains the Beretta on him, utterly deadpan.

"Just don't try to pull anything, fucker."

A kick goes through him like a cattle bolt. Her jaw drops in pleased, scandalized horror.

"Jesus, shit, I'm sorry! I can't believe I said that!"

He can feel the sweat coming off him, smell the stink of it.

He puts up his hands.

"No false moves," he says, as evenly as he can manage.

He waits until they have taken the stuff before he goes down for the cigarettes. When he returns he finds her standing in the cold on his balcony still in her stocking feet, staring into the dark. He comes up behind her, just close enough for the heat of their bodies to touch, like weather fronts meeting, like rivers.

She doesn't turn.

"You'll catch your death out here."

And yet the cold feels far from them, as if a bubble protects them, a private atmosphere.

It has started to snow, small scattered flakes that flash out of the dark.

He knows if he touches her, there will be no going back.

"How do you feel?"

"I don't know. I feel like—I don't know."

"Like what? Tell me."

"Like— God. I shouldn't say." A shiver goes through her. "What was that stuff? Like jello."

Twenty-six storeys below them a cube van pulls into the courtyard and stops at the lobby door. It sits for a moment, idling, then pulls away, though no one has emerged from it.

"Jello sounds right," David says.

He tries to muster a proper sense of the cold. This is how errors are made, how people miss warning signs. He pictures the two of them freezing to death out here, caught in this frozen instant for all time. Millennia from now they'll be sifted from the ash of the apocalypse like the fugitives of Pompeii. The right and the wrong won't make any difference then, they'll be merely history, a story, beyond judgment.

"It's just," she says. "I don't know."

She leans into him then with the near-weightless press of a snowfall or wind, or maybe he is the one who presses against her. The different versions of the evening that have been shadowing each other like light and dark seem to collapse suddenly into one.

"You're freezing," he says, though her body is as hot as a bird's. "Come inside."

What happens next he'll be able to reconstruct afterwards only in the way that dreams can be reconstructed, with always that sense of a logic that can't be recaptured or put into words, of a larger complexity that is forever lost. The air itself has grown gelatinous by then, an ether they move through or water, past tilting doors, down tilting halls, as in the hold of a sinking ship. Time makes its way through here only in flickers, brief gloamings of murky light. There is her dress, the feel of it under his hand like satin, like skin; there is his gun, floating free like a dismembered appendage. Then outside the window, the building snow, slowly whiting out the darkness like an opiate, like sleep.

This much is clear, that at some point they end up in his bedroom and fuck. There is nothing tentative about this, for all the torpor of the drug: he has crossed over by then, to the dark rooms, the unspeakable sanctum, and he fucks her the way he has imagined, splitting her open, crawling inside her. All that matters is that none of it matters, that they are beyond scrutiny here, beyond telling. That that is the point.

Afterwards all he will remember is her body beneath him the merest scribble of flesh and bone, so flimsy he could break it in two.

Smell, emanating from the bedsheets. Julia's but not Julia's: he feels for her beside him but with the sick sense he has done it again, has betrayed her. Then suddenly he is awake.

The place beside him is empty. He taps the dimmer bar on his clock radio to light up the face: three in the morning. His head is pounding from the wine and the Ritalin. For a long moment he sits on the edge of the bed, listening, hears only the whirr of the fridge, the distant clack of the twenty-four-hour streetcar that passes in front of his building.

He checks the bathroom, the couch, the fold-out bed in the den. She is gone.

The snow has stopped, though the blanketing it has left gives the city light through the living room windows a ghoulish glow. The apartment stinks of cigarettes and spilled wine, of the left-over food they never bothered to clear. Open cabinets and open drawers; half a dozen books lying askew on the coffee table and floor. The mortar and pestle. The fresh pack of cigarettes.

David lights one and sits down in the club chair to smoke it.

Fragments come back to him that he can't quite tease out into intelligibility. He must have overestimated their doses, he thinks, then thinks, *Don't think*.

A bottle of sodium oxybate sits on the bathroom counter with its red warning stickers and threats. *Keep away from children! Avoid alcohol!* It isn't like him to have left it out. The thought hangs an instant, then he pushes it away, because of the other thoughts he feels pressing up behind it.

He measures out a dose to get him through the rest of the night. In his bedroom, in the dark, he makes out a lump of greater dark on his dresser: the Beretta. Then he feels something hard underfoot and bends to collect a bullet. There are more, scattered at the foot of the bed and under the dresser. David can't dredge up any memory of how they got there and yet even before he takes up the gun and feels the weight of it he knows that someone—who? at what point? to what end?—has taken the trouble to load it.

He sits down on the edge of the bed. In his brain, just white space.

The panic doesn't really start to set in until Jennifer Lowe fails to show for the afternoon faculty meeting. Until then he has more or less been able to put the matter from his mind. To armour himself with what he tells himself is the truth, that he has broken no laws or university protocols, crossed no uncrossable lines. Consenting adults.

The meeting is in one of the Humanities lecture halls. The minute David sets foot in it the familiar repugnance rises up in him: the factions and cliques, the jockeying, the whispered stratagems; the sense of how low the stakes are, how everything that happens here is only in the service of crushing whatever doesn't fit in. The real reason, he knows, that it was so easy to push through Jennifer Lowe was that there had seemed nothing dangerous in her, no sign of brilliance or heresy, anything that might challenge the dreamless sleep of the status quo.

He ought to have phoned her. The truth is it didn't occur to him to phone, didn't occur to him to do anything at all except show up here at the meeting acting as if nothing untoward had happened between them, and so put them on the light footing that was surely the only workable one going forward.

He keeps his eye on the doors. Despite the extra fistful of meds he has downed he has to fight to keep from nodding off.

It happened once in committee during the hire, on a day that Sonny had sat in to go over procedures.

"Late night, David?" Then the titters around the room, as if there was nothing more laughable, more demeaning, than falling asleep. If he'd had a gun then. Instead, even to open his mouth was to risk the further humiliation of having his words come out garbled like a mental deficient's.

He spots Julia up front but makes a point of blotting her from his field of vision. She had managed to get a new book out the previous fall: all those years that she had languished at home making his ambition seem something criminal, then the instant he was out the door she was back in the game. Meanwhile he has had to return again and again to the start on his own stalled opus as one after another his lines of approach have faltered.

He is already halfway to the door after the meeting has broken up when Sonny's voice rings out from the rostrum above the din of exodus.

"David, wait!" In such a peremptory tone that for a moment the whole room seems to focus on him. "My office! Five minutes!"

He detours outside for a cigarette, huddling in the cold near the garbage dumpsters at the back of the building. When he comes in, Sonny is already waiting for him, his skin the bluer blue-black it takes on whenever he is in high dudgeon.

"I don't even know where to start, David. I don't even know."

It has been clear from the moment Sonny called him out that she has been in to see him. What David can't figure is what she might have said, or out of what madness or malice.

"You could start," he says to Sonny, "by telling me what made you think you could ream me out like a teenager in front of my peers."

"Don't fuck with me, David! Don't play dumb with me! I sent

that girl to you in good faith! Because she looked up to you, if you can believe it!"

The bitterness of this, the sense of personal affront, takes David by surprise.

"Look, Sonny, you're going to have to spell out what exactly you're accusing me of here, because honestly, I'm not following."

"She came in here today trying to get out of her contract! Are you going to tell me you had nothing to do with that? I don't know what it was you did to her, I don't want to know, I don't even want to think about it, but whatever it was you better find a way to make it right, because if it comes down to a choice I'll trade you for her in a second! And don't think I won't find the way to do it! Don't think it isn't already there in your file!"

She is overreacting, clearly, is behaving like a child. All they did was *fuck*, for Christ's sake. And yet her reaction is all he has to go by, really, the only thing that might give a shape to his own blankness.

This much is obvious, at least: she hasn't told Sonny shit.

"You've got to be kidding." He resists the mistake of going on the defensive. "Look, I'm sorry she's changed her mind, but how is that even a problem? Everyone knows she wasn't your first choice."

Sonny's face twists with some emotion David can't read.

"I don't believe it. Here I was thinking all this was some revenge scheme you'd cooked up when you still don't have a clue, do you? She was the choice practically right out of the gate! The only question was how to get the great David Pace to think the idea was his so he wouldn't pull one of his diva acts."

"That's bullshit." This seems too byzantine even for Sonny's tortured power politics. And yet already David suspects he is actually telling the truth, that even now the story is making the rounds of the department. "It's not as if she's some big catch, for fuck's sake! She can't even place her dissertation."

"Do you know how many other offers she's had? Don't tell me she isn't a catch! She'll bring in more funding in a year than you will the rest of your life!"

"You're joking, right? Because she's been to the University of fucking New Mexico or wherever?"

"Because she's Indian, David! Do I have to spell it out?"

"What are you talking about? Not from your part of India. Not from where I'm sitting."

"Jesus, David. *Native* Indian! First Nations or whatever the bloody term is these days. Please don't tell me you didn't know that."

It is as if someone has put a bullet in his head. As if all along the gun has been raised, he has been staring right at it, yet somehow has missed it.

"It's right there in her dissertation, for the love of God, it's not as if she made some big secret of it! Did you even bother to *read* her dissertation before you wrote your report or were you just planning to fuck her from the start?"

David feels like he is back in Dirksen's office in Montreal with that woman and her son, facing the maw.

"What exactly is it you want from me here, Sonny? Why do you think you can just put this on my plate? For all you know she's just playing all of us. Maybe she's just using us to lever-age a better offer."

"David, I'm not an idiot. Don't think I can't tell the difference between leveraging pay scale and running scared. If you'd been here when she came in. Like I say, I don't want to know what went on with you two, but if she walks out after all the work and expense of finding her, after fighting tooth and nail to get money that'll probably just get shuttled over now to Engineering or Business Admin—it's pretty fucking irritating, David. It's pretty dispiriting. So if there's something you did that you can undo, I'm asking you. I'm begging you."

A window opens up into Sonny suddenly, into his own split brain, all the trade-offs he has had to make, all the lies he has had to tell himself to get by. It isn't true that David knows nothing about him. He knows about the wife he never shows in public, probably the product of some arranged village marriage he made when he was barely out of his teens; about the four or five children he never talks about, and of whom not a single photo has ever shown up in his office. About the early promise he has frittered away on pointless monographs and on being an errand boy for upper-level administrators who earn three times his salary for a quarter the effort, though he could easily have defected to admin himself years before instead of staying down with the rank and file. David knows these things but doesn't like to think about them, for fear of letting down his defences.

"I'll call her," he says. "I'll see what I can do."

Sonny nods, purses his lips.

"Look, David, I know you've been going through a lot these years, with the divorce and everything. But I can't help feeling there's something else going on here. Something that's behind this destructiveness you're bent on. If there's a health problem or anything or some kind of mental issue, maybe we need to look at that. Even Lowe asked about it. If you had some kind of condition."

To think David had actually been ready to take pity on him.

"My health is fine," he says, as acidly as he can manage. "It's also none of your fucking business."

He retreats to his office feeling enraged, indiscriminately, at Sonny, at himself, at Jennifer Lowe, unable to think, form a plan, see anything clearly. All these years of waiting for a turnaround, an even break, and now his whole fate seems to rest on a one-night stand. All the years of scrambling for some sort of handhold, anything to stop his free fall. Fudging his students' grades because he can't get through their papers; blowing up at them on the least pretext to bully them out of their complaints. Exhausting the milder fare of the surface web and gradually sinking down into the hard-core filth of the deep one. Avoiding his own son because of what he has become. And spurring it all, the panic, the horror, at this oblivion that trails him, that continues to steal up ever closer at his back like his own death.

All he can see now of Jennifer Lowe is the black hole of her Indianness. As if he had debauched a Holocaust survivor, a child. As if in his split brain that was exactly what he had wanted, to go past some limit, some uncrossable line.

In the accounts he has read of crimes people have committed in their sleep the crimes always get depicted as going against the grain. The gentle giant who drove miles across town to murder in-laws who adored him. The devout Mormon who stabbed a beloved wife of twenty years against whom he had never so much as raised his voice. And yet there is always some detail that points to intent, the gambling addiction the in-laws would soon learn of, the problem at work over which the wife had not shown full support. If intent is there, doesn't blame follow? Maybe all sleep has done is provide the permission the waking mind has withheld.

From those human guinea-pig epileptics whose brains had literally been cut in two a bizarre discovery had been made: that the brain houses within its separate hemispheres actual warring consciousnesses, each so distinct from the other, down to the level of political affiliations, of food preferences, of religious beliefs, as to seem those of entirely different people. In the normal course of things one side dominates and the other gets suppressed, though what this means is that everyone carries within them a shadow self that dogs the dominant one like a stalker, always at odds, always seeking an outlet, awaiting its chance under cover of dark.

David sits in his office at his computer going through Jennifer Lowe's dissertation. Only toward the end of it does he come across the half-dozen pages in which she sketches out her life. It turns out to be so close to the one he has imagined for her that he almost laughs: small prairie town, grain silos, big sky. Her father, a doctor, she describes as pure Scots. The native blood comes from her mother, descended from the Blackfoot Confederacy, though Jennifer's only contact with actual status Indians before she started studying them seems to have been through a high school literacy project at a reserve near her hometown.

None of this ever came up in committee, of course. Despite the expected tokenism, any reference to something as specific as bloodline or race would probably have rung out like the N-word, surely part of the logic behind Sonny's video interviews. Now, though, David can see that the evasions had the added bonus of allowing everyone to skirt the embarrassing truth at the heart of Jennifer's Indianness that was exactly what made her the ideal candidate. Better by far to bring in someone like her, a doctor's daughter, with barely half a black foot in the alien camp, than to risk the genuine article, whose grievances were too staggering by now, whose chances at redress too remote. It was the typical doublethink of academia, scared shitless of what it claimed most to want.

There is a final peroration in Jennifer's bio sketch where she writes of a kind of turning-point moment, a visit to an old buffalo jump near her town where she had a vision of the order that had prevailed in the thousands of years before the coming of the white man. In a few quick strokes she conjures that vanished world with an impressive complexity and breadth, the enmities and alliances, the different ways of life, the farmers with their settlements and divisions of labour and routes of trade and the nomads following the herds, slowly changing the landscape for their sake from woodland to grassland. The description has an authenticity to it that seems to moot the question of her own background. What does it matter if she is Micmac or Mongol if she has been able to make this sort of leap?

Something in the passage rings strangely familiar. When he reaches the end of it, where she compares the invading whites to the barbarian hordes who unravelled Rome, the connection hits him: his own *Masculine History*. He had included in it an account of his own turning-point moment, his visit to Ostia Antica as a child. Now he begins to see echoes everywhere, right down to phrases and words.

So she wasn't just snowing him, then. Somehow this cuts him more deeply than anything else has.

She is merely ashamed, perhaps, something as simple as that. Remembers as little as he does. Or did a search of the drug she found on his bathroom counter, the doctor's daughter, and needs reassurance, something to quash the nightmare version of the evening that might have formed in her afterwards. And yet already he knows that he won't call her. That he can't bring himself to apologize or make light, to face her different version of things or sort out what truths or lies he might have to tell to sway her to his own. Knows he can't pretend he has done with her anything other than what he has intended, or that his first reaction at finding the spot next to him in bed empty was anything other than the old familiar one of plain relief.

She is better off leaving this place while she can. He would do it himself if he thought he had anything in the way of real alternatives.

*Maybe we need to look at that.*

As soon as the thought hits him he wonders how he could have taken so long to come to it. It is Sonny himself who has shown him the way out: all this time he has been busting his balls trying to hide his affliction when he ought to have been flaunting it. That is what his mewling colleagues do, using every wart removal and stubbed toe to milk concessions and excuse their sins. He is sure he can get Becker to paint a picture of his disorder so dire that the university will be happy to put him on paid leave just for the peace of mind of keeping him out of the classroom. So much for Sonny's threats after that. So much for any of this, the enforced mediocrity, the institutional grind.

He calls up his collective agreement online and reads through the disability clauses, making notes. A burst of energy takes him and on impulse he starts packing up his office, grabbing some empty banker's boxes from the utility room and beginning to fill them with his books. It is madness, of course, he can't just walk out; it might take months to plod through all the paperwork. Yet now that the idea has formed he can hardly bear the thought of another day in this place. Shake the dust of it from him, no looking back. All his time free to work on his book, to do it properly now, no more dithering, no more false starts. He is not so old that his best work can't still be ahead of him. He is not so afflicted that he can't rally to the task once he is free of distractions.

Night has fallen. He catches his reflection in his darkened window like his own second self staring in at him and feels a chill. The thought of Montreal floats up again for an instant, the false bravado when he quit, the possibilities that never panned out.

He grabs another box and starts to fill it.

# PART TWO

# SIG Sauer P250

THE SHOP IS AT the edge of a beleaguered island of gentrification bounded by crosstown expressways and the old industrial lands to the south, in a turn-of-the-century clapboard
barely distinguishable from the residences flanking it. Across
the street, the interstate runs where a row of the same clap-
boards must have once stood, raised up on its concrete pillars
above the surrounding rooflines as if part of a separate dimen-
sion. From the online crime maps, which give a snapshot of
crime across the city practically in real time, David knows that
the interstate is a dividing line. It is like being at some border-
land, the fraying edge of the civilized world.

He has landed here, in this dying Rust Belt city, on a year-long
visitor's chair arranged by his former grad-school sidekick Greg
Borovic. Borovic is the one who has ended up at the prestigious
American school David never got to, a Top 20 where he has won
a closetful of teaching awards and oversees a raft of endowments

he seems to manage like a personal slush fund. David would have liked to tell him to go fuck himself except that he needs the money, reduced to living off a credit line on his condo as one by one he has burned whatever other bridges remained to him.

Inside the shop the August heat hangs like a fog. A rifle rack behind the counter holds a couple of Bushmasters and Remingtons, a glass-fronted display case an array of handguns. The walls, in faux wood panelling, are covered with joke signs and bumper stickers. "If you can read this, you're in range." "Make my day." "Protected by gun." It is like the setting for a B movie that takes place in a dystopian near future. Any second the aliens will burst through the walls or the zombies through the windows and the massacre will begin.

The man who emerges from the back room seems to have stepped out of the same B movie, dwarf-sized and slightly humpbacked and trailing an odour of cigarettes and boiled cabbage.

"So what can I do you for?"

David gets him to bring up some of his handguns. A Colt; a Ruger; a couple of Glocks. From a back cupboard the man takes out a SIG Sauer in black polymer that he sets in front of David like some vintage wine he has been holding back.

"Can't beat the Germans for engineering. Believe me, you're not going to find anything sweeter than this biscuit."

The gun is entirely black, right down to its rivets, like a thing forged in the devil's furnace.

"And the best part," the shopkeeper says, "it's completely modular. Don't like the frame, get the bigger one. Want more concealment, take the shorter barrel."

With practised ease he breaks the gun down and reassembles it with different components, switching the parts in and out like shells in a shell game. His fingers, despite the stubbiness of the rest of him, are elegant and long. David wonders how many hours he has given over, sitting alone in his back rooms, to perfecting manoeuvres such as these.

David takes up the gun. For all its space-age efficiencies it is not so far removed from his Beretta, has the same profile, the same frugality, the same weight. Nuclear bombs have fallen since his Beretta rolled off the line, men have walked on the moon, yet this simple design has persisted unchanged.

Already in the short time he holds it he knows his hand will remember the feel of it the way an addict's arm remembers the needle.

"How much?"

The background check, on the phone, takes under a minute. David has brought along the state hunting licence the web sites said he would need in order to get the restrictions on foreigners waived, but the shopkeeper hardly glances at it. He fits the gun into a blue plastic carrying case that looks like it might hold a power drill or wrench set and bundles the case into an old Walmart bag along with two hundred rounds of 40-calibre Smith and Wessons.

David nods at a sign behind the counter that reads "We don't call 911," beneath an image of the business end of a revolver.

"Ever get bothered here?"

The shopkeeper gives him a furtive once-over.

"Nah. Not here."

"I guess you're taking your chances robbing a gun store."

"Well, I'm ready for them, I'll tell you that."

Likely he has loaded weapons stashed in every cranny, awaiting a day of reckoning. It occurs to David that even in this place where the danger is real, it is still also a fantasy, that there is probably a part of this man that dreams only of this, of blowing some hoodlum to kingdom come.

Outside, the heat, the gun at his side, give the surrounding blight the post-apocalypse feel of the first-person shooter games Marcus has lately taken to. The violence of these games, that Julia would allow it, is always a shock to David, the blood spatters, the constant barrages, the enemies mown down in swaths or the innocents dragged from their cars or shot dead or simply run down and abandoned. Sometimes he stands watching behind Marcus as he plays and grows frightened at the silence between them, the weird energy that seems to join them like a third person they have formed.

He has left his car a few minutes' walk from the shop, on a tree-lined side street where in a matter of paces the mood changes from urban menace to small-town idyll, complete with rose bushes and juniper hedges and picket fences. It is like the sudden scene shift of a dream, with a dream's same inscrutable logic. In his drives through the city he has gone, in the space of a block, from the not quite faded glories of robber-baron carriageways to no-man zones that look like they've been pillaged by marauding armies, whole strip malls sitting abandoned, schools defaced, houses with their clapboard worn to the weathered grey of dust-bowl farmhouses.

He finds his car intact, no tires missing, no smashed windows. He puts the Walmart bag on the front passenger seat, where it sets off the seat belt alarm when he shifts into drive like another presence beside him.

*If he had a gun.* In the moment when matters had come to a head it had actually felt possible, easy, just a matter of filling the magazine and emptying it out, of giving in to the him-not-him in his animal brain that acted only on the cold irrefutable logic of stimulus and response.

Instead of buffering him from Sonny's threats, David's

disability application had ended up playing right into his hands. It was David's bad luck that the same week he submitted it he got flagged for double-dipping on his Ritalin, which had become a regular habit by then. Becker, who had sounded ready to write up whatever claim David asked him to, grew suddenly circumspect.

"It's not a joke, David. It's a risk for the doctor as well, this sort of abuse, you should think of that."

This from the man who had been handing out meds as if they were jujubes the whole time David had been seeing him.

Everything began to unravel after that. The university used the charge as an excuse to drag its feet on his application, making David sit through a series of infantile psychological tests, presumably to determine if he was some sort of drug fiend. He had gone on unpaid leave by then to help buttress his claim, and as the matter stretched on he quickly burned through what little he had in the way of savings. He missed a child support payment and had a screaming argument with Julia when he went by for Marcus. The next day his brother phoned.

"We're worried about you, Davie. Julia too. You're the father of her child."

"Are you doing her dirty work for her now, is that it? Can't you see how she's playing you? Are you that stupid?"

Burning his bridges.

Then toward the end of the summer the university announced it had appointed a new dean of arts: Dr. Sunil Krishnan. It was as if all these years Sonny had held off making the leap to admin until just the right time when he could do David maximum damage. Now with each day that went by with no word on his application David grew more obsessed with the thought of Sonny plotting against him. Again and again he had to stop himself from picking up the phone, from sending the emails he composed in his head, from tracking Sonny down in the flesh and doing he didn't know what, something eviscerating, irrevocable. Had to keep reminding himself to save his energies for his book: it was all that mattered now, what all his hopes rested on. It was why he had holed himself up in his condo the whole summer seeing no one and going nowhere; was why he kept begging off his weekends with Marcus, inventing bogus excuses that Julia no longer bothered to call him on. Was what would give the lie to every calumny against him and put him back on top. This time, he would work out a canvas large enough to match the book's ambitions. This time, even if it cost him his life's blood, he would see it through to the end.

The fall term had already started by the time the university gave him an answer on his application. What they offered was a joke, not the full leave he had asked for but a mere thirty per cent cut in duties coupled with a fifteen per cent cut in pay. He could already see what would happen: all his best courses would be taken from him and he'd be left with the shit intro courses and the mountains of marking like an indentured sessional, doing more work than before at less pay. To top if off there was no mention of backdating the claim to cover his unpaid leave or of what accommodation would be made for the fall. He felt a real panic then, a dizzying sense of how vulnerable he was. He couldn't survive another term without pay; in a matter of weeks his benefits would lapse if he didn't return to work and after that his drug costs alone would beggar him.

The kicker, though, was the letter that arrived a couple of days later from the office of the new dean notifying David that disciplinary procedures had been started against him. Apart from the expected charges, which covered nearly every infraction Sonny had ever hauled him in for, there were some that came straight out of his disability files. An infuriating reference to his "medication abuse" was made to seem to apply not just to his Ritalin but to the whole range of drugs Becker had cycled him through over the previous years, all of which were named and described. In amongst the list, sticking out like a dagger, was a bald reference to the "date-rape drug" sodium oxybate.

The thin thread that was all that was still holding David to the world seemed to snap. He packed his Beretta into his car with the notion of blowing off steam at the club, though when he came off the parkway he found himself heading instead in the direction of the university. Thinking and not thinking. Seeing the image play out, the look on the fucker's face. *Just to put a scare in him*, he thought, but not really thinking it, not wanting to know in that moment what he might be capable of.

He ended up in the parking lot outside Sonny's office not quite certain how he had got there, his mind at once empty and filled with a white fury that was new to him, dizzying, enthralling, spinning its not-dreams of the not-him that would be able to do such a thing. Picturing himself opening the trunk, taking out the padlocked case he used for carrying the gun to the club, undoing the lock. Dropping the gun's magazine and pushing in the rounds. The whole time feeling as if he was floating above himself, was already dead or near-dead or in whatever uncanny space you slipped into when you were ready to take a life.

He could hardly have said afterwards who he was in those moments. It was as if the different selves who inhabited him no longer reported to any final authority, like the self who could stab a wife forty-seven times for a tiny betrayal while his alter ego slept, like the one who could drive across town to kill his in-laws to avoid losing their good opinion. Like the borderline case at his old university in Montreal who had shown up at work one day with a couple of handguns and killed three of his colleagues because he felt he hadn't been given proper credit for some minor joint publication. The line that separated such acts from each other, with their same skewed sense of proportion, was starting to feel increasingly thin to David. There were studies that suggested one of the functions of sleep was exactly to mitigate the day's injuries and slights, through an intricate mechanics of deep sleep and dream that gradually wore down every grievance and sublimated every hurt. Who knew what mayhem threatened when the machinery faltered, at what point walking awake became as dangerous as asleep.

Over the next months David would end up making all the same mistakes he had made in his divorce, hiring lawyers he couldn't afford, losing all objectivity, fighting tooth and nail on what anyone could have told him from the start were lost causes. He had taken out his credit line by then, but his legal fees kept mounting ever more precipitously as victory grew ever less likely. What he settled for, finally, was little more than nothing, the university agreeing to call off its inquisition in exchange for his backing off on his disability suit. The catch was a sort of unofficial probation that would keep him on unpaid leave until a reassessment a couple of years down the road, his only wins a concession on benefits and a partial payout on an upcoming sabbatical.

By the end of this gutting Sonny Krishnan had come to seem almost an irrelevance. It wasn't Sonny David blamed anymore but the higher-ups, who cared nothing for Sonny's little agendas or principles, whose only principle was expedience. Yet Sonny was the one who haunted him. David had made up his excuses by then, his explanations, the anger, the isolation, the fatigue, until from a distance what he had contemplated looked almost innocuous, almost comic, almost sane. And yet the shadow of it remained, as if he had touched something in himself that should have stayed hidden.

It was only after matters with the university had been settled that he ran into Sonny again, not on campus, where he barely set foot anymore, but in the parking lot of a big-box mall near his gun club where he'd gone in search of a birthday gift for Marcus. Sonny had three kids in tow, all boys, who stood ranged beside him in descending order in their cheap Michelinman parkas like Russian dolls. At the sight of David, Sonny looked caught out, one minute joking with his boys, seeming unburdened in a way David had never seen him, the next his familiar armoured self.

"David! Ah! Well!"

Not even able to look him in the eye. David felt a stab go through him at the sight of his sprawling brood, of his ancient car even more rundown and junk-filled than his own, that it took him a second to recognize as envy.

"Nice family," was all he said.

"Yes, well. Thank you. Thank you."

David hadn't so much as got out of the car that day outside Sonny's office. And yet what he had pictured in his head had remained etched there as vividly as though he had lived it. The blue autumn sky as he made his preparations; the pellucid air. The weight of the gun in his hand, the feel of each round. The burn in his gut as he knocked on Sonny's door. It was only when a colleague he knew distantly walked by his car and gave him a curt nod of greeting that David came out of the trance state he seemed to have fallen into. His blood was racing. Not with fear, or with horror; something else. He had put it from his mind.

At the end of the first week of classes Greg puts on a mixer for David at his house, a rambling Queen Anne Victorian at the edge of the university zone that back home would have run him well into the seven figures.

"Just the elect," Greg says of the guest list. "The ones whose butts you'll have to kiss now and then."

The old poison is still there. David was hoping to find him aged, pot-bellied, gone soft, but he looks unchanged, right down to the horn-rimmed geek chic he wore like a badge twenty years ago and that now makes him come across like a veteran of the siege of Sarajevo, bristling with ironies. "Still waiting for my share of the royalties on *Masculine History*," he wrote in his first email, making a show of burying the hatchet as a way of planting it squarely in David's chest. At the mixer he goes out of his way to mention the book at every introduction, never failing to work in its time on the American bestseller lists.

"Oh, yes," people say. "I think I remember that."

The real irony is that just as David's stock has been tanking back home it has been enjoying a small rally south of the border. He had put out a collection of essays a couple of years earlier comparing the decline of American democracy to the failure of the Republic, another stopgap he had cobbled together from old articles and blog posts to fill space while he worked on his opus. The book had looked destined to sink like a stone until a belated rave on its paperback release had been picked up by every two-bit affiliate across the country and had pushed it to the bottom rungs of a few bestseller lists. That Greg has never breathed a word about the book even though the course David has proposed to teach is essentially based on it seems the clearest evidence it is what has put David back on his radar.

"Just be careful looking at this stuff as an outsider," was all Greg had said about the course. "You don't want to come across as a dilettante."

Greg's "elect" turn out to be mostly horses' asses from what

David can tell, smarmy liberals to a one, all steeped in the prevailing orthodoxies. After only a week on campus David already feels smothered by the Orwellian atmosphere of the place. At the mixer he downs three vodka tonics in quick succession to get by and chases each of them with a tab of methylphenidate, so that by the time the provost arrives, a crew-cut all-American type who exudes the menacing charm of a cult leader, David is ready for blood.

"Greg tells me you're quite the powerhouse. I hope our students are up to your standards."

David leans in confidentially, shooting Greg a look to make clear he has the matter well in hand.

"To be honest, there's an African-American girl in my class I'm already having a hard time keeping my hands off."

The provost's grin hasn't altered. He claps a beefy linebacker's arm around David's shoulders.

"Dave, I don't know how you do things back home, but down here we don't joke about these matters."

Greg corners him in the kitchen afterwards looking ready to strike him.

"Christ, David! You can't pull that shit with guys like him!"

"Come on, how can you stand it? It's like Pyongyang around here, the PC's so thick."

He knows the nerve this will touch in Greg. Back in their bad-boy days no cow had been too sacred for them.

"You don't have any idea how differently sex plays down here." But already he sounds defensive, petulant. "Try to remember that."

*Round one to me*, David thinks. He has put Greg on notice: he won't be licking his boots for this bone Greg has thrown him.

He doubts Greg would have had him here at all if he'd had any real clue of the depths he had plucked him from. After the lawyers and fights, the paranoia, the constant sense of siege; after the months of being closed off in his condo like a subject in a sensory deprivation experiment. The growing tolerance to his meds, so that bit by bit he had upped his dosages, chipping away at the stockpile he'd amassed from his double-dipping, and which no one had thought to take away from him, until he had lost all track of how much drug was pumping through him. Sleeping in erratic fits, without schedule, pressing himself at his work until he simply passed out at his desk. Weeks had gone by that might never have happened for all he could remember of them; or he could not say for certain if what he remembered had in fact occurred. He had started seeing things by then, at first just flashes at the edges of his vision but then full-blown hallucinations. Visits from Marcus or Julia or his father, some judgment always hanging over him; from Jennifer Lowe, who had packed her bags and left town without David's ever having lifted a finger to stop her. In the end he had agreed to the university's settlement offer mainly just to rid himself of the thought of her, of the prospect of her showing up one day in some hearing room or continuing to haunt him until the men in white suits came.

From the kitchen he hears Greg making the rounds in the living room again.

"You should have seen him in grad school. Like Fredo in *The Godfather*. Banging cocktail waitresses two at a time."

So there will be no respite between them. *Fine.* That is the last thing David wants, some kind of mid-life reconciliation. Anything that might require him to let down his guard.

He slips out to the back yard for a cigarette and finds Greg's wife and daughter there, the daughter practising pliés and pirouettes in the shade of a big oak and the wife sitting in a weathered deck chair as though the party inside had nothing to do with her.

He tries to call up her name.

"Not fond of faculty parties?"

Her eyes flit from his like a nervous teen's. She is not unattractive, fine-boned and pale-skinned and blond like some elf queen or changeling, though from the couple of times he has met her he has taken away only an eerie blankness.

"Dance class," she says. "I'm the taxi."

The phrases sound so cryptic and disconnected it takes him a second to follow her meaning.

"Mind if I come?"

She actually laughs, a short "Ha!" as if she has caught him out.

"Not fond of faculty parties?"

This time she leaves an impression. He has heard she is ABD, All But Dissertation—no doubt Greg plucked her right out of his own doctoral stream, moulding her to his tastes and then quickly getting her with child to keep her out of circulation. It is a common syndrome at these small private schools, the grad programs often serving as spouse farms for the aging male faculty. Then at some point the progesterone haze begins to fade and the old ambitions rear their heads again.

The next morning the wife and daughter show up at the coach house Greg has set him up in behind the university's foreign student centre. He hears their voices from the upstairs office and looks out the window to see the girl playing on a jungle gym that sits next to the house. As soon as he looks out, the girl turns.

"Look, it's David!"

Whatever this is, he thinks, he is sure he doesn't need it.

By the time he gets down to them he has managed to dredge up the wife's name.

"It's Sophie, right?" Cheery and glib, as though to underline how peripheral she is to him.

"We didn't mean to bother you. It was Kateri's idea to come. She used to play here when Sidney lived here."

The girl, like a discreet chaperone, has kept at her exertions on the jungle gym.

"Sidney?"

"Sidney who lived here before you. Sidney who died here, in fact. In the bedroom, I think."

"Mom!" This seems some sort of running joke between the two of them. "You weren't supposed to tell!"

"Funny that Greg never mentioned any of this," David says.

"I'll bet you wish I hadn't either. You'll see ghosts now."

"Don't worry, I brought enough of my own."

They end up inside. Kateri wanders the house calling out the changes she notices since the reign of Sidney while Sophie makes coffee, moving about the kitchen as though it were her own.

It has come out that Sidney was a visiting choreographer the university got saddled with when he fell ill.

"The dreaded you-know-what," Sophie says. "So it took a while."

"I didn't think people died from that anymore."

Another of her laughs.

"People die of the flu! Come to think of it, that's how it started. He didn't have anyone, really, by the end. Just me and Kateri."

There seems no moroseness in this, no sentimentality, just the plain refreshing fact of aloneness and death.

Kateri has drifted up behind him. Belatedly he thinks of the SIG Sauer in a drawer of his desk. Unlike back home, no law here requires him to keep his weaponry under lock and key.

"We used to bring him food sometimes," Kateri says. "This was his place, right where you're sitting."

"What about me? Are you going to bring me food?"

She blushes.

"If you want."

When they leave, Sophie lingers at the door after Kateri has gone out.

"I imagined you differently," she says. "From how Greg described you."

"Well. Sorry to disappoint you."

He feels strangely deflated afterwards. She was expecting David the sex fiend, David the asshole, David the rival. Instead she has found this avuncular middle-aged academic. This Sidney.

Later in the day he gets a call from Greg.

"So. I hear the Welcome Wagon stopped in on you." In a neutral tone David can't read. "Sorry about Sidney, by the way. I hope you washed the sheets."

He invites David for dinner at the house. It is as if he has passed some test.

"Let's aim for next weekend. Sophie's schedule's a little crazy during the week, what with extracurriculars."

*Good*, David thinks. So there was no intrigue after all, nothing to hide. But he also thinks, *I'm no fucking Sidney.*


He puts the visit from his mind. The last thing he needs is distraction. Since his arrival here he feels he has finally turned the corner on his doomsday book, his head cleared of all the static that filled it back home and the ideas starting to flow again. By now he has broadened his scope to take in the Hittite and Mycenaean collapses, which has meant a whole new round of reading and notes, of virtual tours of the important sites, of mastering the prevailing views until he knows them well enough to refute them.

Right from the start he has been logging ten- and twelve-hour days up in his coach-house office, up at dawn every morning to run in the wooded reserve behind his house and keeping a close watch on his meds after the months of abuse. By now he knows that every deviation from routine will cost him, every lost half-hour of sleep, every glass of wine, every extra pill that pushes up his tolerance. Every cigarette: he has cut himself back to three or four a day, and none past supper or he can feel the nicotine coursing through him the whole night. It feels positively monkish, living this way, all his usual habits getting stripped from him one by one until he is no longer sure whether he is distilling himself to some essence or simply erasing himself.

His teaching duties run only to a single upper-level seminar that meets once a week. Because he hardly prepared for it, the first class did not go well—he could see students' eyes starting to glaze, could hear the bombast creeping into his voice in lieu of anything like real conviction. By the second week his numbers have dropped from a full complement of twenty to a mere dozen, as if here too he has failed to deliver the bad boy people have been expecting.

It was the black girl he joked about with the provost who tripped him up the first class. The whole time she sat with the skeptical look of the unconvinced, finally deigning to weigh in when he was rehashing an argument from his book about the imperial trappings of the Obama inaugurations on the Mall.

"But isn't that a little simple-minded? I mean, by that logic the March on Washington would look imperial."

Instead of rising to the challenge he grew defensive.

"You're missing the point. You're talking about an entirely different relationship to power."

He is glad the second class to see that the girl, Abby, is among the returned. He starts by offering an apology, admitting the dangers of mapping the present onto the past.

"Take something like slavery." The reference is so on-the-nose that the air in the room goes heavy at once. "In Rome slavery was what you did, not what you were, something you could leave behind in your own lifetime. But here, even a hundred and fifty years later, right down to the sixth and seventh generations like the good book says, we still can't look at someone like Abby without thinking she came from slaves."

The girl's eyes go to stone. No one dares to look at her.

"What's more, we can hardly even talk about it. In a free country. In a country *built* on freedom. Now that's power the Romans never dreamed of."

All this is standard PoMo 101, maybe as tendentious as his original argument, but it has had the desired effect. The room is charged now; they have stepped beyond the expected.

"So what's your point, exactly?" one of the guys says. Defiant; angry, really.

"I dunno. What's my point?"

The girl shifts. He can almost see it, the bubble that has formed around her. When she speaks it is in the same defiant tone, with the same anger.

"The point is it's true."

This is enough to break the ice. A discussion starts, careful at first, though bit by bit people start to risk something like an honest opinion. For the first time in years David feels a bit of the thrill he had in the classroom when he started out, all these young minds before him ready to be cracked open like eggs. Where did it go, that thrill? How much of it has been lost to his own shutting-down, to the walls he has built to hide his afflictions?

They end up going the whole three hours without a break. Afterwards David keeps expecting the phone call telling him to pack his bags, though the only one he gets is from Greg, confirming dinner.

"B.Y.O.W.," he says, from the old days. Bring your own weapons.

"I've got to hand it to you how you've mastered the digital idiom. I don't think there's a single paragraph in that last book that's longer than three lines."

David has arrived for dinner to find Greg alone, chopping vegetables and seasoning tenderloin in the kitchen like a reality-show master chef. He has the dim sense he has been lured here for some sort of ambush.

"Sophie's just dropping Kateri off at a sleepover, by the way. In case you were afraid I was going to try to force myself on you."

Greg has poured them both double Scotches. The drinks, David knows, are a test: on the several restaurant dinners Greg has treated him to he has had to defend himself against the expensive wines Greg has insisted on plying him with. He makes a show of taking up his glass, of nodding his approval, and Greg makes a show of not noticing it is a show.

"What I don't get," David says, "is how you missed the boat on all that stuff. You were always so ahead of the curve. Now I do a search for you and all that turns up is a plumber in Belgrade."

"My cousin, I think. Don't let the plumbing fool you. And whatever you do, don't ask him about the war."

"If I know you, you've got your reasons. Some kind of theory, probably. As in conspiracy."

"Here's my theory. The only stuff worth looking at on the net is for people who don't need a search engine to find it. Homeland Security, pedophiles, arms dealers. All the rest is just TV on steroids, one more mind-control network to get us to buy more stuff so we can burn through what's left of the world's resources even faster. And don't tell me you don't pay attention to the ads. It's all ads, every word of it. What's your web site but an ad for David Pace?"

"All I can say is, one day you'll wake up and you won't exist. The balance will have shifted. Having a body won't mean shit unless there's some piece of you out there in the cloud."

"That's where you're wrong. It'll be the other way around. Don't think we're not mobilized, we resisters. When the time's right we'll take out the whole system, and everything in the cloud'll just vanish. Think of it, banks, corporations, whole governments ceasing to exist from one minute to the next. Now there's a terrorist act I could subscribe to."

They used to spend hours on riffs like this. It was how they limbered their minds, how they communicated. How the theory of masculine history had got its start.

"Sounds like a great idea for a blog post," David says.

"Go for it. All yours. No charge."

David hears a car in the drive and a minute later Sophie steps in through the mud room.

"Oh!" Her face twisting in surprise at the sight of them as if she had accidentally stumbled into a men's room.

Greg barely turns.

"Traffic?"

"No. A bit."

She slips past him at the stove like a ghost flitting by. Her eyes catch David's an instant.

"How's the Gingerbread House?" she says.

It is what Kateri calls his place. A smile seems to start but she is out of the room before it has a chance to finish.

David waits for the sound of her footsteps on the stairs.

"So I heard she's ABD."

"She told you that?"

"No. Someone at the mixer, I think."

"Right. My trusted colleagues." With more sourness than David might have expected. "Just don't jump to conclusions."

"You mean, former grad student marries mentor?"

"That's exactly what I mean. For your information, she went to the state school across town. In cybernetics, for that matter, so so much for your mentor theory."

"Cybernetics? I would have thought that was right up your alley. AI and all that."

"That's a bit of a misconception, actually." With a hint of pride, almost. "More the study of systems. Games. Brains. Civilizations. Finite universes."

"Right. It makes sense now."

"Really? How's that?"

"How she's managed to survive being married to you. She's smarter than you are."

"At least you got that right."

Greg lets his guard down a bit after that. At supper he sits by like the doting husband while David grills Sophie on their relationship. It turns out she had been a student of Greg's after all, taking a graduate Enlightenment course with him through an interuniversity exchange.

"I figured that was when it started," she says.

"What? Greg's Lolita complex?"

She laughs.

"I mean thinking in systems. Cybernetics. In the Enlightenment."

"You see what I have to put up with," Greg says. David thinks he can feel the impulse in him then to put an arm around her, to claim possession of her. "Total Asperger's. She wanted to spend the whole term talking about automata."

David manages to get through three of Greg's double Scotches without falling asleep or falling down. The biggest surprise is how much he enjoys himself, how he almost feels, even while a part of him keeps waiting for the knife, as if he is among friends. He and Greg will clap arms around one another at the end of the night and all will be forgiven, all the one-upmanship and stupid jealousies, all the dark things that seem to dog them still out of the past.

David's hand rests at Sophie's waist an instant as he leans in to kiss her at the door.

"Tell Kateri I'm still waiting for my Meals on Wheels."

Greg follows him outside to his car.

"Look, David. There's been a bit of a problem." David can't make out his face in the dark. "It seems that black girl you mentioned to the provost has been in to see him."

*The fucker.* David has to fight to keep the rage from his voice.

"So when's the hanging?"

"You can imagine how the provost took it. He said it was a first for him."

David had been so sure he had won the girl over. He can already see how matters will go, how Greg will make a show of fighting for him, will finally shrug his shoulders and say nothing could be done.

"What did she say exactly?"

"That's the kicker. She said you were the first teacher she'd had here who'd actually been honest with her. You can guess how disappointed the provost was, after the stunning first impression you made."

David feels his knees go weak. This is how vulnerable he has become, how needy.

"You're fucking with me."

"Of course I'm fucking with you. When I stop fucking with you is when you should be worried."

He just wants to leave now, to be in his bed, but Greg wants to prolong the moment.

"The best part was the provost's face when he told me. Pouring it on thick. I mean, think what she was really saying to him. That it took an outsider. After all the years of being the fucking outsider, I can tell you, it was sweet."

"I hope this isn't going to cost you your annual increment."

"It's more the Klan I'm worried about. Just don't let it happen again."

Somehow the evening has ended in exactly the absolution David has dreamed of. Yet now that he has it, it only feels like a burden, something to get free of. Now that he has it, all he can think of on the drive home is Sophie's heat against his palm as he bent to kiss her.

When he sees her again it is as a shadow that crosses his path on one of his morning runs, so fleetingly he isn't sure at first he hasn't simply imagined her. It is barely sunrise, the morning light through the trees just a stain of orange and red against the orange and red of the changing leaves. He quickens his pace to go after her, then thinks of the terror that might go through her at the sound of someone pounding up the trail behind her at this hour and feels a strange doubling, as if he were running to save someone from himself.

By then she has already vanished into the labyrinth of trails that vein the reserve.

He mentions the sighting to Greg. They have taken to getting together for squash, a carry-over from their student days, on the court their barbed banter falling away until they are just battling animals, grunting and heaving in the court's intimate space with the same controlled brutality animals have, the same aversion to risk. Then as soon as they are back in the locker room all their jangling weaponry comes out again.

"What kind of man sends his wife out into those woods alone? I hope she's packing."

"Believe me, they've got security guys coming out of your yin-yang in there and cameras in every tree. One wrong move and they send in the drones."

On his morning runs now, David keeps circling back to where their paths crossed. Every day that goes by without his spotting her again he feels the same lag in his energy. He notices now the webcams peering down from the lampposts, the brown security cars parked discreetly at trailheads. The cars give off a mixed air of protection and menace. Inside, high school dropouts and failed cops probably sit with loaded Tauruses or Smith and Wessons in their laps, spinning visions of the one who will give them a reason.

It is several days before he finally sees her again, this time when he practically runs into her as he is coming around a bend. For a second she looks ready to veer right past him.

"Oh! It's you!" With the same startled look she'd had in her kitchen.

"Nice to see you too."

She flushes.

"Sorry!" Her hair is pulled back in a ponytail and the colour spreads in a wave right down to the nape of her neck. "Greg says I do that. He says I wear my brain on my face."

"That makes me feel better. So I really *do* scare the shit out of you."

"It's not that!" But she's laughing now. "It's more like, when something's out of context. Like you jogging here. I dunno."

"I get it. A sort of systems error. Me doing something healthy when I'm supposed to be this chain-smoking badass."

She laughs again.

"You must think I'm awful."

He stays with her for the rest of her run. He can feel his blood thrill at being this close to her again. For many days now the images of her have crowded his head, the thoughts of what he might do to her. It is madness, of course, would put everything at risk again, yet the more he tells himself this, the more the thoughts fill him.

At the end of her run they linger at the stairwell at the far end of the reserve that leads up to her street. A mist of sweat has formed on the down of her cheek.

"Maybe we should coordinate our runs," he says, as casually as he can manage. "So you don't have to be out here alone."

"Oh. Maybe." Her eyes have taken on the look of a panicked animal's. "Do you really think it's dangerous? There's always other runners around."

Her brain on her face. For the first time he is sure that the thought of him has crossed her mind.

All it would take now to move them forward, perhaps, is the right lie, the right excuse.

"Not to mention the cameras."

"Sorry?"

"The security cameras. Greg says they're everywhere."

"Right." Her eyes shift uncomfortably. "I always forget about them."

Her fear of a moment earlier, which had seemed pure, turbid with possibility, feels tainted now. It has been enough simply to bring up Greg's name.

"I guess you better get going. Greg's probably got breakfast waiting."

He begins to vary the times of his runs, wondering at the demon in him that always wants to drive him to the most destructive thing. The days go by without his seeing her again and yet still she is there in his thoughts, is there in his dreams at night. His mind keeps returning to the moment when he might have pushed things with her, to the black wave that rose up before him then that was less conscience or reason or fear than simply the fatigue of a lifetime, the impulse to turn toward what was easy, what required nothing of him. For all his new discipline the fatigue is there almost always now, a wall he has to fight his way through each time he sits down to write or make his way through some tome, each time he starts a conversation or heads out to class. It is born, perhaps, of his disorder and yet is somehow larger than it, seems to take in every wrong turn he has ever made, everything he has ever risked or lost, every delusion he has laboured under or bauble he has let himself covet. Every pat on the back that he pretends to himself now is the sign of a resurgence when perhaps he is just reverting to all the old compromises, all the old lies, to the sleep his life had become before his disorder, in its twisted way, had dragged him kicking and screaming from it.

Mornings, now, instead of running, he drives out to a gun club he has joined, where he fires rounds from his SIG and from a vintage Colt revolver he has picked up to break the monotony of the SIG's relentless precision. With the Colt there is no mistaking what he is at, the fire bursting from the chamber with each shot with an addictive violence. Often he is at the range before sunrise so he can have the bays to himself, letting himself in with his key card and clustering round after round in the kill zone to kick-start the day.

The Colt he picked up at a local gun show. Row after row of banquet tables lined with guns heaped up like underwear in a discount bin, cookie-cutter handguns in black polymer, derringers and revolvers, assault rifles and sniper rifles, semi-automatic shotguns with massive 30-round drums. At the NRA booth he ended up signing on for a free on-the-spot safety class that qualified takers for concealed carry.

"Believe me, it's a whole different experience," the bleached-blond at the sign-up desk told him. "The first time you go out you'll feel like you just swallowed a box of Viagra."

The instructor turned out to be little more than a kid, greasy-haired and scrawny, dressed in an ill-fitting blazer that at the outset of the class he opened with a studied casualness to reveal a Glock 17 at his hip.

"First bit of advice: you want a high-volume mag. The law says, you've got time to reload, you've got time to think. Which means you've just seen self-defence ratchet up to first-degree."

He trotted out the colour code of alertness that was popular in gun circles, Condition White, Condition Yellow, Condition Red. For a few minutes then he almost rose to the poetic.

"Condition White is every jogger or boarder going down the street with earbuds jammed in their ears. It's everyone texting or talking on the phone hardly noticing what's two feet in front of them. Condition White, basically, is asleep. It's what almost everyone is almost all of the time, which is why people like you can't be. Why every minute of every day, as soon as you step out your door, you have to be alert. Because when the time comes to do something, it's on you."

The pitch sounded like an ode to the hope guns imparted. They made of everyone, even this scrawny kid with his Glock 17, a potential warrior, a potential hero.

Afterwards everyone had their photos taken and filled out the paperwork that would get sent on to whatever office it was that issued the permits. David was sure there would be some glitch, that the class had been little more than a hook to get him on an NRA mailing list. But one day he opens his mail and the permit is there, a flimsy plasticized card with the bad graphics and grainy print of something run off in someone's basement. *License to Carry a Concealed Handgun*. A strange charge goes through him. He has been given the right to arm himself like a vigilante, could walk out his door with a handgun in every pocket and enough ammo to take out an entire schoolyard or platoon, and no one could stop him.

For the rest of the day he floats in a kind of suspended animation. Then toward sunset he gets out his SIG and loads the magazine, pulls the slide back to draw a round into the chamber. He'll need to get a holster of some sort; for now he simply sets the gun in a side pocket of his coat. His heart is already pounding. It is the first time outside of a shooting bay that he has carried the gun loaded. Apart from an auto-lock that keeps it from firing if it is jostled or dropped, the gun's only safety is the 5.5 pounds of pressure it takes to pull the trigger.

He steps outside. Despite himself, the instructor's spiel comes back to him, every detail around him suddenly sharp, important, the baring branches, the dying leaves. He starts down the dirt path behind his house that leads into the woods. He can hear every twig that snaps and make out every smell, of earth and bark and decay and something else, vaguely out of place, like the smell that warns a prey or the one that betrays it.

He passes a brown security car. In the twilight all he makes out through the tinted windows is the barest silhouette of a face, featureless and dark like a comic book rendering of a villain or spy. He thinks of the two of them with their guns and a shadow crosses him of what feels like a primordial fear, the sense of what it might mean to live in a lawlessness where every stranger had to be reckoned a threat, like those isolate tribes you heard of for whom every meeting on the road carried the prospect of death. He is only playing at this, he knows it, and yet for the first time he thinks he gets what the real thrall of a gun is beyond the blood lust and compensations, this feeling of being alone on the road without judges or gods, beholden to no authority but your own. The terrible freedom of that, of making the hard choice. Anything less, it seems, is only for sleepwalkers.

Around him the woods stand carved in the sodium light of the lampposts as if a fog that has surrounded him all his life has suddenly lifted.

He is out in the woods the next morning before he can second-guess himself, circling them again and again until she appears coming toward him on the path as though he has conjured her by sheer force of will. At the sight of him, a flash on her face as at a gunshot.

"I haven't seen you," she says, but distant and muted.

"Just work. Trying to finish something up."

For a long time they run in silence, with only the sound of their footfalls and their breaths. They reach the stairwell that goes up to her street but she doesn't slow, and they end up circling back toward his house.

"I think I'm going to head in." Trying to empty his voice of every false note, every hint of casualness. "I don't suppose I could offer you a coffee."

Her face colours like a beacon going off.

"Kateri will be getting up."

He sees it clearly then, her other life, the closed curtains and rumpled sheets, the smell of sleep, the sound of puttering in the kitchen.

"Another time, then."

In the end she is the one who starts toward his house, without so much as a glance at him, only a furtive look over her shoulder as if they were fugitives in a police state, making their escape. Any minute the alarm will sound, the shots will ring out.

"We have to hurry."

It is all she offers in the way of consent.

He is on her the second they are inside. They don't talk now, not a word, only pull at each other's clothes until enough parts are exposed to fuck, which they do on the living room floor, still trailing bits of clothing like patches of skin they have shed. There doesn't seem time to think or plan or take stock, to show consideration or restraint. Afterwards there is no small talk, no fishing for endearments, only her panicked look, her brain on her face, the sense of her fear again like a tidal wave rising.

"I have to go," she says, gathering up clothes like someone trying to piece back together a life after a hurricane or war.

When she is gone it is almost as if he has dreamed the whole episode. He feels rattled, not sure what has begun or if anything has, if he has pleased her or merely terrified her. He has no email address for her or private cell, doesn't dare try to call her at home, so that the whole day he is on tenterhooks. When he doesn't spot her the next morning on his run, he goes into full panic.

"We're doing Canadian Thanksgiving Sunday night," Greg says at their squash game. "If you're around."

David wonders how they imagined they could hide such a thing from someone like Greg in this fishbowl, this place where there are cameras in every tree. But then that is the kind of lie people always tell themselves at the outset, when such lies are needed.

"I'll let you know," he says.

At class that day he is a ticking bomb. He has grown too chummy with the students, too invested in being the hip one, the one not afraid to confront their creeping nihilism rather than dosing it with bromides. Now, all of a sudden, he can't bear his own falseness.

One of them tries to shrug off a missed reading.

"Next time," David says, "read the fucking text or stay home."

The boy packs up his things and leaves the room without a word. With one lapse David has managed to undo all the weeks of hard work he has put in to win the students over.

*Fuck them.*

The next morning, again, there is no sign of Sophie on the trails. It is all David can do to keep from showing up at her door. She has slit her wrists for all he knows, has confessed everything, has slipped town in the dead of night.

At the height of his panic, he gets a call from Julia.

"Don't tell me you forgot, David. We agreed to this weeks ago."

There it is, clearly marked on his calendar: *Marcus here.* Julia had planned to fly him down for the weekend en route to some conference.

"It's bad timing for me. Can't you bring him to your dad's?"

This is enough to send them into one of their spirals.

"Are you still his father, for fuck's sake? Doesn't that mean anything to you?"

He drives out to the airport on the Friday afternoon for the hand-off. His first thought when he sees the boy, going on twelve but still scrawny and small, still full of quirks and tics and obscure intent, is, *Let this be over.*

He can't get the image of Sophie out of his head, of fucking her on his living room floor.

"He's only allowed an hour of internet a day and one of gaming. Don't let him fight you on that."

In the car Marcus's eyes are on him the whole time. Then at the house he is finicky and brooding, avoiding surfaces as if the place seethed with contaminants. He sits hunched over the laptop Julia has sent along with him while David makes supper. Afterwards David manages to find a movie on pay-per-view he is willing to watch, though when he goes through the options for the next day Marcus offers only unreadable twitches and shrugs.

"We'll work something out in the morning. If I'm not here when you wake up I'm just out for my run."

He goes out early, in the cold and dark, scouring the trails for Sophie until dawn has given way to full daylight. Julia would be livid if she knew he'd left Marcus alone for so long. He returns home expecting to find him still in his bed, but from the entrance hall he hears sounds from the upstairs office. A thought shifts at the edge of his brain like a movement in his peripheral vision. Then he starts up the stairs and catches sight of Marcus through the office doorway.

His blood freezes.

"Pee-uw. Pee-uw."

Marcus is panning the room with David's SIG Sauer. Somehow, with a child's instinct, he has known where to look to find the most precious thing, the most forbidden one.

*Jesus fucking Christ, Marcus, it's not a toy!*

But he doesn't say it. Instead he comes up so quietly Marcus doesn't notice him until he is already close enough to reach for the gun.

"Better let me take that."

In an instant David has dropped the magazine and checked the chamber. The chamber is clear, though the magazine still carries six or seven rounds from his last trip to the club. All it would have taken to make the gun live was a pull of the slide.

Marcus looks close to tears.

"Sorry, Dad! I was only looking at it!"

Still such a child, really, still so unformed, something David forgets over and over, always imagining him as this looming fault-finder, this adversary, this judge.

"Nobody's angry at you. It wasn't your fault. I shouldn't have left it unlocked. I shouldn't have left it loaded."

The boy's relief is so palpable it sends a surge of emotion through David.

"I've got another one, too. A revolver. Here, I'll show you."

The guns end up filling the rest of the morning. David shows Marcus how to field-strip them and lets him practise on the SIG until he gets good at it. He is taken by the focus Marcus brings to the task. He can't remember a time when the two of them have shared something so intently.

"I've still got that gun of your grandfather's back home. Maybe it'll be yours one day. I use it for target shooting, like these two."

"Do you think I'd be able to do that? Shoot targets?"

"I don't know, son." He can imagine what would become of the little he has left in the way of visitation rights if Julia ever got wind of any of this. "You might be a bit young still."

Instead of dropping the matter, he looks up the state's minimum age for handling guns. A mere nine.

"Looks like you're in luck. Maybe we'll swing by my gun club this afternoon and you can try a few rounds."

All Marcus's hunched resistance to him has vanished by now. He asks to help with lunch, something he has never done, and the two of them move around David's narrow kitchen bumping elbows like bachelor room-mates.

"There's a couple of safety rules we should probably go over before we head out."

"I know the first one. Don't tell Mom."

David packs only the SIG, which even at .40 calibre is so finely tuned that the recoil hardly registers. He warns Marcus not to be put off by the gun club's clientele.

"Some of these guys, guns are like a religion for them. They're all they live for."

"Why do they like them so much?"

David resists the urge to launch into a lecture.

"I dunno. Why do *we*?"

The club is a no-frills place in a strip mall just outside the university zone. The lounge has all the charm of a halfway house, a battered vending machine, a torn vinyl sofa, a magazine rack where people dump their back issues of *American Hunter* and *American Handgunner* and *Soldier of Fortune*. A couple of regulars, big truck-driver types, sit watching football on a tiny flat-screen. David has a moment of doubt, wondering at what he is dragging Marcus into. Yet it has been enough simply to show some trust in the boy for him to seem to mature before David's eyes.

The video monitor in the prep room shows two shooters already out in the gallery, the soundproofing cutting the noise of their shots down to distant pops. David fits Marcus with goggles and with earplugs and muffs.

"Whatever you do, don't take these off. Once you're out there the noise'll blow out your eardrums."

Then they are through the airlock and in their bay, staring out into the gallery's eerie cave-like space. David can feel the thump-thump of the other shooters in every fibre now.

He has to shout to be heard.

"You all right?"

"I'm okay, Dad!"

He sends a bull's eye out to ten yards and takes a couple of test shots. He remembers the first time he fired the Beretta, how it twisted in his hands like something alive.

"You're up, son! I'll help with the first few shots."

Marcus's shoulders barely clear the counter of their bay. David crouches behind him and wraps his hands around Marcus's to steady his shot. For a second he feels the same panic as when he awakens in some unlikely location from a bout of sleepwalking and can't reconstruct what logic has brought him there.

"Just a steady pull! Like we talked about."

The gun explodes. David, pressed up against Marcus like his shadow, feels the tremor that goes through him.

The bullet has gone wild, missing the target completely.

He squeezes the boy's hands more firmly.

"Don't be afraid of it. Just think where you want the bullet to go and pull!"

This time the pull is smoother and the shot lands just a few inches short of the bull's eye.

"Great shot! Looks like you're a natural!"

Marcus starts to relax a bit now, his next shots clustering around the second one. David is impressed at how quickly he has learned to absorb the kick of the gun instead of fighting it.

David takes a step back.

"Now try a couple on your own!"

Marcus gives him a nervous look but doesn't lose form, keeps the gun pointing forward, like David has taught him, keeps his finger off the trigger.

"You think I'm ready?"

"You'll be fine. Just keep doing what you've been doing."

He pulls up on the first shot and misses the target again.

"Take your time. No hurry. And don't forget to keep breathing."

He takes his time. He is just a kid, holding this lethal thing in his hands.

On the second shot he nails the bull's eye.

"Dad, look! It's right in the middle! It's right on the bull's eye!"

"Like I said, you're a natural!"

The high carries them through the rest of the visit. David can still feel the thrill of it when he hands Marcus back to Julia at the airport the next day. He has made his resolutions by then, that he will break off whatever it is he has started with Sophie, that he will make the six- or seven-hour drive home every weekend to spend time with Marcus. Will look into shooting lessons for him and get him signed on at his club, Julia be damned.

"So what was it?" Julia says. "Computer games the whole weekend?"

Marcus shoots him a look.

"We did some other stuff. Movies and things."

It is only when Marcus is gone that David wonders at the foolish risk he has taken, not just with his son's safety but with his own access to him. He was merely pandering to him, perhaps, risking everything just for the sake of winning him over. Was trying to cast what they did as some sort of rite of passage when maybe all he was passing on was his own darkness.

What matters now is that the weekend not turn into just one more false start. That he keep his resolutions to spend more time with the boy, to be the father Marcus needs, the one he has always wanted to be.

Then the next morning there is a knock at his door in the dark of pre-dawn and every resolution gives way.

This is how it goes between them: she shows up at his door in the lengthening dark of early morning and they fuck. They don't talk about what they are doing or what it means, don't make declarations or plans. There is only the stink of their bodies, of their heat, their sweat, the need that rises in him the instant he hears her knock.

Always, at the door, that last look over her shoulder.

"He can't ever know. Not ever. It would kill him."

What he hears, though, what he sees in her eyes, is, "kill *me*."

She likes him to hurt her. He doesn't see this at first, not even after all the internet smut he has consumed across the whole gamut of depravity and perversion. But then slowly he gathers that the fear, for her, is the point, not that it isn't real but that it is her addiction somehow, what she can't resist. There are no rules or safe words in this, no sense of a game they can step out of, and yet it is still a game, a way of reopening a wound again and again.

Bit by bit, her addiction addicts him, like a drug she pumps into him each time they fuck that he then needs to withdraw from each she time she flees.

"It's always so rushed like this," he says. "We need to work something out. So we can take our time."

She turns away as if he had slapped her.

"This isn't like that."

"What's it like, then? Because I don't have a clue."

"Don't you see? It's like nothing. Like something the instant you talk about it, it has to stop."

But the next morning she is at his door again.

Every day to him now feels like a day won against a lethal threat. Attending faculty dinners, doing public lectures, teaching his class with the same sense of heightened, hidden alertness as when he is walking around with his loaded SIG. Going out of his way to pass by Greg's office to forestall the least hint of avoidance or change.

"Isn't that David Pace of *Masculine History* fame? Right here in our own humble hallways?"

David keeps up the old patter, keeps up their squash games and restaurant meals. This is the hardest part, the cruellest, the one that most makes his heart race, until it is all he can do to keep from shouting, *Fool, open your eyes!*

He has stopped asking himself what he is at, how he finds the way to live with himself. Instead he plunges forward headlong, afraid to slow or look to his side to see what damage he is doing, what devil spurs him on; afraid of the moment of tolerance, when the adrenalin rush starts its crushing decline. Every time he and Sophie fuck they seem to push one step closer to ruin. He fists her and shits on her, ties her up like a pig for slaughter. He fucks her from behind holding his loaded SIG to her head.

"Come or I'll kill you," he says, "I fucking swear it," and she does, as if her life depended on it.

They never discuss these acts or plan them, only move forward like blind things, eating whatever they stumble on, crawling into whatever hole. Afterwards it is always a shock to return to the mundane world, to breakfasts and school drop-offs, to Cato and classes at three. This, too, they never speak of, everything that is left out of the shadowy country they defect to together, what carnage threatens if its borders fail. All the things about her that he doesn't quite let himself take in, how her eyes flatline sometimes, the faded pencil-thin scars on her limbs, on her wrists. How the more he sees her, the more he travels with her to the darkest places, the more she seems somehow lost to him, until bit by bit he begins to crave what he has tried to close out, the small, telling details, the thoughts that run through her head.

He asks her once about Greg, what she does with him, if they still fuck. That is how he puts, purposefully crude, as if it is just another part of their brutality, though she pulls away from him at once.

"Why would you ask that? Why would you want to know?"

"So I don't have to think about it. So I don't have to imagine it."

Instead of answering him she takes up his laptop and goes to a login page whose password runs to a good fifteen or twenty characters.

"What is this?"

"It's what we do. It's what *he* does."

She has entered a cybersex site of the kind David himself has gotten his jollies from, dozens of avatars milling around in a lurid dance-club setting done up in every sort of fetishist gear and getting off on every sort of perversion. Torture scenarios, asphyxiation and cutting, whips and chains, like scenes from *The Last Judgment*. Sophie manoeuvres her POV out an exit door to a blighted suburban landscape where people run screaming, where corpses lie rotting in the street covered in rats.

"So he visits these sites? That's how he gets off?"

She stops at a house with a crumbling turret, a ruined veranda. On the lawn, some kind of dead animal. It takes David a moment to recognize the house as her own.

She kills the screen.

"He doesn't visit them. He builds them."

She was right to resist him. Already he knows too much. Now Greg will be there in his head whenever he is with her, the sense of Greg's strangeness, not so different from his own. The creeping fear that all of this comes down to the two of them, that Sophie is merely collateral damage.

*He can't ever know.* And yet the knowing has always felt certain to David. He has seen it in his dreams, in the telling word he lets slip, the clue he plants that can't be overlooked; has seen it in the visions he has of showing up at Greg's door in the dead of night and fucking Sophie right there on his living room couch, on his kitchen counter, on his front lawn, right in front of the neighbours, in front of his child. Each time he makes love to Sophie that is the real gun that he holds to her head, whatever monster it is in him, whatever god, that keeps needing to push him to ruin.

David is winding up one of his classes one evening when Greg comes to stand at his open door.

"Don't mind me," he says. "Just seeing how it's done."

"We were just talking about the Romans' perfection of ethnic cleansing. Something I think your own people have had some experience in."

Greg's smile freezes. He waits at the door until the last of the students have cleared out.

"What kind of asshole comment was that?"

David knows that with the right barb he might still defuse things.

"I just don't like being checked up on, that's all."

"Checked up on? I came by to see if you wanted to grab a bite, for fuck's sake!"

"Ah. My mistake."

It is too late. Something, some bit of truth, has flashed through.

"You can be a real fucking jerk, you know that?"

"So I guess that nixes the dinner invitation."

"You know what? I've lost my appetite."

The next time Sophie shows up at his house she makes him come to the door to let her in instead of using the key he leaves for her now.

"Come inside, for Christ's sake, it's freezing out there."

"Did Greg say something to you?"

"Not about you. We had one of our spats, that's all. I touched one of his sore spots. Why, what did he say?"

The look in her eyes then, like black water, sends a chill through him.

"I can't stay," she says, and then, with strange candour, not looking at him, "He was looking forward to this so much. To your coming here."

When she has gone the words hang like frozen breath.

Days pass and she doesn't return. He has a cell number for her now and an email address but is on strict instructions to use them only as a last resort. From having consumed him for weeks, the affair seems set to die away like a straw fire. He waits for the relief that always comes at the end of things but every morning he is up earlier, listening for the sound of her key in the door.

He drops by Greg's office.

"Look. About the other night."

"If you're going to apologize, David, then fuck you. The last thing I want is anything to undermine my bad opinion of you."

This is about as close as they are likely to get to a reconciliation. It is only now that he has squandered it that David is beginning to admit the windfall Greg's goodwill has been.

"It wasn't that. I just wanted to mention an ethnic cleansing support group you might be interested in."

He ought to be grateful, ought to count his blessings that the thing has ended without their having aroused any suspicions. Instead he starts running again, along her old route, at her usual time. When the days go by and he doesn't spot her he goes out earlier and stays out longer, sometimes alone on the trails except for the cameras and the guards. Each time he passes the stairs at the end of the woods he thinks of the moment when the thing was just pure possibility. The best moment, somehow. All the rest, he begins to tell himself, was just the diminishing return of addiction. One day, as he pressed his SIG to her head, he would have had to pull the trigger. One day, like the beast-gods of the ancient mystery cults, he would have had to tear her limb from limb.

From the cache on his laptop he manages to retrieve the login data from the site Sophie took him to. Day after day he prowls it using Sophie's avatar. The world of it stretches on and on without apparent end, all in the same ghoulish half-familiarity and half-ruin, every doorway leading to some new torture chamber or snuff scene or orgy. It is like walking around in the darkest underside of Greg's brain. What disturbs him is how at home he feels, how there is nothing here he doesn't understand, that hasn't become standard fare in his own late-night drugged ecstasies.

He starts to get sloppy, forgetting to enter any proxy settings to mask his address or simply not bothering to. Then one day, the site suddenly goes black.

Only a few seconds pass before his phone rings. It is the first time she has called him.

"You can't *do* that!" With a fierceness he has never heard in her. "You can't use my account! He can track you!"

"I need to see you. I'm going nuts here. We need to talk, at least."

"I can't," she says. "I can't."

The line goes dead.

For American Thanksgiving he buys a bolt-action Weatherby and books a spot at a hunting lodge a few hours from the city. By then nearly two weeks have passed since he last laid eyes on Sophie. Already she is fading from him, already he can hardly picture her face or call up the things that they did with any sort of clarity or sureness. As the drug of her drains from him he feels like he is the one who is fading. He has begun to up his meds again, is back to a pack a day of cigarettes. Sometimes at night he drives into ruined neighbourhoods where gunshots ring out and cars sit stripped and abandoned just to feel the fear go through him, as if it is all that still holds him to the earth.

The hunting lodge turns out to be in the back of beyond, lost in a blasted landscape of rundown farms and endless scrub. He has opted for spot-and-stalk, the guide they have set him up with still in his teens, dressed in a ratty parka that looks straight from the Goodwill. They set out at dawn, for a long time trekking through the same featureless scrub David has seen from the roads.

"I thought there'd be more clearings. More elevation."

"Don't worry, man, there's clearings all right. You'll get your buck, that's a promise."

A sprinkling of snow has fallen overnight that slowly turns the terrain to muck as the sun climbs. A dozen times David thinks of cutting his losses and heading back to camp. He ought to have stayed in the city. He ought to have gone home to visit Marcus, like he'd resolved.

"Bit more of a challenge the end of the season like this," the guide says. "They're not so fucked up with hormones anymore."

It is late morning before the landscape finally starts to open up. They come to a valley a good-sized creek runs through and follow it for several miles. Only now does David start to feel the world fall away. On hunts, out in the open like this, he'll go the whole day without meds. For an hour or two he'll feel the ache of withdrawal and then some animal brain kicks in, from the sunlight and air, the thrum in his blood of the coming kill.

They have been following the valley an hour or so when the guide spots a buck near the ridgeline of the far slope. A big one, three or four years old, his antlers rising up like great naked oaks. The guide's whole manner changes now. He smears his clothes with mud to keep down his smell and helps David do the same.

"Last chance for a smoke or a piss before we go in. Bow hunters been up and down this place this last month so you can bet he'll be pretty spooked."

They steal forward like shadows now, avoiding abrupt movements and being careful to keep downwind. The buck moves at a brisk pace, cutting an angle against the wind so he can catch any scent of available does that drifts down to him from their bedding zones. It takes a couple of hours to get within striking distance of him but then they have to scramble to stay out of the wind, losing sight of him again and again amidst the thick brush that lines the ridgeline.

The buck stops and they get in close enough for a shot, maybe three hundred yards. David looks to the guide.

"Too far, man." David is relieved. "Anyway, I bet he moves before you could get your scope on him."

Sure enough the buck turns and heads back into the brush.

The afternoon is waning by the time the buck sniffs out a prospect, a doe grazing alone in a small clearing just beyond the ridge. David and the guide move in to about a hundred and fifty yards and shelter behind a stand of sumac. The doe starts as the buck approaches and edges away; the buck circles, approaches again, and the doe starts again.

The guide grins.

"You can get a shot in if you want it. Some guys like to wait."

The doe has calmed. The buck circles behind her and dips the impressive monument of his head to lick at her calves, her thighs, the wet pink of her privates.

"Let's wait, then."

The delicate push-and-pull goes on for several more minutes. The doe balks again and the buck peers around with what looks like feigned indifference, then starts from scratch again. Finally, with astounding gentleness, he makes an attempt to mount. It is always baffling to David, this mating of beasts, how familiar the protocols look, how human. How, in contrast, the mating of humans seems so much more bestial, more depraved.

Once he has managed a proper coupling the buck is finished in a matter of seconds. The doe holds his weight only an instant before bolting.

"Moment of truth," the guide whispers. "Make it count."

All year the buck has lived only for this, the sole source of whatever sense of purpose he might feel on the earth. The jockeying, the desperate search, the does who resist him, the children he will never know. David would have liked to follow him back to whatever bed of mud or reeds he has made for his home.

"The doe's still too close."

"Take your time," the guide says. "No worries."

The buck turns his head in their direction as if he has sensed them and David takes the shot. He almost thinks he can see in the buck's eyes the sudden realization that something has gone badly awry, that he has made some fatal miscalculation. When his head drops, it drops like dead weight. A single bullet is all it takes.

They dress the thing in darkness, loading as much as they can in their packs and hanging the rest from the trees to come back for. They leave the head with its massive rack swinging from a bough in the dark like a warning.

"Yours if you want it," he says to the guide. "You earned it."

It is late when they get back to the lodge. David feels a blackness by then that he can't seem to shake. Nothing like guilt over the kill yet somehow the kill is the source. The thought of returning to his job, to his friend, to his book, his familiar heap of lies.

He decides to settle his bill and check out. In the car, before he starts back, he sends a text. *Need to c u.*

It is the middle of the night when he gets home. He takes a double dose of his sodium oxybate and falls into a dead sleep, waking at first light to the sound of a key in his front door. But already as he starts down the stairs he knows that he has miscalculated. That the presence he feels in the house is not her.

He finds Greg sitting in the kitchen still in his coat and gloves, the Weatherby propped in the corner behind him.

"I don't want to hear a *fucking* word from you, do you understand? Not a fucking word."

Sophie's cell phone sits on the table. *So this is where it ends,* David thinks. Any minute Greg will pick up the Weatherby, chamber a round. Crime of passion.

David feels a lifting at the thought.

"Here is how things are going to go."

What happens instead is much more predictable and banal. The sanctimoniousness, the bravado, the insults. Above all, the need to save face: Greg actually brings up deadlines and grades, resignation letters, trying to tie up every loose end. David can barely bring himself to listen. The thought keeps forming in his head: *Open your eyes.*

*I put a gun to her head and I fucked her, and she liked it.* In a different world, some sort of wisdom might have come of that.

"Don't think I didn't know everything when I invited you here, you piece of shit. The health issues, the performance review, that girl you practically raped, for fuck's sake. The plagiarism in Montreal, even that. You remember the plagiarism, right? But still I invited you. Maybe I figured you could use a leg up. Maybe I thought, fucking idiot that I am, that we might actually be friends again. But you're poison, David, I should have known that. Everything you touch turns to shit. My only hope is that I never have to lay eyes on you again. And if you ever come within a hundred yards of Sophie again I'll put a bullet in you, I swear it."

Only when Greg has gone does David notice he has left behind a copy of a newsletter from their student days, a compendium of parodies and exposés that the grad students in their department used to put out. He feels something shift in the muck at the bottom of his brain and even before he flips the pages he knows that the article is there, that it isn't merely the phantom he turned it into long ago as a way of leaving open the possibility it didn't exist.

It is the broadest sort of satire, of course, vintage Greg, taking no prisoners, sparing no orthodoxies. A far cry from what David would turn it into, from the possibilities he would see in it, after years of effort and research. And yet the pillaging is clear, right down to examples and subheadings he ended up using in *Masculine History* almost verbatim, and that surely would have been enough to sink him had anyone bothered to make the connection. Even more damning, perhaps, is that the eventual backlash against David's revamp seems already prefigured in the satire of the original.

David doubts it ever crossed Greg's mind to try to ruin him over something like this. And yet it is as if all these years Greg has put his life on hold awaiting his moment of vindication. At least David has allowed him that. At least he has proved worthy of every calumny.

David makes coffee and sits staring into the woods through the kitchen window. It has started to snow. The fall has unfolded like some classic fall of another era, the changing leaves, the shortening days, the gradual cold, almost eerie in its unremarkableness. In Marcus's lifetime or in his own, the days of taking such things for granted may have passed from the earth. He has seen it in the eyes of his students, this sense of an imminent existential threat.

In a hundred years, or fifty or twenty, all this will end up seeming a sleep from which people refused to be roused, guarding their small proprieties and perks, wondering who would get tenure, who had fucked whose husband or wife. *Condition White.*

He has no last resort, no plan, no hope. It is something, at least. Like finally hitting solid ground.

# Beretta M9

HE STEPS FROM THE tempered air of the hotel lobby and at once is in another country. Heat hits him like a bomb blast; the smell of kerosene and cooking fires and dust. The hotel courtyard is crammed with vehicles, the white minivan the journalists use, an armoured Jeep, the black Peugeot that Yusuf, the hotel's owner, keeps on standby. The young driver, Said, some sort of nephew or cousin Yusuf has got saddled with, sits smoking listlessly beneath the lone scraggly palm that rises up against the security wall, his eyes sharpening an instant at the sight of David, then going dull again when David heads toward the gate. The couple of times David has been out with the boy he has been thin-skinned and surly, every smallest inconvenience an affront. By mid-afternoon he will be pumped up on khat: David has seen him chewing wad after wad of the stuff with the kitchen help in the service courtyard beneath his room. It is the same in the markets and tea houses throughout the city, a whole generation of men who sit for hours of every day using the drug to feed their violence or to tame it, David isn't sure which.

Wali stands guard at the gate with his rifle, part of the troupe of thawb-clad cattlemen Yusuf imports from the provinces to serve as his private militia.

"Ah, Mr. David!" Flashing a grin. "Where are you going? I can come with you, is better."

"I think I'm going to try on my own today."

Wali's grin goes wider.

"You are a brave man, Mr. David, very brave!" As if sending him off to joyful death.

It is David's first outing alone. Mostly he has tagged along in the journalists' van, with two or three of Yusuf's cattlemen riding shotgun. Outside the government zone the city is still a jigsaw of clashing factions, each with its own militiamen and checkpoints and tolls. In the neighbourhoods to the north, where the city rises up toward the coastal mountains and every switch-back and corner window and cul-de-sac offers some stronghold or point of ambush, new gangs still form almost weekly, only the sections held by the Malana, a Western-style do-gooder David has been researching with whom Yusuf has promised to get him an interview, offering anything like safe passage.

The street beyond the hotel is deserted, a barren stretch of beaten earth flanked by a jumble of half-built buildings and half-ruined ones. For the first time since he arrived here David feels truly exposed. He has brought sunglasses equipped with a built-in video camera in the hope of putting together some sale-able news items or digital extras for his book, though they only make everything he looks at seem more menacing and veiled.

He turns at the first cross street, following the instructions he got from one of the journalists, Eric, from France. Only now does he begin to see signs of life, men in doorways, cars, open shops. Already the sun is like a hammer blow. He stops at a hole in the wall displaying a motley assortment of hats and picks out a baseball cap that reads *Security*.

"How much?"

The trader sits smoking in the darkness of the shop.

"Twenty dollars."

"I'll give you seven."

The man looks at him so distantly that David thinks he hasn't understood.

"Is twenty dollars. Last price."

He can't read the man's tone. He picks up a fez done in the local pin-hole-style embroidery, in gold and black.

"And this one?"

"Five dollars."

He peels a five from his wallet.

By the time he reaches the main boulevard the crowds have thickened. David has seen pictures of the street from the halcyon days of Soviet backing, the flowered planters and royal palms along the centre island, the office buildings in gleaming glass and gleaming white. Now, the planters and palms have given way to rubble and weeds and rows of crude market stalls obscure the buildings. Textbook reversion—David has seen it in other former satellites as well, modern cities that regressed to primitive villages the minute the empire packed its bags.

David buys a Fanta, piss warm, from a boy hawking them from a water-filled bucket and stands drinking it while the boy waits for the empty. On the roadway, a motorcade bearing the logo of the international delegation in town for peace talks cuts through the traffic flanked by a military escort, a stillness hanging in its wake for a few seconds before the traffic folds back into place.

The Fanta boy is staring up at him.

"America? CIA?"

Anywhere else the question might be a joke. Here, half the guests at David's hotel seem to be agents of one sort or other, selling arms or buying them, gathering intel, playing factions one against the other or paying off the warlords they have failed to depose to kill off the jihadists they once supported.

"Not CIA. A journalist." He drains the bottle and hands it back.

He is headed for the arms market. It is one of the ideas he has pitched for write-ups to various outlets to help offset the cost of the trip and maybe serve as teasers for his book. After years of work he has had to rethink his original concept: it was getting too bloodless, too invested in his own theorizing. What he needs is something more visceral, exactly what served him so well back in *Masculine History*. That is what has brought him here, the hope that this place's reversion, its constant tottering toward anarchy, might give him a paradigm for the failure of states; the suspicion that what is happening here is not some bizarre aberration but the human default, a microcosm of the brutality and blood lust that have spurred human history ever since *Homo sapiens* pushed Neanderthal off an evolutionary cliff.

He looks around to see that the traffic has changed, that the Fanta boy has vanished. This is the other function of his videocam, to act as his brain's backup for everything he misses or forgets, for the blackouts when whole seconds or minutes fail to register. Such lapses happen daily now, no matter how much he loads himself up with his meds. He'll be driving down a highway or standing on a street corner or waiting in line at an airport check-in and suddenly he'll have no idea what he is doing or where he is going or why, as if the thread of time itself, whatever it is that makes a life a continuous whole and not these vanishings his own has become, has been snapped.

If only he can hold out a while longer. If only he can push through to the end. Every morning he tries to convince himself, tells himself the same lies, which by noon have worn thin.

At the back of his mind, always with him now, the locusts of sleep, waiting to swarm.

It had been possible in the end, even easy, to lose even his son. By mere inadvertence, really, as if he had turned his head for a minute and the boy had slipped from him, irrevocably.

In his mind there had always been a time in the offing when he would make the effort, when he would break through. When there was no book to finish, no issue with money; when Marcus was old enough to understand. Then, not long after his return from the States, Julia announced she had taken a job as dean at their old university in Montreal. There was no question of fighting her: he had neither the resources nor the grounds. He had had to sell his condo by then to cover his living expenses and his debt, still in the same limbo with the university as when he'd gone. His new accommodations, a tiny rented condo with flimsy rice-paper sliders to give the illusion of rooms, had no space for Marcus to sleep and so had ended up limiting their time together to awkward weekend outings that stank of obligation. They never spoke again of their visit to David's club. David always meant to bring it up with him, to look into shooting courses, to find a way to broach the issue with Julia, yet at the back of his mind he suspected he would just be laying the ground for some new way to fail him.

It was only when Julia had sold the house that it began to sink in what had happened. The opportunity he had always imagined, the chance to be the good father, to make things up, had passed. Julia moved into the sprawling manse her father still lived in and enrolled Marcus in the same old-boy private school her father had attended two generations earlier, so that visiting him now was like travelling into enemy territory.

David had stopped in to see him on his way over here, taking him out to a restaurant in the old city that had once been a favourite haunt of his. It was the first time he had seen him since Christmas and he had grown half a foot since then, looking more like David and yet also, in some way, in some new bearing he had, more separate from him.

"School all right?"

"You'd have to ask Mom about that." In a tone of complicity. "She seems to have her own grading system."

This was the boy who used to squirm at every question as if it were an awkward piece of clothing he had to squeeze himself into. Almost overnight, he'd turned adult.

"Do you like that place? All that pretension?"

"It's not that bad, really. For a school, I mean."

The boy was managing him. *Old enough to understand.* This was the day David had been waiting for, when they might sit as equals.

"You never told me where you were going exactly," Marcus said.

"Research trip. For my book."

"Ah, yes." Aping a plummy Oxford accent. "*The book.*"

It took David an effort to realize the boy had meant no insult. If anything there had been almost a deference in him, an underhanded pride.

Every moment there had ever been between them seemed suddenly to flash in front of David, every failure.

"We should go away together this summer. To Europe, maybe. Or a beach."

Marcus's adultness fell away and he was the squirmer again.

"I dunno. I usually have camps and stuff. You'd have to ask Mom."

*You're still his father*. Already this seemed less some right he had, some last vestige of hope, than a debt he would never repay.

There had been only a single time since the divorce that Julia had truly turned to him as a father. A boy Marcus had known since kindergarten had begun to bully him, and though Julia had confronted the boy directly, then had spoken to his teacher, then to the principal, matters had only worsened with each intervention. She had finally called the boy's parents, who had accused her of being on a witch hunt and threatened legal action if she called again. All of this she had kept from David until it came out in a barrage one afternoon when he went by to pick up Marcus for the weekend.

"I just want it to end, David, I can't tell you how this eats at me. I just want it to stop. All I can think of now is ways to hurt this kid. I think of burning his house down. Of running him down in my car."

David spent the whole weekend in a fury, imagining how he would ream out Marcus's teacher, ream out the principal, how he would go to the school board and show them what a mockery all their rhetoric was, how they hadn't a clue. It was still the same as it had been in his own day, the same cruelty, the same insidiousness, the same idiotic adults who imagined children innocents. There was nothing more brutal than a child. David would show the kid brutal. He would hire some older kid to give him a beating. He would turn up at his house with the Beretta and give him and his asshole parents a taste of what real fear was like.

He tried to discuss the matter with Marcus.

"Was there something you did to this boy? Was there a reason he stopped being friends like that?"

"I don't know why." Already close to tears. "I didn't do anything. Do we have to talk about it? I already talked to Mom."

He had taken exactly the wrong tack. That was the worst of it, what made it impossible to see the thing clearly, that beneath his rage was his own sense of shame. He was back in the schoolyard again watching Danny get picked on, feeling stigmatized along with him, feeling marked. Wanting to say to him, *For fuck's sake stand up for yourself.*

David kept running through every possible option, what could be done that would work, that would make the kid pay. Yet the more he thought, the more he felt stymied. The truth was that Julia, too, had taken the wrong tack. She had branded Marcus as weak by fighting his fight for him. Meanwhile the other kid, in being singled out, had gained status. There was no way to defend against that kind of primal algebra.

"We have to keep at this," Julia said when he dropped Marcus home. "We have to fix this."

David drove by the kid's house. The front curtains were open and he could make out the father reading in an armchair in the living room, half turning from time to time as though calling out passages to someone in a further room. Something in the look on his face, a certain maleness, vaguely repellent, reminded David of himself. Then, as if on cue, the boy came into the room, not whining or sneering but only holding out a notebook that his father took from him and scanned the pages of before handing it back with a curt nod of approval.

David had already seen too much by then. He had wanted monsters, something to feed his anger. Instead he might have been looking into his own house back when he had one, at his own family. Whatever violence was being bred here was likely not much different from what had made David imagine taking a Beretta to a child and Julia running him down in her car.

In the short run it was Julia who solved the problem, insisting the boy be suspended for a few days after he was caught defacing one of Marcus's notebooks. It was the first real punishment anyone had thought to administer to him and afterwards he left Marcus alone. Who knew what it was that had first set him off, maybe just brute animal impulse, something he could no more be blamed for than for the colour of his eyes.

David, though, knew even then that the only solution that would have made any real difference for Marcus was the one he had never quite had the patience for: that he be a better father. The kind who passed on inner resources. Who taught his son to be strong. The father he had vowed to be, again and again, until every chance had passed.

The gun market runs for several blocks, a string of tin-roofed stalls and patched-over shops selling M16s, Kalashnikovs, Uzis, RPGs. There is a hair-trigger feel of danger but something muted as well, a sense of lethargy, of boredom almost. On the walk from the hotel David passed hardly a doorway that wasn't watched over by some young clansman with a rifle, but here half the stalls appear abandoned, rows and rows of lethal weapons spread out on their crude display racks without so much as a child to keep watch over them. Meanwhile men in robes sit smoking Marlboros and drinking tea under the shade netting of the tea houses that flank the street as if all this has nothing to do with them.

The gun laws here are even more draconian than back home but in practice are a farce, used only for shakedowns and bribes. In the face of recent abductions even some of the journalists have taken to carrying guns, despite the taboo against them, buying them outright if they have ways to get them home or using buyback schemes that amount to a sort of rental system. One of the Americans showed David a full-auto Glock he'd picked up, with a magazine the size of an assault rifle's.

"Twelve hundred rounds a minute, if you could manage to feed them in fast enough. The only other people in the world with this thing are the Austrian anti-terror cops."

The gun was overkill, the kick on it probably enough to break the man's wrists. David had done self-defence courses at a camp outside Buffalo before coming out here and has some notion by now of the difference between the fantasy of lethal force and what happens in real time. In real time, the one round you can control is better than the thirty you can't. In real time, in that first second of blind panic when your life hangs in the balance, the gun you'd thought you'd mastered, landing round after round in the kill zone at twenty-five yards, becomes the bucking animal it had been the first time you'd held it.

His first morning at the camp he was given an eighteen-round Glock and put in front of a huge rubberized screen designed to reseal itself from a bullet's friction when it was shot. As he watched, a shooting rampage unfolded in front of him that was like one of Marcus's shooter games blown up to life size, so realistic he could make out the colour of people's eyes, the sprays of blood on the walls. People running screaming in every direction; others lying bleeding or dead on the floor. The setting, a classroom building in a university, was custom chosen, every detail hauntingly familiar. The scene moved him down hallways, around corners, through open foyers where he stood fully exposed, with each step the sickening pop, pop of the shooter and the grating howls and pleas getting louder. The whole time, people running at him wild-eyed, the fear in them so bald and real he could hardly bear to look at it.

From a doorway, a man ranting at him, a girl in a chokehold, the flash of what might have been a gun. David's heart was pounding; he was drenched in sweat. At the back of his neck, the first time it had ever happened to him with a gun in his hands, a premonitory shiver.

The screen went black.

His instructor stepped out from a monitoring booth at the back of the room.

"Sorry, man, you're dead."

David had signed on for regular courses after that, for a while going down almost weekly, sometimes for two- or three-day sessions. The place offered training for every setting and every scenario, from back-alley muggings and home invasions to hostage takings and guerrilla-style ambushes. In the course of a day he might fire a thousand rounds, doing the same drills over and over, building his muscle memory, training his animal self to make decisions his thinking one was too oafishly lumbering for. After a while he started getting flashes of the simulations he'd done as though he had truly lived them, had been through rampages and war, was a seasoned killer. At the back of his mind, the constant obsession with raising the odds. The actual stopping zones on a human body were infinitesimally small: there was the brain stem's medulla, about the size of an egg, which could shut the body down like a light switch; there was the heart, the size of a fist. The prospect of making these shots on a moving target in a state of agitation without having hardwired them into your very being was next to nil.

From up the street, the rat-a-tat of a Kalashnikov being tested and right away the smell of powder, sharp as ammonia. All along the market the AKs predominate, all with the weathered, indestructible look of having been through it, wars and guerrilla uprisings and coups, jihads, terrorist massacres. Some of them might have come off the lines right back in the first days of the Cold War, might have made the rounds since then of Cambodia and Vietnam, Angola and Afghanistan, Bosnia, Rwanda, Iraq, to end up in this backwater failed state still ready for service. David had had a few goes on an AK at his gun camp. Even in full auto, when it could slice off an arm in a matter of seconds, it had the simplicity of a Nerf gun, and about as much kick.

He pans the street with his video glasses, but when he tries to engage any of the traders they shake their heads, either not understanding him or not wanting to. David can feel the street watching him, the barefoot boys, the alhajis in the tea houses, the young men who sit chewing khat in the shade of tamarinds. He has already seen how easily matters can turn here. The journalists' driver had tried to force their van through a throng of pedestrians once and people had begun to shout insults and pound at the windows with what felt like real violence.

"Mr. Man!" One of the traders is holding out a beat-up AKM whose folding metal stock has the look of a crude prosthetic limb. "This way, come, you can shoot this one! One bullet, one dollar!"

The man is thick-necked and hulking, with none of the desert leanness that is the norm here. He wears a bright yellow T-shirt that reads *Pirate*.

"Who do you want to shoot today, Mr. Man? Who do you want to kill?"

A dozen rifles dangle like sides of meat from the front of his stall. A couple of M16 knock-offs; a hodgepodge of Kalashnikovs with markings in Cyrillic, in Roman, in Arabic, in Chinese. David, playing along, takes the AKM the trader holds out.

"How much?"

The man grins.

"For you, my friend, only your life."

"The price is too high, I think."

"You are smart, my friend. You don't want to die in this place."

The trader goes by the name of Madman. David tries to

draw him out, not sure if he is con man or sage but glad to be getting some footage.

"You are journalist, yes? *New York Times.* You can put my name there."

He goes through his guns, reeling off prices. David tries to get him to talk more generally, about sources, about his bosses, about the city's factions, but he grows cagey. David asks about the Malana, whom the Western press touts as someone trying to rise above the sectarianism and violence, but Madman acts like he has never heard of him.

"People from your country, they come here, they say factions, they say clan, is a way to say we are not civilized. But we are civilized, my friend, many thousands of years. Before the Romans, before the Greeks. They say guns, they say killing, but where are there more guns, more killing? In your own country."

David doesn't quibble. For all he knows the man has committed atrocities, nearly everyone has in this place who has survived, but he seems to have understood the lesson of history, that in the long run such delinquencies hardly matter.

David has spied a crate at the back of the stall that holds a collection of handguns, piled in a heap like discarded auto parts.

"What about those? Are they for sale?"

Madman's eyes brighten.

"Aha! So I have found you out! You like to have pistol, not so?"

He dumps the crate unceremoniously onto the counter of his stall. A Jericho, a Taurus Millennium, a couple of Glocks. The others are mostly cheap knock-offs or types David has never seen.

"Which one, my friend? I give you best price, to sell and also buy back."

David eyes the guns, hardly daring to take one in hand. At his camp, once his reflexes in the simulations had sharpened to the point where more times than not he was making the kill, fear had given way to something else: anticipation. The slow burn in his blood, better than any drug; the incredible focus.

"Is that all you've got?"

Madman smiles.

"You are right." As if they are no longer playing at things. "You are a man of knowledge. Those are only for boys."

He brings out a basket with what is clearly his premium line. A Heckler and Koch. A Springfield. A Walther. It is the last one, though, that holds David's eye: a Beretta. It looks like an idealized version of his own, the same red dot by the safety, the same hatching on the slide, the same monogrammed grip, but sleeker and darker and more substantial somehow, with the flawless finish of something engineered to standards slightly beyond the human. He picks it up. It sits more squarely in his hand than his own does, feels more perfectly balanced. He checks the markings: US M9. American military issue.

He drops the magazine and inspects it, pulls the slide back to check the chamber and barrel. Clear.

Madman looks pleased.

"I think you know this one."

David points the gun skyward and slowly squeezes the trigger to test its resistance. This is the instant he loves, the one just before the hammer strikes, when the gun is still all potential, poised at the balancing point between intent and loss of control.

Click.

"How much?"

The question of buying or not feels already moot. Even Madman, taking his time, playing David out, seems to know this.

"This one is special, my friend, is only one in all of the market. You can see for yourself. Is from your own soldiers, when they came."

The gun has clearly seen service but doesn't look old enough to go back to the American presence. More likely some recent clandestine has been parted from it, though under what circumstances David doesn't like to guess.

"I'll give you three hundred."

In the end he agrees to five, probably more than the gun would cost new, and to a buyback of a mere hundred and fifty. He hasn't dared to come out with that much money on him and will have to return to his hotel for it. Now that business is being transacted Madman has turned no-nonsense, his eye perpetually scanning the street.

"I will come with you. Is better."

Madman wraps the gun in burlap and twine together with a box of the same 9x19 Parabellum soft points David uses in his Beretta back home, making a parcel that resembles those of the local bootleggers. He calls a boy over to watch his stall and pops a banana clip into a Kalashnikov.

"We are safe now, no worries."

Madman waits behind at the cross street when they reach the hotel, to avoid problems with the guards. In the hotel courtyard, Said is berating one of the kitchen boys.

"Animal!" he says, reaching out theatrically to smack the boy on the back of the head when he sees David passing.

The hotel is bustling today because of some sort of peace forum sponsored by the international delegation. David manages to get in and out without interference, glad he has squirrelled away some of his cash in his room and spared himself the awkwardness of needing to get into Yusuf's safe. Only when he is back in the street does he realize how reckless he has been, rushing out unaccompanied and unarmed with his fistful of cash like the merest rube.

Madman stands waiting for him with his parcel in the shadow of a ruined building.

"You managed it?"

"All there."

He draws into a doorway to count the cash.

"Is good." Already elsewhere, already gone. "Go with God, my friend."

This time Yusuf spots him as he enters the hotel, his eye going straight to the burlap package.

"Mr. Pace! Where have you been? Is very foolish to go out alone!"

He is decked out in all his finery today like some oil sheik.

"As you can see, I've managed to survive."

David heads for his room. In the hall he passes the flinty Reuters woman he met the night before at the hotel bar, a new arrival, dressed in a low-cut top that in a country like this might be enough to earn her a stoning. Tasha or Tara, something fashionable like that. At the bar—a snakepit of gonzo journalists and black marketeers that Yusuf opens up only well after supper, presumably to keep it from corrupting the locals—she had barely given him the time of day, matching the men drink for drink and holding court the whole night with her war-zone tales.

She raises an exaggerated eyebrow at his parcel, clearly taking it for the bottle it has been made up to resemble.

"Any to share?"

*Fuck you*, David thinks, though something in him responds to her despite himself, as though the insect swarm that has been massing at the back of his head is starting to clear.

David gets one of the boys in the service courtyard to bring a jar of kerosene up to his room and sets about cleaning the Beretta, stripping it down on his flimsy desk. Fine desert sand has worked its way into the gun's every cranny. The slide shows a good deal of wear, though the barrel, which he scrubs by pulling a strip of kerosene-soaked hand towel through it with a shoelace, is fairly clean. All this suggests the gun has come straight out of the military, which uses only fully jacketed rounds, not much given to fouling. In the delicious logic of war, jacketed rounds are considered more humanitarian than the soft points favoured by civilians because they pass through flesh more cleanly.

Partway into the cleaning, someone comes knocking. The air conditioning has died again and the smell of the kerosene has filled the room.

"Is everything all right, Mr. Pace?"

It is Yusuf. David doesn't get up.

"Fine. Everything's fine."

The barest pause.

"I'm told you have something to clean." It seems everyone here is Yusuf's spy. "If I can help you, Mr. Pace. On account of the smell. For the other guests."

"Be done in a minute. Just an old clock I picked up."

The evasion is so flimsy that Yusuf doesn't even bother to acknowledge it.

"You mustn't go out on your own again, Mr. Pace, I beg you. It's very dangerous. You must let the hotel look after your security."

When he has gone David reassembles the gun and goes through his drills. He has brought a holster with him that fits inside his waistband and he practises drawing and holstering, watching for snags and checking the drape of his shirt. He tests the alignment on the sights; he works the trigger. The trigger pull is heavier on the first shot if the gun is uncocked because of the added resistance of having to pull back the hammer. David dry-fires again and again with the hammer both forward and back so he doesn't get caught botching a shot because he has miscalculated the weight of the pull.

His room looks out over the razor wire of the hotel's security wall toward the distant slopes of the northern neighbourhoods. A lone low-rise in concrete and silvered glass a couple of blocks over breaks the view. David can't tell at this distance if it is occupied or abandoned. Someone could be standing at one of its windows that very minute angling to get a bead on him. In the city's worst days gangs of boys had made a game of such sport, targeting random strangers for casual killings.

David takes aim at one of the upper windows and in his mind's eye sees a shadow move behind its mirrored surface. He pulls the trigger and a black throb goes through him.

Click.

At the camp it had come to seem that threat was no longer something he prepared for but what he needed to conjure. Now, in this place of threat, the scenarios keep playing out in his head until it is becoming hard to distinguish what he craves from what he fears.

In the hotel dining room Eric, the Frenchman, calls out to him from a table the journalists have colonized at the back. The Reuters woman is there, scrolling through her phone.

"Petra, have you met David yet?" For some reason Eric has made a point of taking David under his wing. "He's working on a book about failed states. You must know his work."

"We met at the bar, I think." Barely looking up from her phone. "Sorry, I never caught the last name."

"*Pah-cheh.*" Eric rolls the name out like an aria. "As in '*Si vis pacem, para bellum.*' Though maybe you know him as Pace."

"David Pace? You've got to be kidding."

As if on cue her phone rings.

"Sorry, guys, I have to take this."

David hates the hard turd of ego in him that still clings to the least sign of recognition. That gives in to Eric's blandishments, though for all David knows he comes here to diddle young boys. That itches now for Petra's return.

"It looks like the prospects are good," Eric says. "I am talking about the truce, of course."

"Don't tease me with false promise."

"Ah, yes. If there is a drug here even more dangerous than khat it is that one. Hope."

When she returns her whole manner has changed.

"So. Professor David Pace. *Masculine History*, right? Julius Caesar?"

"Excellent," Eric says. "So you know it, then?"

Petra laughs.

"Oh, I didn't say I'd read it. But I had this history prof at Harvard who used to go on about it, if you can believe it. Small world."

David resists the urge to ask the professor's name.

"So this is the sort of work Harvard gets you these days?"

"Oh, I didn't say I'd graduated."

This time David laughs as well, too loudly.

The others have begun to drift off. Eric asks about David's trip to the gun market.

"I picked up some LAVs and a truckload of M16s. I'm taking the city tonight after supper, if anyone's up for it."

"If it means I'd be able to get a drink in this place before midnight," Petra says, "then I'm in."

It comes to David that this is his cue. *Any to share?* He is glad of the mickey of gin he scrounged in his first days here on a booze run with some of the journalists.

"I've got a bottle back in my room you're both welcome to."

Petra lets the offer hang a few beats.

"Can't say I'd mind. Eric, you in?"

Eric holds up his hands in a show of Gallic helplessness.

"Sadly, some of us have to work for a living."

Petra draws a cigarette from her pack and David leans in to light it. She takes a long drag.

"I guess that leaves me and Mr. Pah-cheh, then."

David pours a couple of generous shots of gin into the room's plastic bar glasses and tops them with a splash of nearly flat tonic from an open can in his fridge. There is an ice machine down the hall but David has yet to see any evidence that it works.

"You need the fucking secret service to keep track of the supply line here these days," Petra says. "I had some duty-free coming in and the bastards actually confiscated it."

"I'm sure Eric can set you up. Or Yusuf."

"Not Yusuf, the snake, he draws the line there. The whole not profiting from sin thing. By which he means what a sin it would be to cut into his profits from his price-gouging bar."

David doesn't let himself think how long it has been since he has had sex. More than once he has had to pay for it; more than once he has failed to finish. The last sex he had that actually mattered was with Sophie, also something he doesn't let himself think about.

He has hardly set the bottle down before Petra is reaching for it to refill her glass. He catches a whiff of something as she leans in that seems too chemical, too deep, to be just the lingering alcohol breath of her previous night's bender.

"So Harvard," he says. "How was that?"

For a second she doesn't seem sure what he is referring to.

"Shit, that was back in the dark ages. But totally Darwinian, you know, like in that movie, what the fuck was it? About social media. Kill or be killed."

"Like here," he says.

"No, this is civilized. At least here they use guns."

The air conditioning is still out. From the service courtyard comes a burst of laughter and the tinny whine of a ghetto blaster playing Eminem.

"So. Failed states. I guess you've come to the right place. I've been to armpits but this is the asshole. The fucking colon."

From the gin they move on to lines of Ritalin and from there to a few grams of sodium oxybate that David cuts with the last of the tonic. By the time their clothes come off, they are lost in a haze of not-quite-presence. It is clear by then that the smell coming off Petra is the acetone stink of the committed alcoholic. David has to fight to stay hard, trying to use his disgust as a way of rising above it.

Petra is already dressed and settled into the lone armchair with a cigarette before he has had time to so much as wipe the jism from him.

"Jesus fucking Christ, it felt like you were drilling for oil down there."

He resists the impulse to say something cruel. She has fucked him for the sake of a bottle of gin without the least hint of apology or shame. There seems something almost admirable in this.

"You never said who that professor was. At Harvard."

From the grin on her he knows at once he should have held his tongue.

"You're shitting me, right? I thought you were on to me. Can you really see me at Harvard? Doing Roman history like some fucking princess?"

"I'm not following." But he is beginning to.

"I was having you on, for Christ's sake. That phone call?" She keys a few numbers on her phone and it rings. "It's programmed, you idiot. For when I want a quick exit. Very handy. It gave me a chance to search you."

He knows he ought to laugh the matter off.

"Why the fuck would you do that?"

"To tell you the truth I wanted to get at that pretentious fuckface Eric. The fact that it got me to your gin was a bonus."

He just wants her gone now.

"I figured it was the liquor you were after from the fumes coming off you. But I'm the one who got the bonus. I'd have settled for a blow job."

She shoots him a smile that drips malice.

"Fuck you too, Professor Pah-cheh. Or no, maybe not professor after all—looks like you lost your job. Oh, and here's news, something about date rape. That wouldn't have to do with that drug you were dosing me with, would it? Amazing what you can learn on the internet. If it's any consolation, I knew all that and still let you fuck me."

The only bearable part of this whole encounter for him now is that it will soon be over. Petra, though, takes her time with her cigarette as if this is what passes as connection for her.

"What are you, anyway? Forty-five? Fifty?"

"Are you going to sell me insurance?"

"It's just, what the fuck are you doing here? I mean, seriously. I just hope you still have a real job somewhere. I hope you have a family or something, in which case, my advice? Get the next plane back to it. People die here."

By the time she is gone he feels ready to peel off a layer of skin just to be free of her. It had taken her a matter of minutes to piece together all the sordid half-truths that dog him these days across encyclopedia sites and blog comments and academic forums, bits of innuendo and implication and lie that join up like a puzzle into a portrait of depravity. Greg's handiwork: that has grown clear from the frequent allusions to plagiarism, which are all the more damning because they are always couched in a vagueness that makes them irrefutable. For a while David was spending hours of every day trying to put out every fire, though usually he only ended up feeding them. Bit by bit he had had to cut himself off, eventually even shutting down his web site.

Exhaustion takes him over and he stretches out on his bed. His stay feels poisoned now. By evening, when Petra joins the others at the bar to regale them with more war stories, he will be a laughingstock. *People die here.* He ought to get on a plane like she suggested and go home. Then he thinks of the cubicle that passes for home now, of his life, of the man he has become.

For days he holes himself up in his room, getting the kitchen boys to bring him his meals and seeing no one. He goes through his video footage and tries to get a start on some of the articles he has pitched; he goes through his book files, the palimpsest of notes and outlines and drafts inscribed into his hard drive going back more than a decade now. The numberless sections he has written up, then excised, then reinserted; the introductory chapter he has reworked a hundred times, polishing and repolishing, then losing faith and restarting from scratch. A million words or more, enough for a dozen books, for a project on the scale of *Decline and Fall*; as ambitious as that, as vast in its reach. His last hope.

He starts writing, in longhand, beginning at the beginning. It has been years since he has worked this way and the process feels incredibly primitive at first, the ink stains, the cramping, the snaking lines. But slowly he finds a rhythm. It is a relief to be forced to commit to a thought and move on. Then there is the pleasure of watching the pages begin to accumulate, these tangible objects with his tangible mark.

He cuts back on his meds to keep from burning himself out and tries to manage his sleep by napping for twenty minutes in every two-hour stretch. That, he has learned, is the rhythm of his disorder, corresponding roughly to the rhythm of lab rats in whom the neurotransmitters that govern waking and sleep have been knocked out of service. In their absence, mechanisms precisely tuned to calibrate darkness and light, to modulate metabolism, to pump the body with the stimulants that make possible the nine-to-five day humans take for granted cease to function. Instead, from the first moment of wakefulness the craving for sleep begins to build.

The routine breeds its own peculiar brand of altered consciousness, until he starts to lose track of the days. He has the sense he is devolving, regressing to what creatures might have been back when there was only sleep in the world, only the protozoal heave and stir of sensation and reflex. Then one afternoon he goes down to the lobby in search of paper and finds the hotel strangely deserted, as though he has slept through some apocalypse. He wanders into the courtyard and sees that no one is manning the gate, which sits ajar.

The light from the street beckons him. He steps through the gate and follows the street in a direction he hasn't taken before, away from the downtown. With each step the neighbourhood grows more desolate, the houses more tottering and ruined, though he feels no sense of danger. An old man who sits smoking a pipe on his front step offers it out to him and laughs and David acknowledges the gesture with a wave and walks on.

He comes to a cross street. In the distance an arched gateway like the portal of a walled city looks out to a vista of such unearthly blue it looks like a painted backdrop. It takes David a second to make sense of it: the sea. He passes through the gate and the sea lies stretched out in front of him to the horizon, edged by a ribbon of white beach. After the days of being holed up in his room he feels dazzled. Some children are playing in the surf, running back and forth as the waves break, holding their sarongs up to keep them dry, and it is all David can do not to join them.

Back at the hotel, Yusuf accosts him in the lobby.

"It is all arranged for tomorrow, Mr. Pace! After afternoon prayers. My driver will take you."

David has almost forgotten by now: the Malana.

"Fine, fine." He still sees the children at the beach, their black, black skin, their coloured sarongs. It seems almost impossible now that he hasn't merely imagined them. "Will any of the others come?"

"No, no, Mr. Pace, there is only you! The talks have finished by now."

David can't quite take this in.

"I'll have to see."

"No worries, of course, of course. In the morning everything can be settled."

He is already back in his room before he realizes he has forgotten to get paper. On his desk, his finished pages sit waiting for him. He slips them into a drawer.

At breakfast the dining room is nearly deserted. Yusuf is on David at once, making arrangements.

"You can take two of the guards, I think. It's better."

"Just one. Just Wali."

"Of course, Mr. Pace, of course, you are right."

David negotiates the use of Wali for the morning as part of his price so he can get more video footage of the downtown, giving in to the beginning-of-the-day optimism that still dogs him, that still makes him feel there might be a point. They go on foot, making their way to the central boulevard and continuing north to the presidential palace, where the provisional government sits. All that is visible from the street is the high stucco wall that rings its compound, studded with watchtowers and topped with a double row of razor wire. David stares up into one of the towers to get footage of it and a soldier turns his rifle on him with what looks like real intent. David can feel the Beretta pressing against his hip beneath the cover of his shirt.

"No worries, Mr. David," Wali says. "The only one they will shoot is the one with a gun."

They keep walking. Farther along the wall a service gate swings open suddenly and three cars come shooting out of it in quick succession, not the usual armoured government sedans but the sort of rattletrap Asian imports the streets here are filled with. Almost at once they disappear around a corner.

Wali looks ready to spit.

"Is the government," he says. "Always the same. Every morning they go like this to the town to drink tea, to show that the city is theirs. No fear! But then why every time they are using different cars, different gate?"

"Where do they go?"

"Downtown. Different places. I can show you. Like children, I tell you, playing their games."

David takes the risk of hailing a street taxi to try to track them down, thinking it might make a good clip if he got some of them on camera touting their fearlessness, then edited in Wali's scathing commentary. Wali directs the driver to what looks like the bohemian quarter, every second shop a tea house or eatery or internet café. The streets are the usual mess of torn pavement and blockages, the taxi moving at a snail's pace. They pass children touting Marlboros and Coke, begging lepers, a cluster of hut-like tents of bent branches and rain sheeting that spills into the roadway from an empty lot like a misplaced village.

It is Wali who spots the cars, parked at the bottom of a short side street that gives onto some sort of hotel. The street is blocked at their end by a small street market.

"Is one of their places," Wali says. "Come, we can walk, is faster."

They have to thread their way through the market. David nearly trips over a boy with stumps for legs who has been plopped down on a mat like a sack of goods. Behind them a taxi has turned into the street and is trying to force its way through the crowd, people shouting and pounding on the hood though still the car keeps inching forward. David gets a glimpse of the driver's face as he goes by, impassive as if the crowd were just weather he needed to get through.

It is only when the car is free of the market and has begun to accelerate that the strangeness of it begins to come clear. By then it is too late. The explosion is over in such a flash that David registers it only as a kind of blankness, a hole in the centre of things that there is no way to think about or know. For a moment, in the blankness, he isn't sure that he is still alive, that whatever it is that is him is still somehow attached to his flesh and bone. Then the noise and the dust come at him like a wall and the world reasserts itself, a barrrage of indiscriminate sensation.

He is on the ground, breathing dirt, and some ghost is pulling at him.

*Mr. David!*

Shouts and wails, car alarms, points of pain, the chemical smell of spent explosives and burning fuel. Everywhere smoke and dust and rubble, twisted metal, uncertain lumps of things his mind can't take in. Where the hotel stood, there is only fog and flame.

"Mr. David! We must go!"

People run screaming in every direction, jostling him, falling and not getting up. A big man in flowing robes looms up out of the murk clutching a bloodied sack that turns out to be a boy.

From somewhere, utterly distinct, the wail of a child.

A soldier is shouting at him.

"Why have you come to this place, you stupid man! Get back!"

The ghost is still at his elbow: Wali, entirely grey with dust.

"Mr. David, we must go! Someone can hurt you! Someone can take you!"

They hurry back through the market, in chaos now. The wail of the child follows them up the street, then goes silent.

They have to fight their way back to the hotel on foot, through streets grown frenetic. Sporadic checkpoints have sprung up but they seem only to heighten the tension, the soldiers manning them paranoid and green and on edge. Wali has called the hotel on David's pay-and-go to get Said to come fetch them, but they see no sign of him.

"I think he is sleeping," Wali says with disgust. "For khat he can leave his own mother to die."

As they near the hotel the streets grow quieter, until there are no soldiers or crowds and they have reached a kind of eerie normalcy again. Only now does David realize how filthy he is, how his whole body aches like a single bruise. He touches a hand to his head: his video glasses are gone. He waits for the disappointment to set in at the footage he has lost, at what he might have done with it, but feels only a dim relief.

Yusuf comes hurrying out of the hotel gate to greet them.

"Such a terrible thing, terrible! Thank God you are safe! It's very bad, what has happened, maybe six or seven ministers, dead! I sent the car for you, of course, but the checkpoints turned it back."

In his room David showers at once, trying to wash away the grit and the smell, though they cling to him like a second skin. He isn't sure if the dullness he feels is indifference or shock or something else. He keeps expecting some upsurge of emotion or understanding, something to make him feel he is on the inside of what has happened instead of at this strange remove.

He sits at his desk to clean the Beretta. Grit has entered every crevice again. He wipes down the guide and the spring, the receiver, the slide, scrubs the barrel again. The work seems to calm him, to bring him back to himself, to his body, as if all this time he has not quite dared to make a commitment to it again. Now the images begin to come back to him, though it strikes him as odd that what he most remembers are the things he most turned from, the glistening bits in the street, gut or limb or severed head, the fallen heaps like shattered manne- quins. All of it familiar from the news yet utterly foreign, with none of the quickening that catastrophe brought at a distance, only the turning away and the guilty blood rush—irrepress- ible, obscene—of having survived.

David checks the time: not yet noon. It is hard to believe that less than half the day has passed. That the rest of his life still stretches in front of him.

In the fevered light of afternoon he wanders Ostia Antica. The handsome guide is there, walking ahead of David with the patrician air of someone who knows he will be followed. Past the tombs outside the gates, past the warehouses and the baths and the forum, to a construction site where he is building an apartment block amidst the ruins. In one smooth motion he edges a brick with mortar and sets it in place. The precision of it, the artistry, leaves David breathless.

Someone is pounding at the door.

"They are expecting you, Mr. Pace! You must come! On account of the curfew!"

Yusuf.

"Just a minute, for Christ's sake."

Somehow the interview is still on. David has to fight to make sense of this.

"What about the roads?" he says. "The checkpoints?"

"It is not a problem, sir. Only there is the curfew now, you must return before dark."

He ought to be gone, like the journalists. Ought to pack his bags and head home instead of risking his life for an interview he doesn't need for a book he will never finish.

"Give me a few minutes."

His clothes of the morning are ruined and he has to pick from the few clean ones he still has on hand. An aging pair of chinos, a light blazer; a dress shirt he'll have to wear untucked, to cover the Beretta. He tests the gun for concealment and snags, then chambers a round and sets the safety and tucks it into his holster.

His mind keeps returning to the blast. To that sense of being there at ground zero at the crucial instant yet somehow unable to take it in. There seems some lesson in that, if only he could make sense of it.

Wali is squatting in the shade of the guardhouse eating some kind of stew from a battered tin bowl. At the sight of David, his grin, like manna falling.

"Mr. David! We are still alive, isn't it?"

A boy darts out from the kitchen courtyard and sets a cup of milky tea at Wali's feet. David recognizes him as the one Said delivered a backhand to some days earlier.

"Is my son," Wali says. The boy is five or six, dressed in a dirty white thawb that is a miniature of his father's. "Name is Wali. Same like mine."

David remembers the hard set of the boy's shoulders when Said struck him, the glisten of tears held back. That he himself said nothing.

"Wali is a good name." He hands the boy a coin as if he were merely the good-hearted foreigner Wali seems to see him as. "Your father is a good man."

Wali beams.

"Ah, Mr. David! I think you are joking! I think you want to kill me!"

There is a sound of raised voices from the lobby and Said and Yusuf emerge in the midst of some heated argument. Said slumps into his chair beneath the palm and Yusuf picks up a stone and flings it at him, hard.

"Why are you sitting, fool? The customer is waiting, can't you see that? Didn't you sleep enough in the morning?"

Said rises like a sulking schoolboy and makes his way to the car. He kicks out at Wali as he passes him and knocks over his teacup.

"Move, animal! Open the gate!"

They set out. David sits in back and Wali up front with his rifle. The streets feel less frenzied now. At the checkpoints Said flashes a permit of some sort and they are let through without a word. But when they reach the central boulevard, they find it clogged with traffic. Taxis and crowded minibuses, army transports, big tankers and semis whose stink of diesel fills the Peugeot. It is hard to tell whether people are simply going about their business or fleeing for their lives. They pass a stake truck laden with bulging burlap sacks watched over by half a dozen riflemen, a single phrase in English sticking out amidst the lines of Arabic that cover its panels: *Road to Heaven.*

Said tries to skirt the traffic by detouring along side streets and back lanes. They go past courtyard kitchens, communal latrines, rows of battered tin lean-tos built against the backs of ruined buildings. Past areas of blight where the houses look cobbled together like children's creations, of mud and tin and coloured plastic; where whole city blocks have been flattened to nothing as though a giant jackboot had stepped on them. Toddlers play naked amidst the ruins; a gang of boys sit perched on the shell of a burnt-out LAV. To the east David thinks he can make out the intimation of the sea, a kind of heightened glow at the horizon line like the blue nimbus of a computer screen.

Wali keeps his eyes peeled. David has yet to see him engage the safety on his rifle.

"I think we must join the main road again. Is dangerous here. Someone can stop us. They can take the car."

Said shoots a smirk back at David.

"Take the car? What is that fucking gun for then, man? What are you doing here?"

The flat grid of the downtown gradually gives way to the slopes of the foothills. As the land rises the streets grow harder to navigate, more and more tortuous and steep and riven with gullies or ruined by war. These were the Strangers' Quarters, emptied out by the waves of cleansing, then reduced to rubble during the jihadist occupation. Here and there, though, lengths of street remain eerily intact, houses with curtains still billowing through their open windows, shops with their signs still hanging and their doors in place as if their owners have merely stepped out for the afternoon pause.

When they finally rejoin the main road it is no longer the grand divided boulevard of downtown but a single stretch of pocked asphalt flanked by open sewers and by the usual string of crumbling storefronts and street stalls. There is habitation here, though the traffic is mostly bicycles and carts and the street life seems to cling to doorways as if afraid to come out in the open. There are no trees, nothing green in any direction, not so much as a weed, everything reduced to the rust colour of the barren mountains that rise up in the distance.

They have left the government zone. It is only a matter of minutes before they come to a roadblock, an old plank laid across two oil drums. It is watched over by a handful of boys who look barely past puberty, dressed in a mishmash of hip hop and army surplus and sporting what look like Chinese M16s.

Instead of his permit Said flashes an American ten. An older boy wearing a hood despite the heat peers into the car, smiles, shakes his head. A twitch of anger crosses Said's face and he and Hoodie exchange a few words. A couple of the other boys shift, moving in closer, and Said finally adds a second ten to the first.

The boy flashes an unfriendly grin in at David.

"Thank you, G.I. Joe!" And waves them on.

They have barely gone another half a mile before they spot a second roadblock. Said curses under his breath and makes a quick turn onto a dirt side street that climbs up over the main road. Wali is unable to hold his tongue.

"You must use the main road! I'm telling you!"

Said scowls.

"Is this your city? Tell me that!"

The street looks at first like it might let them bypass the roadblock but only ends up taking them higher up the slopes, into a neighbourhood that grows ever more haunted and desolate and ruined. They are the only traffic here, the only thing alive. Said takes a turn, then another, but each seems only to lead them farther from the main road.

"You must go back!" Wali says. "Is the only way, you stupid man!"

The veins in Said's neck bulge.

"Watch your fucking tongue, do you hear me? Watch your fucking tongue!"

"For the love of God," David says, "just do what he tells you and go back!"

Without a word Said does a lurching three-point turn in the narrow street to wheel the car around. But at the first intersection they come to he stops short, seeming already unsure what direction they have come from.

Wali cranes suddenly forward.

"Look! Over there! In those buildings!"

"What?" Said says. "What is it, for fuck's sake?"

"There! You can see! There is someone! We must go quickly! Go back!"

David peers into the skeletal patchwork of ruined buildings but can make out only the criss-crossing of darkness and light.

"It's probably just some fucking beggar!" Said says.

"Go quickly! I'm telling you!"

Said manoeuvres them down a steep lane that ends in a square overlooked by the ruins of a small church. Several streets come off it. Said hesitates, then takes the first one.

"You are only guessing now, isn't it?" Wali yells. "Is not a joke, my friend! They are coming, I tell you, more than one!"

"Who saw them? Only you! A child, seeing ghosts! A frightened woman!"

Said brakes.

"Fucking hell!"

A trench has been cut into the roadway, a good four or five feet across. It might be a leftover from the jihadist occupation or something more insidious, some warlord's attempt to make these streets impassable, to trap the unwitting in them like rats in a maze.

Wali is shouting.

"Why did you want to come here, in these streets? I said to you, go back! Is the only way!"

"Don't raise your voice at me, bushman! Don't tell me my fucking business!"

Said hits the gas and backs up toward the square. As he rounds the corner, one of the tires catches on something and the car swerves. There is a sickening jolt and crunch of metal and the car comes to a wrenching stop. Said puts it in forward and guns the engine but the tires merely spin and spin, spewing grit and burning rubber.

The back end of the car has got lodged on a slab of fallen wall from the church. David and Wali push while Said guns the engine again, but the car refuses to budge. From somewhere, the smell of gasoline.

Said gets out of the car and Wali is on him at once, shaking his rifle at him as if ready to shoot him on the spot.

"You useless, useless man! How can you save us now? Do you want to kill us, to do this?"

"Shut your fucking mouth, old man! I'll kill you anytime I want, if it comes to that! I'll snap your fucking throat!"

"You think you can kill me? Such a useless man? When can you kill me? Try it now! Try it!"

Somehow it all reads as slapstick to David, even as Said lunges for Wali, even as he grabs for his gun. He is no match for Wali, who is all muscle and sinew, all reflex. Except that Wali hesitates. David sees it, the flash of uncertainty, maybe just a reflex born of years of servitude or the sudden under-standing that there is no way, for an outsider like him, that this matter can end in his favour.

As soon as Said has hold of the gun his finger is on the trigger, even before he has got it properly away, so that for an instant he seems as shocked by the barrage that comes out of it as David is. But then once it has started, everything that follows has a grue-some air of inevitability.

"Who's killing you now, you fucking son of a whore? Who's killing you now?"

"For Christ's sake, stop!"

There will be no way afterwards to parse the next seconds with any sureness, if Said shifts the barrel in accident or with intent, if David makes a decision or simply gives in to an impulse no more conscious or chosen than sleep. He will remember the sensation of bullets whizzing by, close enough, it feels, to scorch his skin, but not the deciding.

At the camp they called it the Failure Drill, the one that tar-geted the stopping zones. Two shots to the heart, then one to the head. Like taking breaths. Click, click and click.

It is done.

There is a long moment like after the bomb blast when there is only undifferentiated sensation. Then time pushes forward again and everything begins to reassume its unbear-able separateness. The mad echo of the shots still hangs among the ruined buildings. Slumped on the ground near the back end of the Peugeot, some object he doesn't quite look at.

He has the dead feeling he recognizes from dreams, of no going back.

*Jesus fucking Christ.*

Somehow, he needs to clean up this wreckage. Needs to find a doctor, police, all the structures he takes for granted.

Wali's chest is a mess of blood.

"I'll get help. Just hold on." David sits in the street holding Wali's thin frame against his own. "Someone will come, they'll fix you."

The blood pools at Wali's belly, gets on David's hands, his clothes, seeps into the dirt.

"Mr. David," he whispers, his voice already the barest rustling.

David tries again and again to reach Yusuf on his phone until the keypad is caked with blood, but he can't get a signal. He tries to stanch Wali's wounds, but there are too many. *Think*, he thinks, as if there is something he has overlooked, some solution. *Stop the bleeding. Call for help.* But the blood comes from everywhere. The help is worlds away.

"Fuck! FUCK!"

The car keys are still in the ignition. David opens the trunk to check for some sort of tire iron or jack to try to get the car free. From somewhere a sound of movement, ghosts or the wind, then a voice in his head.

*G.I. Joe! Why have you killed those men?*

A crack and a hiss of split air, a puff of dust.

*G.I. Joe! Why can't you kill us?*

Laughter, from the shadows. The laughter of boys. It comes to him: the boys from the checkpoint.

Another crack, a ping of metal. The thought forms in his head like a stage direction that they are shooting at him.

"G.I. Joe, why can't you pay us?"

He has to find cover. He heaves Wali up from the dirt and carries him to the church, clambering with him over the rubble of the ruined foyer trying to reach the beckoning gloom of the nave. As he moves, another shot. Pain shoots through his leg like a spike.

"G.I. Joe, can we come to your church? Maybe the priest can pray for us!"

He props Wali against a wall that looks like it is out of any line of fire and checks his leg. There is a livid gash just below the knee. He bandages it as best he can with a torn shred of pant leg, then sets about trying to bandage Wali, tearing strips from his blazer and from Wali's tunic. The task feels hopeless. He can't seem to fashion bandages long enough or tie them tight enough to stop the blood.

Wali's eyes have dimmed like a sleepy child's.

"G.I. Joe, we are coming!"

He can hear them talking amongst themselves in lowered voices, part of his mind reverting to training mode, trying to gauge how many they are, what direction they're coming from. There are a dozen rounds left in his Beretta, which is still at his hip, where he must have returned it with the same trained automatism with which he drew it; there are another dozen or so in Wali's rifle out in the street, which he could make a run for. Then one by one he could pick them off. Except this is no simulation. There is no math here that can make things add up.

The behaviour of children.

"Are you there, G.I. Joe? We are close!"

He needs to go. There isn't any question of bringing Wali, who is no longer conscious, though the failure weighs on him more than any other. He moves as quickly as his leg allows him, slipping out a side door of the church and up a narrow lane that runs between the backs of houses. It brings him out to a street a block over, from where he works his way through the ruins until he has put another block behind him and the boys' voices have receded.

His leg is dripping blood.

"Don't shoot now, G.I. Joe! We will kill you, no joke!"

They are closing in on the church. There is shouting, gunfire, the sound of smashing glass. Then a final shot, muted, as though from inside a building.

"G.I. Joe!" The tone is so buoyant, so good-natured, it is almost heartening. "Where is your friend now? Why can't you take him?"

David ducks into an abandoned tenement, his leg throbbing. He manages to climb to the top floor and finds a back staircase that leads up to the roof, where he tries to get a signal on his phone. Still nothing. The roof is lined with a row of tin shanties like the garrets of Roman insulae and David huddles up in one. It is the merest oven, stripped of everything except its smell, human and stale, though through the doorway he can see out over almost the entire city, past the ruin and blight of the surrounding neighbourhoods all the way to the presidential palace and the telecommunications tower and the little cluster of high-rises along the central boulevard. Farther out, the empty warehouses and abandoned factories, the rusting freighters moored at the docks, and then the sea, which stretches to the horizon.

He ought to tend to his wound. Ought to bind his ankle, which has started to swell from some misstep.

The blood on his hands, on his clothes, has started to set.

He can hear the locusts gathering at the base of his brain, reassuring almost in their quiet suasion. Somehow he has misplaced his pill pod, has left it behind in the tattered remains of his blazer or in his pants from the morning, so that there is nothing for it but to let them swarm.

"G.I. Joe! Is useless to hide in this place, we will find you!"

Hide and seek.

The sun has begun to fall, precipitously, though it has hung at the midpoint for what has felt like hours, days, millennia.

From his perch David tries to gauge the angle of its descent, but it is hopelessly out of kilter, off its axis perhaps or the building is, or the whole city. The city has changed somehow: he hadn't noticed the hills before, or the tombs that line the decumanus outside the gates. How every district is colour-coded, red or purple or green, the hyper-blue of the sea an absolute border that cannot be crossed. In a glance he is able to take in the whole of the city as though it were no larger than a screen, than his own brain, every street and speck of dust and shift of afternoon light, every murder, every cup of spilled tea.

He thinks of his phone again and then it comes to him, the one call he could make.

He hopes he isn't too late.


David awakes to find a boy no older than Marcus staring down at him, with the same liquid eyes as Marcus, gleaming with life.

"G.I. Joe!" Looking genuinely pleased to see him. "So we have found you!"

The boy is dressed in full army gear, his uniform perfectly creased, immaculate. David knows he should be afraid and yet the situation has the air of a pleasant game.

"How did you know where I was?"

"How? Is too easy! The blood! Can't you see it, my friend? Is there, every step, like you are showing the way."

It is true. The back of his leg is a mass of oozing blood. He can't believe he hasn't taken better care.

"I think you are taking a bullet there," the boy says. "You must be a soldier, my friend! You must be marine!"

Somehow they make their way down to the street, though each time David glances at his leg it seems more bloated and ruined.

"You look like my son," he says to the boy. "Marcus."

The boy grins.

"Is also my name! Marcus! Come, I can show you the way."

There are more boys on the street, in the same immaculate gear. Marcus leads them forward, the other boys flanking David like an honour guard. The streets are better now, surfaced with paving stones in the Roman fashion and leading up and up, into the very clouds. The buildings are the same ruined ones, except that gradually the heaps of rubble scattered amidst the wreckage reveal themselves as encampments, the clusters of burlap and tin that cling to the upper storeys as makeshift hovels. It is like a city camouflaged in the ruins of a city. And everywhere boys, who begin to emerge in the tens, in the hundreds, an army of children ranging from toddlers to strapping teens. Boys scrubbing clothes, fixing old furniture, stirring cauldrons of food over huge firepits, though wherever he and Marcus pass they break away from whatever they are doing to follow along. Slowly a chatter builds, an energy.

"They are happy to see you," Marcus says. "That you are safe."

He leads David to a cliff face where a cave stretches back and back into shadow, jammed floor to ceiling with rows of packing crates, steel drums, pallets piled high with cartons and bulging sacks. They walk through the narrow aisles, deeper and deeper into the cave, but still David can't make out where it ends. They pass a stack of bakers' trays filled with the cigar-shaped rolls David's mother used to buy when he was a boy. Marcus hands him one, still warm. The smell of it seems to hold the whole of David's life.

"Is very old, this place," Marcus says. "They say my people have lived here a million years. But still we are children."

They climb higher. Up a great stone staircase like those of the pyramids of the Mesoamericans, the hangers-on swelled to a rabble by now, trailing alongside like the cheering crowds at a triumph. With each step David feels lighter. At the summit, a boy of five or six sits in the shade of a canopy of old lumber and tin, dressed in full military regalia.

"Is our leader," Marcus says.

David wonders what he has done with the bread Marcus has given him it, if he ought to have brought it as an offering. If the David who has appeared here is one he can trust.

"What do I say to him?"

"Ask him your question," Marcus says. "He has been expecting it."

The leader comes forward. Any second now he will emerge from the shadows with the answer David has been waiting for all his life.

Shouting, frantic, and a boy in a dirty wife-beater, no more than eight or nine, is jabbing him hard with the point of a rifle.

"Stay there! Stay there! I will shoot!" Wild-eyed, so that no response seems the right one.

An older boy stands laughing behind him.

"Is not a goat, to poke him like that!" He is dressed in a torn Public Enemy T-shirt that shows a swath of bony ribs. "Is not a chicken!"

But he pokes David in turn to make him rise.

"You see, we have found you, G.I. Joe!" Up close like this there is nothing buoyant in his tone, nothing heartening. "Now we can kill you!"

They force David down to the street at gunpoint, paying no attention to his leg. Three more boys are waiting there, just as ragtag, all with rifles. None looks any older than David's own son. One has a second rifle slung over his back: Wali's.

Public Enemy pulls David's Beretta from his own waistband. David hadn't even noticed it was missing.

"Is nice gun, G.I. Joe, how much in America? Two hundred? Two-fifty?"

"I bought it here," David says.

The boy ignores him. He aims the Beretta at his young side-kick's head and the whole group seems to ready itself for whatever antic is about to follow.

"Boom!" Public Enemy says. Then he raises the gun ever so slightly and pulls the trigger.

The air explodes and a look a terror crosses the boy's face before he erupts in fury, pounding his fists at Public Enemy and trying to wrest the Beretta from him. The other boys are doubled over.

"Boom!" they say, again and again, reliving the moment.

Public Enemy leads the way, up streets that rise higher and higher yet only keep repeating the same landscape of ruin. Two of the other boys flank him at a distance. David's leg has purpled and swelled from his ankle to his knee, but they offer no help.

"G.I. Joe!" Public Enemy says. "Why are you walking so bad? Come now, we are almost there!"

From a distance come urgent shouts and imprecations. They pass what look like the remains of a school and come to a dusty playing field: a group of boys are playing soccer.

"I think you know this game, G.I. Joe. Can you play it?"

The boys crowd around them at the edge of the field as if David were some prize game animal Public Enemy had bagged. Public Enemy spins out his story until he has everyone in stitches.

"'Stay there, stay there, I will shoot you!'"

Some of the boys are as young as four or five, all with the same anemic look of having been out too long in the open. It jars David how close it all is to his dream, the company of boys, the laughter and jokes. Public Enemy has got to the part about the Beretta.

"Boom!" he says, and the sidekick pounds at him again, and everyone laughs.

There is a sudden hush, and the boys part to let someone through. It is the older boy from the checkpoint, still in his hood but looking larger now, more the leader, no longer just a kid extorting petty cash at the side of the road. He ignores David and goes straight to Public Enemy, meeting his expectant grin with a backhand that nearly knocks him over.

"Is this how you bring in a prisoner? Did you think to tie him? What if he runs? What if he grabs for your gun?"

Before he has finished saying it he has pulled the Beretta from Public Enemy's waist. Public Enemy looks close to tears.

"Sorry, sir."

"And then you go bragging! How long did it take you to find him? Why did you let him kill that man? What of the car they were driving, what has become of it? We are not playing here, you fool! This is no game!"

Only now does he turn to David. His cheeks are gouged with tribal markings David hadn't noticed before, just healed-over gashes, really, so crude they look self-inflicted.

"So you don't want to pay the tolls, G.I. Joe. But now you will pay."

There is barely enough time for David to think of the pettiness of this before the boy cracks the butt of the Beretta against his skull and his mind goes blank.

In the old stories it is only in hell that the hero learns what will set him free. The trick is remembering. The trick is making it back.

These are the things that David can no longer remember: What it felt like the first time he made love to Julia. The first time he held Marcus. When he learned his father was dead. The images are there, the memories of the events, but not the important thing, what mattered most. As with history. *Only to show how it actually was.* A joke.

Even now, after so many years, he still has his dreams of returning to his father's hometown. The dream is always the same and yet never quite; there is always the train that pulls into a station, made up of luxurious sleepers or the filthy cattle cars of concentration camp transports, or there is no train at all, just an arrival, a sense of walking through streets at once familiar and utterly foreign. People greet him and smile, then stare after him from behind closed curtains. Tell him nothing. Tell him everything. Tell him he is lost, has made a mistake, has taken a wrong turn, or wonder how someone who claims such an interest in history has not even bothered to understand his own.

He is the man of history who wants to stand outside it. Who wants to think he is born out of nothing. Who doesn't want to pay.

He must remember to save a coin for the ferryman for the trip back.

David opens his eyes, to the taste of blood.

He is on his knees at the edge of the playing field, under the slanting afternoon sun. He tries to move but feels strangely encumbered, realizes his hands are bound, his ankles are. That the sun is like daggers.

He tries to remember what dream this is. If only there were a clock, or a mirror, or a book.

"G.I. Joe, you have come back from the dead!" The boy in the hood stands over him, haloed in the sun but somehow not blocking it. "You are welcome, G.I. Joe, you are welcome!"

Laughter and jeers. The whole troupe surrounds him now with their rifles and rags, dozens of them, a republic of boys, their leader's joke rippling through them. *G.I. Joe! You are welcome!*

"Do you think is a game, G.I. Joe? Do you think you have come here to play? You can join us for football. You can show us American style."

More laughter. David knows he has to make the effort to think more clearly, to understand, yet the more he understands the more his leg throbs, the more his wrists and ankles burn, the more the sun pokes its daggers.

The boy still has the Beretta. He makes a show of inspecting it, flicks the safety on, then off again.

"US M9," he says. "Very fine, very fine. How much, this gun, in your country?"

The question feels more freighted this time.

"I bought it here," he says, as before.

"Here? I think you are lying, my friend! Is not possible here, this gun. Only American soldiers and CIA."

"Maybe some soldier left it behind. Maybe only his body went home."

He regrets his tone at once. There are some titters among the boys and then screaming pain as Hoodie cracks his skull again.

"You think we are joking here, with your lies, but is no joke! Tell me why you have come here, G.I. Joe. Who has sent you?"

He needs to tell them about the Malana, about his book. About Wali's son waiting for his father's return in the kitchen courtyard; about his own. At bottom, though, he knows the boy is right. Knows he is steeped in lies, that there would be no end to the unravelling of them.

He can't shake the dream he had of these boys before they took him, the feeling that he is the one who has chosen which version is dream and which is real.

"I'm a journalist," is all he gets out, and then another hammer blow.

"Lies, my friend! Where is your press card? Where is your recorder? Where is your pen? The truth is you are a killer, isn't it? The truth is you are a spy, CIA!"

There it is, finally, the ludicrous charge, almost heartbreaking in its insufficiency.

The mountains that rise up at the end of the playing field seem to hold them here as on a stage. David imagines all his separate selves massing in the wings like a chorus, readying for the final turn.

The boy presses the gun to his head.

"Last chance, G.I. Joe. Only the truth!"

The sun beats down.

In his last years of high school David had developed a small trade in pot and hashish in his neighbourhood so he wouldn't have to go begging for cash to his father. Once he crossed a dealer in the Jungle by underselling him and the dealer showed up at David's school in his beat-up Olds.

"No funny business. Just to talk. Man to man."

David got in the car. That was how green he was then, how arrogant.

They drove out to an empty parking lot and smoked a joint. The dealer had such an easy manner it was hard not to like him.

"Back home we fix this kind of problem very quickly," he said, as if setting up a punch line.

"And how's that?"

"It's very easy."

He reached in his glove box and pulled out a small silver-plated pistol. David knew nothing of handguns in those days and thought at first it was some kind of toy.

He put the gun to David's head.

"You see how easy? Before you can close your eyes, the problem is solved."

Click.

David felt wetness beneath him.

"No worries, man. Stay out of the Jungle and your secret is safe."

The fear before the hammer had fallen had been like black poison going through him, like a blinding flash in the darkest corner of himself. Yet even then there was that part of him that had thrilled, awaiting the bullet as if there were already a phantom space in his brain set to receive it.

The accusations move through the boys like a wind or a fire, killer, liar, spy. Then the refrain. *Make him pay.*

With the gun to his head David sees things more clearly. The stark contours of the mountains at one end of the field, the vivid blue of the sea at the other. That he can take so much in, that his brain can hold it, is a wonder to him.

If he walked far enough through the desert that stretches out beyond the city he would reach the outposts of ancient Rome, the still-standing custom houses and theatres and city walls, and then beyond them the pyramid tombs of the pharaohs, the ziggurats and ruined temples, the valleys that were the very birthplace of the human race. All of this he has wanted to give a shape to, right back to the animal past that was still almost all of what humans were, back to the shifting continents and striking meteors and drifting orbits that made every notion of virtue and blame, of progress, of hope, an irrelevance. Thinking it his job to breach every protocol and wake every sleeper. As though, if he cast wide enough, if he took in enough of the muck and the gore, the animal stench, the cold mineral sheen of indifference, even the likes of himself could be accounted for.

The sun has begun to drop behind the mountains, giving them the unworldly look of a planet in its end times, a place where no one has yet spoken the words and yet day by day, the certainty grows.

Hoodie's finger is on the trigger.

"What can we do with this liar, this killer? Why should we save him?"

Make him pay.

Any minute now, David is sure of it, he can feel the urge growing in him like the howl of all his disparate selves, he will do the thing that will land a bullet in his brain. He has never felt more awake.

# Acknowledgements

For their material support during the writing of this novel I am extremely grateful to Antanas Sileika and the Humber School for Writers; Sheila Bauman and the Edna Staebler Writer-in-Residence program of Kitchener Public Library; Professor Anthony Cicerone and the Canadian Studies program of Bridgewater State University; Steven Hayward and the Creative Writing program of Colorado College; Greg Hollingshead and the Writing Studio of the Banff Centre; Professor Jeremy Adelman and the Canadian Studies program of Princeton University; Andrew Westoll and the Writer-in-Residence program of the University of Toronto Scarborough; and the Canada Council for the Arts.

For their generous permission to use a reproduction of Alex Colville's *Pacific 1967* for the novel's cover my sincere thanks to Ann Kitz and the Colville estate and to A.C. Fine Art Inc., which owns the copyright.

I am deeply indebted to my agents, Anne McDermid and Martha Webb, and to my U.S. publicist, Saverio Mancina, for continuing to take me seriously; and to my incomparable editor at Doubleday Canada, Martha Kanya-Forstner, for always being a reader I could trust.

Of the many sources I consulted in writing this novel, Jeff Warren's *The Head Trip: Adventures on the Wheel of Consciousness* was particularly helpful. Special thanks also to John Montesano for his insights on Toronto's neighbourhoods and history.

The poem by Gaius Petronius Arbiter cited in the novel is from Chapter LXXIX of the *Satyricon* and is a liberal translation from the original Latin indebted to many other translations from across the centuries as well as to Google Translate.

My greatest thanks go to my children, Luca, Virginia and Sarah, for helping to spare me the fate of the protagonist in this novel, and to my wife, writer Erika de Vasconcelos, for her indulgence, advice and support, and for filling my life with beauty and love.

A NOTE ABOUT THE TYPE

The body of *Sleep* has been set in Palatino, a typeface designed by Hermann Zapf and originally released by the Linotype Foundry in 1948. Based on the humanist fonts of the Italian Renaissance, Palatino is named after 16th century Italian master of calligraphy Giambattista Palatino. While Renaissance faces generally feature small letters with long ascenders and descenders (imitating the forms produced by a broad-nib pen), Palatino's larger proportions and generous width make it readable at small sizes. Palatino is one of the most widely used text typefaces in the world today.